SHADOW MERCHANT

A JACK MERCHANT MEDICAL MYSTERY

BRUCE HENNIGAN

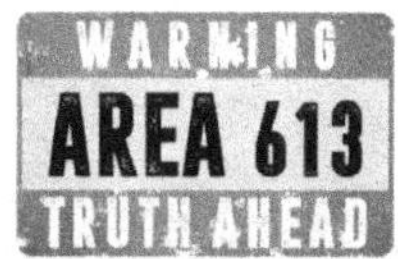

SHADOW MERCHANT

A JACK MERCHANT MEDICAL MYSTERY

BRUCE HENNIGAN

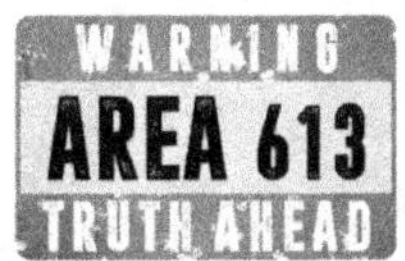

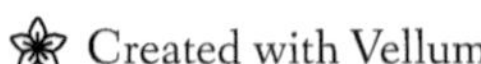 Created with Vellum

Books By Bruce Hennigan

Hope Again Books:
The Homecoming Tree
Our Darkness, His Light
With Mark Sutton: Hope Again: A Lifetime Plan for Conquering Depression
Area 613:
Death by Darwin (Jonathan Steel Prequel)
The 13th Demon: Altar of the Spiral Eye
The 12th Demon: Mark of the Wolf Dragon
The 11th Demon: The Ark of Chaos
The 10th Demon: Children of the Bloodstone
The 9th Demon: Time of the Cross
The 8th Demon: A Wicked Numinosity
The 7th Demon: The Pandora Stone
The 5th Demon: Demoneyes

To everyone in my radiology practice who made the past 38 years such a pleasure in the midst of the chaos. Thanks to my retired partners from whom I have chosen the best qualities to dress my characters. Especially thanks to the real Roger and Debra Montana, Cliff and Diane! You're the best!

Also to Sally and Robert who often asked me to share my stories at the table in the doctor's cafeteria.

Most importantly, in memory of Johnny Blake who passed away on March 10, 2022. He was a good friend and a good brother in Christ. He was the inspiration for the character of Gill.

FOREWORD

"Just remember one thing. You're nothing but a *expletive deleted* photographer!"

I was a resident in radiology at the time and this lovely admonition directed at me came from a well known local cardiothoracic surgeon. Was I nothing but just a "photographer"? I knew it wasn't true but this person echoed many of the falsehoods about radiologists perpetuated by many physicians. That was almost 40 years ago and the field of radiology has changed more drastically than any other field of medicine thanks to the huge leap in technology.

I have worked on this story for a number of years. I am a radiologist and I once was told to "write about what you know". Who would every think the life of a radiologist would be of any interest to anyone? Who would want to hear about a medical "photographer"?As I sat at the table in the doctor's cafeteria one day, a fellow physician sat across from me and said, "Bruce, tell me your latest story." I realized that our lives as physicians are filled with stories, not just of our patients, but of the drama of trying to do our job for our patients in a rapidly changing field of science. Medicine has become so technical, so scientifically grounded it has been stripped of the "art of medicine". What do I mean? The art of medicine is the most essential ingredient now missing. It is time a doctor takes to truly connect with the patient. To talk to the patient. To listen to the patient. To understand the fullness of the patient's story.

There are many stories I could tell. Most involve very special, amazing patients I have had the honor, the privilege, no, the blessing of working with for the past 38 years. But many of the stories are about doctors and their personal struggles. About hospital nurses and technologists trying to thread the needle of income and needs in an ever-changing world of decreasing reimbursement. About administrators struggling to keep their hospital at the cutting edge so they would have a competitive edge over another hospital. It's about heart and drama; life and death; triumph and defeat. It is about life and death.

Over the past few years I have worked hard to keep the stories neutral in my mind. To avoid telling stories that are about specific patients for the sake of privacy. I have worked hard to disguise physicians who would be instantly recognized by anyone in my local medical environment. Encouraged by Sally, that doctor I mentioned, I am going to tell some of those stories. The details will be changed but the drama and the impact will be preserved. Some of my partners may see a bit of themselves in these pages. That is entirely intentional because I am only using their most positive and endearing "eccentricities". Any negative portrayal of an individual paralleling a real world position is completely fictional. If I offend you, accept my apology in advance. I have poured over this book for ten years to make sure I do not offend anyone who would see themselves in these pages.

At the same time, I want to pull back the curtain on the

world of hospital based medicine. I want the patient to see the struggles and trials their doctors, nurses, technologists, and support staff face every day in bringing healing to the world. Be warned because my works always include a spiritual foundation. For we are more than just sacks of meat. We are divine creations made in the image of God; creatures a little lower than the angels; beings born with intrinsic value, dignity, worth; beings of light and love. Let us never forget that as we move through our world of scientific discoveries so profound they often seem magical.

Dr. Bruce Hennigan

March, 2022

ONE

Colorado Springs, Colorado

I HAD RETURNED to the scene of the crime. Thunder rattled from the distant mountain peaks as I tried to figure how to get past the housekeeper. She stood in the doorway to the motel room, her cart blocking the walkway on the second floor. I studied the doorway from my car and shivered. Number 212. It all looked the same. Exactly like it had a year ago, the cheap, cheesy motel we had chosen for our honeymoon ten years previous. The black soot and broken glass were missing. They had remodeled. It was as if she had not died that day.

The housekeeper moved into room 210 and I slid out of the car. I hurried up the outside stairway six doors down from the room. A year before I had run up them, desperate to get to my wife. I hadn't been quick enough. I walked to the open door to room 210 and stopped.

"Excuse me?" I looked in through the open door.

The maid came out. "Yes?"

"I left something in my room. Do you mind?"

The maid looked behind her and shrugged. "This is your room?"

"Yes. I'm Mr. Smith. Room 210." I held up the keycard from the year before. The fire hadn't destroyed it because it had been in my pocket. I couldn't tell her my real identity. She might check with the front desk. The maid stepped out onto the walkway and pulled her cart away from the door.

"Sure. I'll wait right here."

"Thanks." I said, slipping into the room and I paused to think. How could I get into the next room? I walked back out.

"How silly of me. I'm in 212, not 210." I held up the card. She looked at the number on it and I stepped up to the door to 212 and placed the keycard in its slot and withdrew it. The door didn't open.

"I don't understand. It worked a while ago." I looked at her with the most plaintive, innocent look I could muster.

She sighed. "I'll open it for you. But you need to go down to the front desk and get a new key." She slid her card through the slot and the door popped open.

"Thank you. I'll do that. I'm going back down for the continental breakfast in a few minutes." The door clicked shut behind me and I turned and looked out the peephole. The maid turned away and went back into 210. I drew a deep breath and turned.

The room was perfect. Clean. Walls papered with a forest scene from the mountains. A picture of Pike's Peak hung above the king-size bed. We had planned to ride up the mountain for our tenth anniversary. My heart raced. I looked at the bed. There was no curdled blood on the floor. No charred blood on the wall. I drew in a deep lung full of air. No smoke. The white-tiled ceiling was not stained with soot.

I crossed to the window and pulled back the curtain. The

glass was intact. That evening, it had exploded from the heat of the fire. My reflection stared back at me. Unruly black hair. Unshaven face. Bleary eyes behind gold-rimmed glasses. The eyes of an exhausted Dr. Jack Merchant. This is who am I now. So, why was I here? What did I hope to find? Answers?

I went to the sink, took off my glasses, and washed my face and looked at the thin man in the mirror. My skin still looked tanned and healthy, thanks to the genes I inherited from my grandmother. She had been full blood Choctaw Indian. But my skin was loose and sagging and dark circles under my eyes matched my dark hair. Was that a patch of gray at my temples? I wasn't THAT old! It wasn't the years. It was the mileage!

I glanced down at a toothbrush and toilet kit. Clothes hung in the closet. Someone was using this room. They might come back any minute. I turned and looked at the bed. Janice had been lying in bed, no doubt watching her favorite cooking show. The fire investigator said she had been smoking in bed. I knew she never smoked in bed because I made her go outside. Someone had started the fire. Someone had killed Janice. In my heart, I knew it. But no one believed me.

The firemen had found her body on the bed. I went over and sat on the edge. My life had become a mess in the past year. I had lost weight. I had lost respect from my partners in our medical practice. I had become a shell of a man. And, I had lost the money.

The door suddenly burst open. I put my glasses back on and squinted into the light as a woman stepped into the room.

"You are so predictable." The familiar voice echoed in the empty room. I stood up.

"Detective Sanchez?"

The tall, willowy woman wearing jeans and a leather jacket stepped away from the door. Her reddish blonde hair hung in a ponytail and her deep brown eyes gleamed with victory. "I knew you'd be back. I've been waiting for you."

"Good. Then maybe you can tell me why you haven't solved my wife's murder."

"Murder? I wasn't expecting that." Sanchez studied me for a moment and then started laughing. Behind her, the maid stepped into the room, rattling off something in Spanish. Sanchez replied, flashed her badge and waved the maid away.

"If you're finished breaking into someone else's hotel room, Dr. Merchant, we can take a little ride."

"You're going to arrest me for breaking and entering?"

Sanchez smiled. "No. I'm taking you to breakfast."

TWO

Moisture frosted the windows of the small diner. Fake Christmas wreathes hung from rubber suction cup hooks. I wiped the moisture away so I could see the distant peaks of the Rocky Mountains. Janice and I planned to celebrate our tenth anniversary retracing all the places we had visited on our honeymoon, starting with the motel. When we got married, I was nearly broke, just out of fellowship and joining what would become a lucrative practice. Now, I was broke again, but for different reasons. And Janice was dead on what would have been our eleventh anniversary. Clouds had rolled in over the peaks and the first wave of snowflakes drifted down from the gray sky.

"This is my favorite place to have breakfast." Sanchez said as she sat across the booth from me. "I highly recommend the huevos rancheros."

"I'll just have coffee." I glanced at the server who had appeared at the table.

"The usual?" She pushed dark hair out of her eyes as she glared at Sanchez.

"Sure, Gladys. And bring my friend a side of your French toast."

"I said I'm not hungry." I protested as Gladys walked away.

Sanchez sniffed. "You should eat something. If you don't want the toast, I'll eat it."

"Whatever." I shrugged.

"So, what are you doing back in Colorado Springs?"

"I told you. It's been a year since Janice died. And I don't have any answers."

Gladys arrived, placing mugs before each of us. She sat a carafe of coffee on the table and left. I poured cream into the cup and a couple of packets of yellow artificial sweetener.

Sanchez looked at me with distaste. "How can you drink that stuff?" She poured an inch of sugar into her cup.

"You get used to it." I said, sipping the coffee.

Sanchez stirred her coffee and studied me. "Looks like the diet is working." She tapped her spoon on the edge of her cup. "And you have your answers. You had them a year ago."

"The weight loss isn't from a diet." One of my eyelids spasmed because I had not slept well the past few days. I glanced back at the coffee cup. "Detective Sanchez, I believe my wife was murdered. A year ago, I asked your department to investigate it and all I've gotten is the cold shoulder."

Sanchez studied me for a long minute. "Funny you should say that. I believe someone murdered you wife." She gulped her coffee, emptied the cup, and sighed. "Caffeine. I might make it until lunch."

"What?" My heart raced. "You believe me? You believe it wasn't an accident?

Gladys showed up with two plates of food and placed a plate full of thick honey and brown sugar laden slabs of French toast in front of me. She placed a platter of scrambled eggs heaped with peppers, onions, and molten cheese in front of Sanchez. "Anything else?" She asked.

"Yeah, Chalupa sauce." Sanchez dove into the eggs. Gladys retrieved a bottle of red sauce from another table and handed it to Sanchez.

"Want me to get a fire extinguisher ready?"

Sanchez shot her an acid look. "No. Get lost." She did.

I took a small bite of the toast. It was delicious and I suddenly realized how hungry I was. It had been a long time since I had been hungry. Since Janice had died, I had lost over fifty pounds. "If the department thinks my wife is murdered, why have they been avoiding my calls?"

Sanchez slurped a grilled pepper and wiped red sauce from her mouth. "Because the department doesn't agree with me. The medical examiner, who is an idiot, signed off her death as accidental. Said she died from a fire started by cigarettes."

I sipped coffee and watched Sanchez attack her eggs. "And you disagree?"

"Yeah. Your wife was murdered. The fire was huge. But there were no cigarettes anywhere in the room. I talked to one of the firefighters. He said he smelled some kind of accelerant. But there was no evidence of an accelerant on investigation. I know Manuel. He's been with the fire department for thirty years. I trust his nose more than I do a test tube. But the investigator insisted no chemicals. Do you know what was in that hotel room that could have caused it to go up in flames like it did?"

"We just had luggage."

"Your wife use a curling iron?"

I gasped as the memory of Janice's hair, straight and blonde, burst into my mind. Her smell. The feel of her hair cascading across my shoulder. Her face pressed close to mine. I groaned and pushed the toast away suddenly nauseated. "She wore her hair straight."

Sanchez scraped the last of the eggs off the plate. "Bad memory?"

I glared at her. "No. Good memory."

Sanchez wiped her hands on a napkin and pointed to the toast. "You going to finish that?"

"No."

She placed my plate in her empty one and sliced at the toast. "Dr. Merchant, your wife's death is surrounded by mystery. I am the only one on the force who is remotely interested." Her eyes sparkled with mischief. "I knew you would be back today. I was watching you."

"What?" A trickle of dread ran through my unsteady stomach.

"I had a hunch. An intuition you would come back on the anniversary of your wife's death. You see, I've found some additional evidence. If I could just get someone to look at it, I could change this into a homicide investigation."

"What kind of evidence?" I sat up, suddenly alert.

"There were no cigarettes by the bed or out in the room. We found a pack in your wife's purse. But the purse was in the bathroom."

"It was a pretty bad fire." I swallowed. How could I talk about this? "Seems to me any cigarettes would have been burned up."

"We can still tell, Doc. Your wife smoked, didn't she?"

"Yes. She tried to quit, but the stress at work was too much." That and other things. "She went back to smoking when I wasn't around."

Sanchez sniffed. "I found some of those cigarettes from her purse in the evidence box. I had them analyzed by my friend Manuel. He found traces of a chemical that might have come from an accelerant." She leaned toward me. "You see, the fire department conducts its own investigation. They never asked for her purse."

"So, there was an accelerant?" My pulsed quickened.

Sanchez looked down at the toast. "Yeah. Maybe. But unfortunately, Manuel didn't exactly follow a proper chain of evidence. It's not admissible." She stabbed a piece of toast with her fork and glanced at me. "And then, there is the matter of the life insurance policy."

A chill ran down my spine. "What about it?"

Sanchez grew very still, taking the time to finish chewing the toast. "A half a million dollars. Taken out just a week before she died. Naming you as the beneficiary."

My stomach churned. "What are you saying?"

Sanchez pushed a pepper from between her front teeth with her tongue. She sat back and crossed her arms. "I think you killed your wife."

I froze, my mind reeling. Why hadn't I seen this coming? Nausea gripped me and I fought to keep the coffee and toast down. "That is ridiculous." For a second, I felt maybe it wasn't so ridiculous. If Janice had known what I was doing behind her back that day, it would have killed her!

"Then how do you explain the life insurance?" Sanchez's intense gaze bored into mine.

"I knew nothing about it. It wasn't until after Janice died, I found out about it."

Sanchez made a grunting sound and poured a second cup of coffee. "Where were you when she died?" She said evenly as she poured sugar into her coffee cup.

I stared straight ahead. "I was at the motel."

"But not in the room." Her' gaze shifted from the cup to me. Something predatory gleamed in her eyes; the cat playing with a mouse. She reached beneath the table and picked up her satchel. She placed it on the table beside her. From within, she removed a file folder. She opened the folder in front of her and was silent as she studied the papers within. Sweat popped out on my forehead and fogged my glasses. Sanchez sipped her coffee and nodded and retrieved a toothpick from a nearby dispenser and slid it out of its plastic wrapping. She placed it in the corner of her mouth.

"You told the investigating officer you left the motel room to run down the street to a convenience store."

"Yes. I drove down to the corner. Janice wanted some chips and some soft drinks."

Sanchez reached into the satchel and removed a tablet. She tapped the screen, and it awoke, illuminating her face. Outside the windows, the morning had grown darker, and a thick blanket of snow fell from the sky. The wind moaned against the window and tossed snow into a whirlwind in the parking lot. Sanchez turned the tablet around so that I could see the screen. A small window in the corner showed the motel parking lot from a high vantage point.

"Security camera on the roof of the motel. It took me nine months of wrangling to get this footage. They had already erased the tape. Old school system. You really should have gone to a more modern motel. But then you might have planned to stay in an old motel with outdated security. It took me a while to dig around and take the manager to dinner. He thought I was interested in him. Nope! I was interested in his computer with a backup digital file from all the tapes. Turns out his son, a computer nerd, of course, had put in a backup system."

She took the toothpick from her mouth and drank more coffee, allowing what she had said to sink in. It did. I swallowed the nasty aftertaste of the toasts and the coffee.

"Found out his son was using the backup digital file for a little blackmail on certain clients. When I threatened to throw his son's butt in jail, the dad gave up the file of that day." She tapped the video window, and it played. My heart raced.

A car pulled into the parking lot and paused at the far corner just behind the office that sat across from the rooms. It was my car. I could barely make out the movement of two figures inside the car. The passenger door opened, and a figure emerged, poorly seen due to light conditions and the proximity to a row of bushes lining a breezeway that led into the office. I got out on the driver's side and paused to say something to the other person. I walked around to the passenger side of the car out of the view of the camera. I returned, still taking to the person obscured by the bushes with a sack in one hand and a cup of coffee in the other. The bushes shifted, and the figure disappeared down the walkway.

I watched myself turn and lean against the car door. I watched my gaze travel up toward the motel rooms. A bright flash of light illuminated my features as the fire exploded through the front windows of our hotel room. I ran out of the camera range. The video ended.

"Who were you with, Dr. Merchant?" Sanchez asked, her voice flat.

I gulped for air. The memory was seared into my brain. "I, uh, met this guy at the convenience store who was staying at the hotel. He had walked down to the store, and I offered to give him a ride back."

Sanchez leaned back in the booth. "I see. What was his name?"

"I don't know, uh, his name." Careful, I thought. Don't say "her".

"You picked up a total stranger?"

"I had met, uh, him at one of the continental breakfasts. I recognized him at the checkout counter at the store. We talked, and he said he had walked down to the store. I offered him a ride. End of story." I kept my eyes riveted to hers and tried not to blink.

I felt her gaze bore into my head. She put the toothpick in her mouth and chewed it. Quietly. Waiting. "What did he buy?"

"I don't know. It's been a year."

She glanced at the tablet. "I couldn't see this person clearly but there is one thing I'm certain of. He handed you a bag and a cup of coffee."

I shifted my gaze to the computer screen. Anger boiled inside of me. "I have no idea what he bought. I can't remember if he had his own sack. I had left my sack on the console, and he handed it to me. Sanchez, my wife died that night, and everything is a blur." I looked back at her; my face flushed with anger. "If you want to ask me any more questions, get a warrant."

Sanchez smiled, shifting the toothpick with a flick of her tongue. "How much of the money do you have left, Dr. Merchant?"

My face blanched. "I'm not answering any more of your questions."

Sanchez leaned across the table, pushing the plates aside to plant her hands in front of her. Strands of her hair had escaped from her ponytail holder and her eyes shone with fervor. "I know you had big debts to pay, Dr. Merchant. I know you have a huge problem with gambling. And I know you are broke. You blew through a half a million dollars in the last year. Now, you either came back here because of your guilty conscience or you've returned to the scene of the crime. Save us all a lot of trouble and just tell me what I want to know."

I clenched my teeth and leaned into her face, my nose almost touching hers. "I did not kill my wife."

Sanchez held my gaze for a moment and then blinked. "Fine. Who would want to kill your wife, then?"

I sat back, keeping my gaze locked on hers. "I don't know. I wasn't aware that my wife had enemies."

"Then why do you think she was murdered?"

"Call it a hunch. An intuition. Something about her death isn't right."

Sanchez relaxed and placed the tablet and folder back into her satchel. "Then you won't mind if I have the body exhumed."

I drew a deep breath. "No."

"Good. You have a new medical examiner in your area. I know their reputation well. They can tell me how your wife died, Dr. Merchant." Sanchez slid out of the booth and stood up. Her gaze shifted to the window. "Of course, since I do not have an official case yet, you'll have to sign a permission slip to have the body removed. Are you willing to do that?"

"Yes." My voice shook with indignation and rage. Or was it fear?

Sanchez looked back at me and smiled as the toothpick wagged up and down. "Then you have nothing to worry about. I'll send the papers to you in a few days. You sign that paper, and I might consider that you didn't kill your wife. You don't sign it and I will come after you, Dr. Merchant." She turned and started toward the door. She paused and glanced back at me. "Oh, thanks for the breakfast." She exited out into the snow filled air.

I shook all over. Gladys came and placed the ticket on the table. I handed her a couple of bills without looking at the ticket. "Keep the change."

She smiled and pocketed the money. "Thanks, sir. That's more than Sanchez ever leaves me."

"How long have you known her?"

The waitress shrugged. "She's been coming here every morning for the last three years. She's a regular."

I wiped sweat from my brow with the napkin. "She a good cop?"

"They have a nickname for her. They call her 'Jaguar', a tenacious hunter." She leaned toward me. "And once she sinks her teeth into anything, she never lets go!"

THE INCOMING SNOWSTORM delayed my flight back to Louisiana by two hours. November storms were notorious, but the early skiers loved it, the airline attendant had told me at the gate. I hugged my backpack to my chest and stared out at the swirling snow billowing around the shrouded shadow of my airplane. Why had I come? Because it was a year? Or because of something else?

My cell chimed with an incoming text. I glanced at the phone number and hesitated before answering. "Yes." I texted.

"Are you OK?"

"No, I'm not." I texted.

"What did the police say?"

"How did you know about Sanchez?"

"I came to the motel to see you and saw you leave with her. I knew you'd be back. It's been a year today."

I paused, staring at my reflection in the window. I guess I was very predictable. "They think I murdered Janice." I texted.

A long pause came before the next reply. "I can vouch for you."

"No! I'm not dragging you into this."

"If you had not been with me, Janice might still be alive." The text said.

"We might both be dead." I replied.

"Jack, let me go to the police."

I wiped sweat from my face and sighed. I typed. "No, give me some time. They're going to exhume Janice's body and then I'll have some answers."

"Promise me that if you get in too deep, you'll let me go to the police. I can clear you."

I sighed, my head pounding, my heart racing. I could not let that happen. I tapped on the phone screen. "I promise. I'll let you know something. Just give me some time."

I waited as the tiny dots oscillated with the reply. "Thank you, Jack. Love you."

I stared at the words and shut off the phone.

THREE

Talako, Louisiana

MY NAME IS JACK MERCHANT. I am a radiologist. No, that isn't someone who fixes radios. And yes, I am an actual doctor. After getting my M.D., I spent five extra years after medical school in radiology residency and another year of fellowship in body imaging and nuclear medicine. I sit around all day and interpret shadows, shades of gray, images produced from the human body with various kinds of radiation or magnetic energy or ultrasound waves. Along with my eight partners, we work in the shadows.

Our group covers three major hospital radiology departments in the Fairmont Medical Center system. The main campus is called Fairmont Central, referred to simply as Central, in downtown Talako, not far from the Choctaw River. Talako is a Choctaw word for eagle.

Fairmont East was the newest hospital on the northeast side of the city in the ritzy part of town. It was built to compete with the oldest and most prestigious of Talako's hospitals, St. Alexander, also called St. Alek. Since it was in stiff competition with the Fairmont hospitals, we called it Smart Alek. In return, physicians at Smart Alek referred to Fairmont East as the Death Star. It would amaze you at the level of vicious competition between the two competing health care systems in a moderate metropolis like Talako. In north central Louisiana, Talako didn't rank with the likes of Dallas or New Orleans or even Shreveport to the west. But, as one native put it, Talako was a great place to visit from. Two universities and the oil industry provided the economic foundation for the city. Of course, oil wasn't the black gold it used to be, so other industries had moved in along the river.

Bayou City sat on the west side of the Choctaw River. Rumor was Fairmont administration planned to build a new hospital in Bayou City to beat Smart Alek to the punch and take business away from the smaller city run Bayou City Medical Center. Bayou City thrived because of its riverboat casinos. That's the other industry I referred to. And, finally, there was General University Hospital-Talako and its associated Institute of Biotechnology south of the interstate in Bayou City. Medical students rotated through GUT, as it was called. The aging hospital sat on the other side of the new Institute from the local private medical school.

My flight returned late on Sunday evening, and I tossed and turned all night as sleep eluded me. I was torn between anger that Sanchez would accuse me of murdering my wife and relief that someone agreed with me she had been murdered. But Sanchez said she had solid evidence. Problem was, other than the hint of an accelerant, the only other evidence was my mysterious passenger, and I knew she had nothing to do with Janice's death. Perhaps the exhumation would yield something new. I could only hope so.

Monday morning came and my rotation that day put me at the main campus of Central, a hodgepodge of old and new buildings shoved together in a dizzying maze of modernism and old medicine. The radiology department took up half of the basement area and one could tell the transition from old to new just by walking through the double doors into our department. On one side of the doors, cool, shiny marble floors reflected soothing wallpaper and expensive paintings for the patients to see. On the other side of the door, old granite tile stained from 50 years of abuse led down a dingy corridor into the department of radiology.

Most people don't realize the importance of radiology. It is the hub of the hospital's diagnostic system. Every patient eventually passes through radiology, sort of like they will one day pass through the morgue. We hope our destination is more desirable. During the pandemic, I came in a side door manned by a no-nonsense nurse. I had left my ID and my white coat in the car that day. Truth be told, I was a bit overhung by an all-nighter at one of the casino riverboats. She stopped me and asked who I was and then enquired if I had any patients in the hospital.

I glared at her. "All patients in the hospital are mine. I am a radiologist and I see anybody and everybody!" I had stormed away down the hallway half expecting security to come haul me back out into the parking lot. Yes, any inpatient could be my next "victim". And there were lots of outpatients, too. I say victim because someone having a radiology procedure usually has to swallow something or have it infused in another orifice or be at the receiving end of a large catheter or needle.

Despite my perceived importance to the care of the hospital's patients, life in radiology is a continual struggle for funds from the hospital and respect from the physicians. Without the power of patient referral, we are at the mercy of the referring physician. All we can offer is service and quality diagnosis. As one internist once told me, "I don't care about service. It all boils down to money." He had just put an ultrasound machine in his office to perform his own studies. In just three months, he sold the machine after his "technician", a secretary who attended a one-week course on performing ultrasound, caused a patient to suffer a fatal stroke when she pushed on his carotid artery a little too firmly.

"Welcome back, Dr. Merchant." A cheery voice echoed behind me. I turned around to see Chloe, one of the nuclear medicine technicians. She was small and wiry with short brown hair, a triathlete. Her most astounding characteristic was her unfailing optimism.

"Hey, Chloe. Busy day?"

"Ah, no. The cardiologists have another camera in their office and that has cut our treadmills in half."

I stopped and swore. "When did they get another camera?"

"Just last week. They hired a dedicated cardiology imaging doctor. I've heard she's good at interpreting heart scans and cardiac MRI." Chloe frowned.

I rubbed my tired eyes. "There goes my job." Each person in my group had an area of the department we oversaw. In the years I had been at Fairmont, I had quadrupled the size of the Nuclear Medicine department. But, now with over half the studies disappearing into the hands of the cardiologists, my area would no doubt started getting cut back. I had taken a week off and my career had imploded.

"Oh no, Dr. Merchant. There are still plenty of nuclear studies." Her bright-eyed smile failed to cheer me up. "You still have the PET/CT scanner to look forward to."

"Let's hope so." If we ever got one. That was another story! Competition had grown between Fairmont and Smart Alex for the newest PET/CT scanner. Right now, the only PET/CT scanner was at the Institute and the load of research scans outnumbered the needed private patient scans. PET/CT scans were the gold standard in looking for cancer response to therapy or cancer recurrence. Whoever received the second scanner in town would get the mother lode of cancer imaging in the region. Right now, cancer patients who could not get a scan at the Institute in a timely fashion had to drive an hour or two to Shreveport for their scans. Their cancers could not wait for a two-month window on scheduling!

I made my way through the doors and paused outside the "reading room." It was here that members of our group sat before large high-definition flat screen monitors reviewing imaging studies from all three hospitals. I drew a deep breath and stepped through. The dark, depressing room occupied the old film storage space. That room had a recessed floor and rolling shelves to sort and hold all the Xray film folders dating back years and years.

When the hospital system had transitioned to digital imaging and PACS reading stations, the department moved the folders to an outside temporary building and renovated this room as our "reading room." That renovation merely comprised of putting a noisy, creaky wooden floor along with some cheap carpet. Walking across the floor sounded like trying to survive a trip across a rickety rope bridge draped over a deadly chasm.

Two of my partners sat on opposite sides of the room. Our main interventionist, Rolly McBride, ran a hand through his dense, red hair as he spoke on the phone. He loved violating any body cavity he could find with a needle and catheter.

"Rounding up business, Rolly?" I said. Rolly smiled and kept talking. He hated an empty procedure list.

Maximillion Wu sat in the other corner. Of Asian descent, he had a Chinese mother and a British father. The man was brilliant in neuroradiology, the study of the imaging of the nervous system. He was currently clutching his chest while looking at two monitors filled with MRI images.

"Morning, Max." I said, going to the center station. Max glanced at me, a look of ecstasy on his face.

"Is not this the most elegant and enchanting sight you have ever laid eyes upon?" He motioned to the MRI. "Our new MRI is astonishing. It rivals a romantic evening with a ravaging woman."

Rolly laughed as he hung up the phone. "Speak for yourself, Max. Pictures produced by a magnet do not compete with last night."

I shuddered. I didn't want to hear about Rolly's latest conquest. A single and very active bachelor, Rolly's escapades were legend.

"We are using a new updated MRI protocol, Jack." Wu's eyes glistened. "Wait until you see the new proton density images. The sagittals through the pituitary are exquisite."

I sighed. "So, what does today look like?" I asked as I sat before my monitors and logged into the PACS system. The procedure list appeared in the information window on the monitor.

"Fourteen interventional cases." Rolly rubbed his hands together. "And one of them is a TIPS, and the other is a Y90."

I recoiled at the thought of sticking a stiff, metal cannula down someone's jugular vein, through their heart, and out into the liver where one would literally rotor-rooter a new channel between the portal vein and the inferior vena cava to relieve the pressure of engorged veins from the scarred, cirrhotic liver. And the Y90 procedure he referred to required the placement of small, serpentine catheters into branches of hepatic arteries so the radiation oncologist could inject radioactive particles into tumors in the liver. It was a tedious and very long procedure with LOTS of radiation to the radiologist, the technologists, and lest we forget, the patient. I performed many low-level interventional procedures. I left the more difficult ones to Rolly and our other interventionist, Dr. Taylor.

"I'm glad you're here, Jack. Like I told Max, when you're here, I don't have to worry about reading the regular stuff." He winked at me and went back to his phone call.

"Max, how many pulses sequences did you add to the current MRI procedure?"

"Only twelve." He raised his eyebrows. "And I can't wait to see them."

Great! That meant these new sequences increased each MRI study from sixteen hundred up to two thousand individual images. It would take Max forever to examine each image! On the one hand, I was glad I had not gotten extra training in neuroradiology because of the extra strain on the brain and the eyes from having to look at so many digital images. On the other hand, I knew that Max's attention to details and minutiae meant I would take up the slack on other studies. That was okay by me, but it meant an endless day. No, a very long week!

AROUND NOON, I slid out the door and headed for lunch. Rolly had finished four of the fourteen cases and I was on call that night. That meant I would stay after 5:30 to finish up the day while the CAT scans and ultrasounds from three busy hospital emergency rooms piled up for the call person until midnight when the rest of the images were offloaded to our Nightrad partners. Each of us had a home station for reading images but, if I was in angio catching up the day's workload, I could not keep up with the ER cases. Relief would come at midnight when we would pass the ER studies, a pot load of

CAT scans and ultrasounds, off to our Nightrad service of radiologist reading from their comfortable beach houses in Tahiti and Europe.

But, until midnight, I would read studies as fast as I could and pray I wouldn't miss something in the barely contained chaos. And yet, most doctors thought we lived the life of a banker coming in at ten and going home at two. I wished.

I picked up a sandwich and a drink from the cafeteria and went off to hide in my secret place. Thirty years prior, the hospital had built the chapel, a small room just off the old part of the hospital. The chapel had six rows of pews separated by an aisle that led up to an altar table and a huge Bible. Stained glass windows let in the bright sunshine. The portrait of a young doctor graced the foyer. The hospital built the chapel in the memory of Dr. Fairmont, the founder of the hospital system. Supposedly, he died at a young age from a brain tumor. As I studied the face of this man, I wondered what he was like living in a time before CAT scans and MRIs. Someday I would like to find out more about him.

I slid into a pew and munched on my sandwich. The chapel held no special significance for me as a center of religion. I used to go to church. Back when Janice and I first married, we attended a local church. But, over the years, my endless nights of call and exhausting schedule destroyed my desire to get up on Sunday morning and sit in a pew. Janice's research at the Institute had become more demanding and she was rarely home at night. And there was the other issue! The weekends became our only time together. I decided God could wait for me. Someday I'd find the time for him.

In the months after Janice's death, I searched for answers to why she had died. If there was a loving God, why had he let her die? I could find no answers from God. And so, without a God to blame, the conviction grew week by week that her death had been no accident. There had to be someone responsible. Right? But why someone would murder her was beyond me for now. Maybe I was being paranoid. Wouldn't be the first time.

A noisy commotion descended on the quiet chapel as a group of people burst through the doors. I turned and watched an entourage of suits walk down the aisle. Leading the pack was Dr. Robert Lamb, chief administrator of the Fairmont Medical Center. Tall and gray-haired, he exuded an air of confidence and leadership that came from many years in the surgery suite. Twenty years ago, he had assumed the position of administrator and had built an imposing medical empire that, for the first time in decades, had passed St. Alek and left it choking in the dust.

Behind Lamb, Murray Washington scribbled on his notepad. Chief administrator of Radiology, he had risen from the position of an Xray tech to the head of the Imaging Department of three hospitals. The stress and strain were telling on him. He seemed anemic and thin; his short, curly black hair now shot through with gray. Behind Murray, Janice's former boss, Dr. Richard Korskin, walked into the room. He wore a perfectly pressed suit, and he had combed and contoured his hair to matching perfection. He smiled at me.

"Is that Jack Merchant?"

Lamb seemed to notice me for the first time. "Dr. Merchant? Are we interrupting you?"

I stood, raking the remnants of my sandwich back into its container. "No, not at all. I was just taking a short break for lunch. This is a quiet place to catch your breath."

Murray looked like he had swallowed a cat. "Dr. Merchant, they're looking for you downstairs. They can't find Dr. McBride or Dr. Wu." He delivered this in a stage whisper so as not to alarm Lamb.

"I'm done, so I'll just run on down." I tried to push past him. But Korskin put a restraining hand on my chest.

"Not so fast, Jack. I haven't seen you since Janice passed away. I would like to extend my condolences." He turned to Lamb. "Dr. Merchant's wife was Dr. Janice Manning. She went by her maiden name. Brilliant geneticist. She chaired our department of nanotechnology over at the Institute." He said the word with such reverence I almost gagged. The Institute of Biotechnology had become an icon in the last decade. Affiliated with the local medical school, the Institute had grown out of a huge monetary donation from a local oil tycoon. It housed different branches of biotechnology, including the only PET scanner affiliated with GUT. Korskin was the head of the department of PET scanning and a professor at the medical school.

Lamb studied me as if he had seen me for the first time. "I didn't know your wife was a doctor?"

"A Ph.D." I stated, growing uneasy about the subject. "Now, I really must be going."

"Wait." Lamb stopped me. "We're here to evaluate this potential space for a new PET scanner. What do you think, Dr. Merchant? Since you are the clinical director of nuclear medicine, you should be interested."

Here was the elephant in the room. The competition I was not supposed to be aware of.

"You mean a PET/CT scanner here? At Fairmont?" I feigned surprise.

I glanced at Murray's tortured features. If Korskin was here, it could mean only one thing. He would run the PET department even though he was an employee of the Institute leaving my radiology group out in the cold. I tried to think of how to best handle this delicate political situation. If Korskin made inroads into Fairmont, what was to keep the rest of his imaging staff from coming over?

"I would be interested. But only if our group is in charge." I said, and Korskin frowned. Before he could say more, I gestured to the room. "I really hate to see the chapel go away. They built it in memory of Dr. Fairmont." I looked at Korskin. "He started the Fairmont clinic fifty years ago. It became what you see today." I glanced back at Lamb. "Thanks to Dr. Lamb's leadership."

Murray's face softened. I had said the right thing.

"I know this chapel is important, Jack." Lamb placed a comforting hand on my shoulder. He had called me Jack. "But we have plans to move the chapel to a location elsewhere in the facility. This room is in the perfect spot for a PET scanner. It is close to outpatient registration and far enough away from vital structures so that the radiation issue wouldn't matter."

"What's wrong with putting it downstairs?" I asked. Murray's face paled, and he shook his head slightly at me.

"It would cost too much money to renovate in the basement. The chapel is next to the street and the cost would be a tenth of what it would be downstairs." Lamb said.

I ignored Murray's warning glances and looked at Korskin. "I guess that means you will be in charge of the scanner, then?"

"To begin with." Korskin answered in an oily voice. "Of course, in time, we could train you and your partners on how to interpret PET scans. And, who knows, one day you may take over."

I looked up at Lamb and frowned. "I already know how to read PET scans. If you'll excuse me, I have work to do." I gently pulled away from Lamb's grasp and exited into the hallway. I heard heavy breathing behind me, and Murray ran around in front of me.

"Do you realize what you just did?"

I closed my eyes. "I don't really care, Murray. Lamb's going to do what he wants no matter what I or Roger says." Roger Montana was the hard line, no-nonsense head of our group.

"Well, let Montana fight this battle. Lamb is after part of the federal grant money the Institute received for PET scanning. It could bring a few million dollars into the system."

I looked him in the eye. "And will any of that money go to help renovate Radiology? Murray, we have three fluoroscopic rooms downstairs and two of them are as old as I am. We need another CAT scanner that can do coronary digital angiography and a second angio room. The last thing we need is to be spending time and energy on a PET scanner to be run by the Institute who would, by the way, take all the income while we supply the technologists."

Murray rubbed his eyes in a tired gesture. "I know. You're right. But you must play the game if you want to get ahead. If I support the PET scanner, Lamb promised at least some of the money to Radiology."

"Talk to Montana." I said as I pushed past him.

"You know what he'll say." His voice sounded pained. Montana's response would be one best not repeated in delicate company.

FOUR

By 5 p.m. that afternoon, Rolly had finished only eleven of the fourteen special procedures. I stepped into the Special Procedures room and looked up at the Board. It contained all the cases for the day.

"What do we have left?" I asked an Xray tech swathed in a blue surgical gown, mask, and gloves.

"We have a triple lumen catheter, a PICC line, and an Uldall left. They need the TLC and the PICC for infusion and they can't wait until tomorrow. And the Uldall patient is in severe renal failure with a dangerously high potassium." She answered. Latoya Williams was our chief special procedures tech. I glanced at the clock on the wall. Thirty minutes until my call started. My phone would go wild.

"What is Rolly doing?" I looked through the lead glass window into the angio suite.

"He's finishing up his TIPS. Anesthesia has already left, and he's just doing his last run of films to make sure it's patent." Latoya answered, stripping off her gloves. "The TLC is on the way down." A TLC was a triple lumen catheter placed in the big jugular vein of the neck. A PICC line was a peripheral vein catheter placed just above the elbow with the tip positioned in the upper part of the heart. The Uldall was a dialysis catheter placed in the jugular vein in the neck. Looked like my evening was a series of pains in the neck!

"And you're sure the Uldall has to be done tonight?"

"Her potassium is almost 8." Latoya uncovered her face. "When is Murray going to get us some help, Dr. Merchant?"

I shrugged. "I don't know. It's not up to us, unfortunately. He says there is a nationwide shortage of techs. Just like there is a shortage of radiologists. You know, a practice our size should have fifteen radiologists and we only have nine."

The phone rang and Latoya closed her eyes, snatching the receiver off the wall. "Angio. This is Latoya. He's right here." She handed me the phone. Had they started already? Maybe the rads at East had gone home early.

"This is Dr. Merchant."

"Hey, man, this is Ron." Ronald Charles was one of my partners. "How are you doing?"

"With three angios left, not so good."

"Well, I have a deal for you. Why don't you let me take call tonight and you can take my Friday call. This has been a tough day for you since it has been a year since Janice passed away. I thought you might want to have a little break from the stress."

I stared at the wall and drew a deep breath. "Ron, thanks. I'll take you up on that offer."

"Good. Tell Latoya I'm on my way from East and I'll be there in 15 minutes." The line went dead. I hung up the receiver and looked over at Latoya.

"Charles is going to take call tonight."

"We'll be out of here in an hour." She smiled. "Hey guys." She stuck her head into the angio room. "Charles is taking call."

I heard a collective whoop of joy. Latoya turned back to me

and frowned. "Sorry. You weren't supposed to hear that. It's just that Charles is so fast."

"I've heard. You call him Turbo Rad." I left the angio suite suddenly devoid of anything to gripe about. I wandered out to my car and slid beneath the steering wheel. Now where was I going to go? I could go back to my one-bedroom apartment, reminding me once again of how I had ruined my finances and had to sell the dream house Janice and I had built. Instead, I went to the one place I could find some temporary solace. I headed for the boats.

PARADISE CAY WAS the only riverboat casino on the Talako side of the Choctaw River. Bayou City boasted two boats on its side of the river. Neptune's Lagoon was the less ritzy of the two Bayou City boats. I rarely went there, preferring the casino with the higher payoff and the higher stakes. After parking in the garage, I walked across the street into the towering Paradise Cay Hotel. The sights and sounds of the casino flooded over me, taking me into a different world. The hotel had spared no expense in putting up Christmas decorations a week before Thanksgiving. An enormous tree towered over the foyer covered with colorful gambling chips, playing cards, and miniature roulette wheels.

I ignored the restaurant and walked across the gangway into the boat. Under Louisiana law, gambling could only take place on the river. While the riverboats floated in the water, they were far from freely roving riverboats. I headed for my favorite area, the slot machines. Before I sat at my favorite machine, I stopped at the bar. A tall, African American man stopped in front of me.

"Evening, Doc."

"Evening, Ben." I slid onto the bench. "I need the usual."

He studied me. "It's been a year."

I was getting irritated. "I didn't know I had sent out a press release."

Ben frowned and turned away to get my drink, a whisky sour. He sat the cold, sparkling glass in front of me. It had been weeks since I had been to the boats. I looked at the liquid beads streaking down the side and the amber fluid within. Time to deaden a few brain cells. Time to quash some unwelcome memories. Five drinks later, I sat at the slot machine down one hundred fifty dollars. My eyes were blurring. I glanced at my watch. Nine o'clock. I really needed to stop and go home because I had to work tomorrow. But I had to give the machine one more pull. Just one more pull.

"Jack?" I heard a familiar voice. I glanced up and focused on a short man in a Talako Police uniform. His dark eyes filled with suspicion as he studied my posture. The last time I had seen him, he had a mullet. Now, his black hair was short and very thin on top.

"I didn't do it." I protested.

Lieutenant Jerry Langley's suspicion lessened, and he finally grinned. "It's been a while since I saw you. How are you doing?"

I motioned to the machine. "I've done better."

He looked down at my empty glass and up at the machine. "How much have you lost?"

"A buck fifty. I didn't know you gambled."

"It's kind of hard to gamble when you're the chairman of the deacon board at Burnside Baptist Church. I'm here on a call. Found a body in the river caught on the paddle wheel of the boat. Could be a homicide or a suicide. We've had two jump from Texas Street bridge in the last month."

I shook my head, contemplating the prospect. "Maybe that's not such a bad idea."

Jerry looked away and wiped his mouth with his hand. I tried to focus on him, and he frowned. He placed a hand on my shoulder. "Look, remember when we were seniors in college?"

I tried to reach through the fog shrouding my brain. "What about it?"

"One night I was pretty wasted, and you were sober. You drove me back to the dorm. I've signed off on the call and turned everything over to Homicide. Why don't I return the favor tonight?"

I pulled the lever one last time. The last of my money was gone. I looked at Jerry. I think he had been at Janice's funeral. "It's been a year, Jerry."

"I know. Come on. I'll drive you back home and my partner can follow us in your car. What do you say?" He gripped my shoulder and for a moment, I felt reassured. Old Jerry. Good old Jerry. I tossed my empty money cup in the trash. "Easy come, easy go. Take me home, Jerry."

JERRY PULLED the cruiser up onto the interstate and I watched the receding lights of the casinos. Tension was heavy in the front seat of his squad car. His partner was following in my car.

"Aren't you going to give me a lecture?" I mumbled.

Jerry was silent. Low level chatter over his radio filled the deafening silence. "Look, Jack, there was a time when you and Janice were close to me and Sally. I understand how busy a doctor can be. And both of you are doctors."

"But?"

"But you just stopped coming to church. You stopped taking our calls. What gives?"

I looked straight ahead and tried to swallow back nausea. "You know why."

"We would have been there for both of you. I know what you went through was bad."

"Bad?" I slurred my words. "You have no idea."

"Jack, I'm sorry. I really am. But what have you accomplished with the gambling? You're throwing your life away. You know Janice wouldn't want you to do this."

"Don't tell me what Janice would have wanted." Instead of a scream, the words came out in a senseless blubber. I wiped my face and drew a deep breath. "You're right. I've got to quit gambling, Jerry. I know I have to."

He was quiet for a moment. "I can help you. You could come talk to Brother Mark."

"No!" I shouted. "I'm sorry. I have little use for God these days. Janice is dead. My life is a shamble. I'm almost broke. How can you believe in God when these things happen?"

Jerry sighed. "I think it's the opposite, Jack. How can you believe in man?"

I turned away from his answer, refusing to consider the possibility of any alternative to my anger. Already, the alcohol was lifting from my brain and a dull ache made its way up my neck. Tomorrow's hangover would be a doozy.

"Jack, you're a doctor. You can't afford to lose control. People's lives depend on you. Just like they depend on me." Jerry said.

"I should have known my good luck was gone, Jerry. I've lost everything."

"Not everything." Jerry said. "I'm still your friend. You still have your job. Unless," he paused, "you've messed that up, too. Grief can do horrible things to you."

Leaning back in the seat of the patrol car, I sighed. "I guess you're right. I've got to go on living. But it is so hard."

I wasn't paying much attention to where we were going until Jerry pulled up into a driveway and stopped. Outside the window sat my old house. Red and white Christmas lights outlined the ceiling and dormers, making it look like a gingerbread house. Huge red bows hung from the gaslights on either side of the double front doors. Glittery red wreaths hung from the doors. Through one of the French doors to the right of the front door, blinking colored lights covered a tall Christmas tree. My heart pounded, and I gasped for breath.

"This is our house." I stuttered, my eyes blurring with tears. "This was our house. Oh, my God. She's gone." Tears flowed from my eyes and my breath came in shuddering sobs.

"What's wrong?" Jerry asked.

I looked at him through tear-filled eyes. "I don't live here, Jerry. I don't live here anymore."

Jerry backed out of the driveway and motioned for his partner to stay behind us. I cried while Jerry drove aimlessly around the neighborhood. The tears stopped, and I was exhausted and wiped snot from my nose. "I had to sell it, Jerry. I lost all the money. I don't know if I can go on without her."

Jerry had been speaking into his radio and must have gotten my new address. We pulled up in front of my apartment complex. "Where's your apartment, Jack?"

I pointed toward the back of the complex and rattled off my number. Jerry pulled up in front of my row of apartments and turned the car off. He turned in his seat to look at me and took a card out of his pocket.

"Jack, I want you to promise me you won't try anything stupid. If you need to talk, call me." He handed me the card. "I mean it. Any time, day or night."

I studied the card. "How can you care about me, Jerry? We haven't been close in so long."

Jerry patted my shoulder. "Friends forever, remember? In high school, we promised we'd be friends forever."

I smiled. I remembered the picture in our high school yearbook and his inscription. When we graduated from college, we had recreated the picture and signed the same inscription. "Take it easy, greasy. We've got a long way to slide! Friends, forever!"

"Friends forever." I looked at him. "I'm sorry. I didn't ask how you and Sally were doing." I swallowed hard and said it. "How the kids are."

"They're fine, Jack. We're fine." He gripped my shoulder. "And you are going to be fine. Go to bed. Get up tomorrow and try to have a good day. Put the past behind you. And promise me you'll get some help."

I grabbed his hand like a drowning man losing his last grip. "I promise, Jerry. I promise."

I got out of his car and his partner parked beside us and handed me my car keys. Jerry's partner climbed into the front seat of the cruiser, and they drove off into the still, cool night. I went upstairs to my private hell.

FIVE

The next Monday I walked into the reading room at Central after working my butt off the week before. Friday night's call had been one call after another, and I had spent most of Saturday in bed recovering from the night call. The only good thing was I had survived my hangover and had stayed away from the booze and the boats for the rest of the week. Not to mention the stress of work had kept my mind off the trip to Colorado Springs. My late wife. And Sanchez. And the text message at the airport. It was Thanksgiving week, which meant I had Thursday off and we were only half-staff on Friday. I had taken my holiday call over Memorial Day weekend and Labor Day weekend. I should have taken Thanksgiving as my holiday. I had no family to spend it with and nothing to be thankful for. My partners had much to be grateful for.

Wu and McBride were gone. This week I would work with Roger Montana, head of our group, and Moondog Taylor. Yeah, his name was Moondog. We called him Dog, and he came from southern California. He still wore his long, blonde hair in a ponytail, and he was the only radiologist in the group with body piercings. But, beneath his "Hey, dude." demeanor, he was a hard-working radiologist with the quickest acumen I had ever seen. And he had training in interventional radiology.

Montana, on the other hand, was laid back and quiet. He was a tall Texan with short, curly salt and pepper hair. He wore cowboy boots and jeans to work. Currently, he was kicked back in his chair with his boots propped up on my console, reading a radiology journal.

Moondog was shifting from foot to foot while studying one of Wu's MRI's. He had his reading desk elevated so he could stand. The man never sat still! "I'm telling you, man, this chick has pseudotumor cerebri. You can see the flattening of the posterior eye globe. And look, you can see fluid all the way down the optic tracks."

Montana shifted his gaze up to me. "Dog is convinced she has PC. I think it's MS." He tapped his book. "I'll find that article with the images."

"Good morning to you, too. You might try Google." I said.

Montana gave me "the look" and if his eyes had been lasers, I'd have holes bored through my head. The man was almost a Luddite in his hatred of advanced technology.

Shaking it off, I stepped up behind Moondog. "You shouldn't argue with the boss man, Dog."

"I'm telling you I'm right. Look, she even has herniation of the optic chiasma into an empty sella. Tell him, Jack. I'm right. I'm always right."

Problem is, he was always right. "I think you'd better give up, Roger. I think Dog is right."

Montana slammed the journal closed and tossed it across the room. It slid across a counter and came to rest up against a pile of old journals. "I hate it when he's right."

A man stepped through the doorway into the reading room, and he paused. He was of medium height, dressed in maroon scrubs. His head was totally bald. He had two cups of coffee in his hands.

"Is this a bad time?" He asked.

"No. You got our coffee?" Montana said gruffly.

"Yes, sir." He said, bringing a cup of coffee to Montana. He carried the other cup to Moondog. "Would you like a cup, Dr. Merchant? It's fresh."

"Yeah. Two creams and three yellows."

The man left the room. "What was that all about?"

"One of the transport guys. Came in here and offered to bring us coffee." Montana sipped his cup.

"They don't make them like that anymore." Moondog picked up his microphone to dictate the MRI report. Our voice recognition software would render his dictation into a final report for the ordering physician. "Dudes don't give us any respect anymore."

The door burst opened, and Murray rushed into the room. His face was red with anger. "Merchant, I hope you're satisfied."

I turned around and watched him open and close his fists in anger. "I just wanted a cup of coffee."

He ignored my comment. "You made a fool out of this department last week in front of Lamb and Korskin. You can kiss any new equipment purchases goodbye. Just because you guys wanted to keep the PET scanner in your little group doesn't mean you have to jeopardize our chances of growing the department."

Montana stood up slowly and towered over Murray. "I had dinner with Lamb Saturday night. I convinced him to hold off on the PET scanner for now. He doesn't want any money going out of the hospital. Korskin wants Fairmont to renovate the chapel, pay for installing the machine and then let Korskin's group collect all the money for the exams. Fairmont would get nothing out of the deal but would pay for the whole thing except for the scanner itself. Federal grant money is paying for that. But the cost of the machine is a onetime deal. Maintaining the facility and losing money isn't very attractive to Fairmont. So, Lamb agrees with us. No scanner unless we have total control."

Murray blinked. "Korskin didn't tell me that."

"Of course not. Murray, you don't trust us to help you out with these things."

Murray sighed. "I try not to drag you into the administrative cesspool. I know how you feel about the politics. And you have problems with your temper."

"You know what he would say." I interrupted. Montana glared at me. "Face it, Roger, when you're upset, sailors around the world are blushing."

Montana swore. I blushed. He turned to his satchel, reached in, and took out two sheets of paper. He slapped them down on the counter. "Here. A signed purchase order for a second CAT scanner. And a signed purchase order for a second angio room."

Murray's eyes bulged and his mouth fell open. "How did you?"

"Like I said, Murray, let us help you. Next time you want to buy some equipment, come to us first." He turned back to his seat, sat down, and nonchalantly put his boots back up on the console.

Murray grinned. "I can't believe this." Behind him, the transport guy came into the room carrying my cup of coffee.

"Here you go, doc."

I took the cup and sipped it. Tasted fine. "That's just right. Thanks." I glanced down at his shoes as I took another sip. Odd. Most health care personnel wore tennis shoes or walking shoes. His huge, clumsy boots reminding me of combat boots.

And he had been kind enough to bring us coffee. He had to be new. Once his feet hurt, he would get rid of the combat boots. And, once Murray got through with him, he would no longer be kind. The transport guy left the room. Murray never noticed, even though he was the guy's boss. His smile slowly faded as he studied the papers.

"What's wrong, dude?" Moondog asked.

"Now that we're going to get a new room and new scanner, I've got to find personnel to staff them. Do you realize how hard it is to find good techs nowadays? Where am I going to find more people to make this work?" Murray shook his head and mumbled to himself as he left the room. "Not enough FTEs!"

"He'll never be happy." Montana commented as he sat forward and scrutinized a set of CAT scan images on his monitors. I finished the coffee and tossed the cup in the trash can.

"If it's not one problem, he'll invent another."

Moondog finished dictating his MRI report. "It will be nice to have two angio rooms. After all, the cardiologists have six new cath labs upstairs."

"They also have control of the patients." Montana commented. "We don't have any political pull."

I sat in my chair and belched. The coffee wasn't going down well. "How did you pull it off?" I loaded a set of ultrasound images on the monitor.

"Impression: Unremarkable CT examination of the brain." Montana finished dictating and placed his microphone on the counter. "I told him what was good for Fairmont was good for us. And what was good for us was good for Fairmont. I also told him an orthopedic group was putting in an imaging center out by Fairmont East. And reminded him we were three weeks behind on scheduling outpatient CAT scans and MRIs. I pointed out if we didn't add a CAT scanner and a second MRI, we would lose those patients to the ortho group who have contracted with the radiologists at Smart Alec for interpretation. I also said we could use a second angio room and let him know it would be cheaper than an MRI. He went for the angio room and signed the purchase order and said he'd wait on the MRI." Montana smiled, a rare sight. "We really don't need a new MRI."

"You gotta know how to play the game!" Moondog laughed. "Good work, man."

My stomach churned with the acidic coffee. "Unbelievable."

Montana grinned. "The two bottles of wine helped."

Lydia, the main receptionist from the front desk, stepped into the room. "Dr. Merchant? I hate to tell you this, but there is a sheriff outside with a certified letter for you."

My stomach did a flip-flop. A certified letter meant I was being sued for malpractice or subpoenaed to testify in court. I didn't like either option. "Great! And things were going so well."

I stepped out into the hall, and the first pain hit me. It started in my right flank, over my kidney, and radiated down into my groin. I almost doubled over. I drew a deep breath and leaned against the wall. The sheriff saw me and ignored my distress.

"Are you Dr. Jack Merchant?"

"Yes." I managed through suddenly trembling lips. What was happening?

The sheriff shoved the letter into my hands and walked away. The pain hit again. It had to be a kidney stone. I'd had two attacks in the past, but it had been years. I stumbled across the hall into the waiting room and leaned against the counter at the front desk.

"Get Montana." I managed through trembling lips. Lydia's eyes grew wide, and she hurried to the reading room. It is a sad commentary on the state of medical malpractice that the crippling pain I was suffering didn't deter me from ripping open the letter. I pulled out a sheet of paper. It was the release form for the exhumation of my dead wife. The third pain doubled me over and I fell backward onto the floor. Montana's face hovered over me.

"Jack?"

"Kidney stone." I managed.

He picked me up and walked me into the CAT scan room. He put up the "hand" to the CAT scan techs to get the current patient out of the room. The "hand" was a frequent ploy used by Montana. Whenever he didn't want to talk to someone, he merely had to put up his hand and that person would meekly go away.

"Jack, we're going to scan you and I'll give you some contrast, so if you have a stone, it will wash out your kidneys." Montana said. I was in too much pain to respond.

"Dude, I'll call one of the ER doctors and we'll get you registered with them." I heard Dog's voice through a cacophony of pain.

"Get me an IV kit and some contrast." Montana barked. Techs scurried. "Get Jean in here." Jean was our no-nonsense Marine sergeant of a head technologist. She burst into the room, eyes wide. Montana grabbed an IV canula from a tech. "Jack's having a kidney stone. Call back to Specials and get the nurse to bring some pain medication, Vitamin D!"

I barely felt the pain of the needle stab in my arm, the pain in my side was so intense. Vitamin D was coming, our euphemism for our preferred pain medication, dilaudid. Nausea hit me, but I only retched. The coffee didn't come back up. Another tech appeared, carrying a syringe of contrast. "Sir, do you want a scan first without contrast?" I'm a radiologist through and through and I answered the question for Montana.

"We'll see the stone even with contrast." I said. "Just get on with it."

Montana hooked the syringe to my IV site. I felt the cool caress of the contrast as it flowed up the veins in my arm. It coursed into my chest and I immediately started having trouble breathing. Heat exploded across my lungs, and I gasped for breath. Sweat poured from my skin. I looked at Montana.

"I can't breathe!" I gasped.

"He's having a reaction to the contrast. Get the crash cart!" Montana shouted.

Montana slowly receded down a long, dark tunnel. The mayhem and noise around me ceased. Confusion. Near the ceiling. Looking down. Montana. Dog. Jacobs from the ER. Going now. Out, out. Through the ceiling. Past an ICU bed. An empty hallway. An empty room. Out the window. Red shoe. Red shoe? Sky blue. Tunnel of light. Coursing, swirling. No pain, now. Light everywhere.

The man stood before me, bearded, his long hair surrounded by a halo of light. He looked amused. He turned and glanced at another figure, Janice in a flowing white gown.

"Hello, my love. It happened on Mickey's birthday. Go back now. Stop him." She motioned me away with a wave of her hand and something jerked me, pulled me like a towel being wrung of moisture and I was back in the noise, the confusion, the pain. I had gotten my unconscious wish. I had died.

SIX

"Why are you still here?"

I faced a wall made of glowing rock. It gave off a faint blue glow. The voice had come from behind me.

"Janice?" I said.

"Don't turn around. Face the wall, dear." She said.

"What is happening?"

"It's not your time. This wasn't what you think it was. You must go back." She said behind me. Light and shadows of colors I did not know existed moved across the wall. "Was that Him?"

"Yes." She said. "If you turn around and see Him, you will never want to leave."

"You're here. That is enough for me to want to stay." I said.

I felt pressure on my back. It wasn't exactly a touch, but it felt like she was moving her hands along the muscles of my shoulders and upper back. How I missed that! "You can't. You must find the truth." She said.

"I love you." I said. "I screwed up my life."

"I love you, too, Jack. It's time for you to go."

The pressure lessened and colors appeared on the wall before me and swirled in a hypnotic pattern, and I was falling slowly. Falling and falling, but there was no fear, no anxiety, only tranquility. As I fell, I wasn't aware of the passage of time. It was like when you are on the verge of a dream and then you wake up only to discover you were never asleep. And then that becomes the dream. There were harsher lights and more strident sounds and the deep rhythm of someone's heartbeat.

I OPENED MY EYES. The face of a woman came into view. Dark skin. Dark hair cascading around her face. Warm brown eyes. A smile that lit up the cosmos.

"Hey, are you with me for real this time?" She said.

I blinked in the bright light. My heart raced. It was her! "Am I dead?"

"They say you were for a while. But right now, I think you're very much alive." She smiled, and I realized how impossibly wrong this had to be. I tried to sit up and felt a profound weakness in all my limbs. "Glasses?" She handed me my glasses. I put them on and she came into clearer focus. It was still her! "What are you doing here?"

"Someone had to come check on you."

"You came from Colorado?" I glanced around the hospital room. "You're not supposed to travel. Someone might see you."

"There's no one here who would have the slightest interest in me." She said.

"No, no, no! You must leave. Now!"

"Jack, you've been out since Monday. Today's Wednesday. I texted you on Monday and when you didn't answer, I called your phone."

"You're not supposed to call me!" I wanted to scream, but my voice was too weak.

She smiled. "Jack, calm down. When I called someone named Dog told me you were in a coma from a contrast reaction. What was I supposed to do? Nothing? So, I came in yesterday afternoon on one of those direct flights with Legioncy. They have three a day to Denver." She sat in a chair next to the bed and put her hand on mine. I pulled away, but realized just how comforting her touch was. I really missed it! "Jack, you have no one. It's Thanksgiving week."

"You can't stay here. It's too dangerous." I whispered.

She looked around the room. "No surveillance cameras." She picked up a surgical mask. "I had this on coming in. People are still wearing masks even after the pandemic. Every time someone comes in the room, I put it on."

I closed my eyes and tried to calm my nerves. I had been asleep for almost two days? I had a contrast reaction and almost died? My mind raced, trying to process everything. What was that weird dream with Janice? Did I see a bit of heaven? And *she* was here?

Someone knocked on the door. "Mask!" I said.

She put on the mask. "I'll just wait in the bathroom." She hopped up from the chair and ran to the bathroom.

The door to my hospital room opened and Detective Sanchez peeked in. Sanchez? How did she know how to make these timely entrances? I slumped back onto the bed. "Not you!"

"Dr. Merchant?" She asked as she slid into the room and closed the door behind her. I got the distinct impression she had just violated a 'No Visitor' sign.

"You're the last person I ever expected to see. Don't tell me you flew down here from Colorado because you wanted to bring me flowers."

"Three nonstop flights a day to Denver. Ski season. You really like snow skiing in Louisiana, don't you? The flights are cheap. You have to pay for the peanuts. They're not comple-mentary." She walked over to my bed. Her hair was down around her shoulders and not up in its usual ponytail. "It's been almost a week since I sent you the release to sign. I told you I would come find you. Where is it?"

I squinted at her. "You came to Louisiana to pick up a release? No wonder they call you Jaguar."

Her face reddened, and she gritted her teeth. "Okay, so I'm tenacious. Where is it, Merchant?"

"I don't know. I'm recovering from near death. Give me a break. Look, Monday they delivered the letter just as I was trying to pass a kidney stone."

"They were supposed to deliver it Friday." She crossed her arms over her leather jacket. "If you want something done right, you got to do it yourself." She glanced at the bathroom. "Who is in your bathroom?"

Before I could answer, she appeared through the partially open door. "Hi."

Sanchez raised an eyebrow and glanced at me. "Well, it has been a year. Can't say I blame you for moving on." Sanchez offered her hand. "Hi. I'm Detective Sanchez. Colorado Springs Police Department. And you are?"

She glanced at me and managed a weak smile. "Keri. Keri Merchant. I'm Jack's stepsister." She shook Sanchez's hand.

Sanchez looked at me and then back at "Keri." "You're his stepsister? You don't exactly have the same, well, external appearance."

Keri nodded unconvincingly. I sat up weakly in the bed and tried to tell Sanchez something truthful. "My father left shortly after I was born, and my mother remarried." I licked my lips. "Uh, Keri and I had the same father. Different mothers." Or, should it have been the other way around?

Sanchez nodded. She scrunched up her lips and raised an eyebrow. "Where are you from, Keri?"

Keri looked at me. "New Orleans."

"You don't sound Cajun." Sanchez tilted her head.

I tapped Sanchez on the arm, and she looked at me. "How would you know what Cajun sounds like?"

"I just got through talking to one of your partners downstairs. Sonny Robicheaux. Said he's from LaPlace, Louisiana. Is he married?"

I nodded. "Got two kids."

Sanchez swore under her breath. "I just love that accent."

"I've only lived in New Orleans for a few months. You won't even find my name in the phone book." Keri said.

"Phonebook? There are no phone books anymore." Sanchez pulled her phone out of her pocket and studied it. "But you might be on the internet."

"Sanchez!" I said out loud. "Stop interrogating everyone."

"Don't you want to find out who killed your wife?" She glanced back at Keri. "If you are telling me the truth, I wouldn't worry. But if you are hiding a romantic interest in Dr. Jack Merchant, beware. His last true love burned to death."

Keri's eyes widened. "What? How dare you! What kind of witch are you?"

Sanchez was unfazed. "The kind that tries to protect women in dangerous relationships, innocent or not."

"Are you accusing Jack of murder?" Someone said as he entered the room. My urologist, Dr. Bolaski, came in and was a welcome interruption. He had taken care of my two previous kidney stone attacks. His knobby skull had pushed its way through his graying hair a long time ago. He wore thick glasses that made his eyes look twice their normal size and his piercing gaze was directed at Sanchez. "Are you the cop that's been bugging everybody?"

"Yeah. What of it?"

Bolaski motioned toward the door. "The sign says 'no visitors'. Get out or I'll call security."

Sanchez laughed. "You mean Barney downstairs? I'm shaking in my boots." She pointed a finger at me like a gun. "You haven't seen the last of me, Merchant." She left.

Bolaski shook his head. "She's been hovering like a vulture since yesterday. Where did she come from?"

"Colorado. Long story. She is looking into a, well, suspicious death."

"Crazy! Look, I'm glad you're awake. How are you feeling?"

"I don't know yet." I relaxed back into the bed, ready to put Sanchez behind us. "I just woke up." I glanced at Keri. "Keri said I've been out since Monday."

"Keri?" Bolaski glanced at her. "I thought you said your name was Leanne?"

Keri stiffened and looked helplessly at me. I shrugged, and she took her time pulling off her mask. "Well, you see, Keri is my middle name and everyone who knows me calls me that." She said weakly. She cleared her throat. "You know how it is to have a middle name everyone calls you by? But every legal document has my first name. That's how I know a call is spam. They call me by my first name, Leanne." She nodded, as if trying to convince herself. "Yeah, Leanne and I hang up."

"I can't believe I've been out all this time." I interrupted the awkward pause. Bolaski shrugged and turned his attention back to me.

"You had your reaction on Monday. Today's Wednesday. The reaction was pretty bad. Montana insisted on putting you in ICU where you got better monitoring. Your vitals got better yesterday, so we moved you out to the floor." He frowned for a moment. "I will not lie to you, Jack. You must have had a whopper of a bender recently. That reaction almost sent you into liver failure. The CT showed fatty infiltration of the liver. What's up with that?"

"It's been a year since Janice died." I mumbled.

"Oh!" He averted his gaze to the computer tablet he hastily pulled from his pocket. "Okay, so, uh, latest lab is all clear. Your liver functions are getting back to normal. You need to make sure you never get iodinated contrast again."

"Don't worry. I'm a radiologist. We ask every patient if they've had a reaction before we give contrast. What about my kidney stone?"

Bolaski looked up from the tablet. "Couldn't find one. You probably passed it after the reaction. We gave you a pot load of saline to bring your blood pressure back to normal. I think we flushed the stone right out of your bladder."

"Heck of a way to cure me of a kidney stone. Can I go back to work?"

"Roger said 'no'. Told me to tell you that you owed Dupuis a week." Renee Dupuis was another one of my partners, a life loving woman from Lyon, France. This was supposed to be her week off. I would owe a lot of people a lot of payback. Fortunately, tomorrow was Thanksgiving. I was looking forward to a quiet day with nothing to do but sleep.

"So, what's next?"

"If you're up to it and you walk around between now and this afternoon, I'll let you go around 5."

"Great."

Bolaski reached out and patted me on the shoulder. "Take it easy but try to move around some. We don't want you to get blood clots in your legs." He left. I exhaled a huge breath and turned to Keri.

"My stepsister?"

"It's the best I could come up with in a pinch." Keri, said.

"Leanne?" I tried to hide a smile. "You named the dog Leanne."

Keri looked away. "I had to put Leanne down last year."

I drew a deep breath. "Sorry." I watched her face soften, watched her eyes glow in the room's semidarkness. "You've got to go back. Sanchez has seen you. It won't take her long to snoop around."

Keri stood up. "If we get you to your apartment this evening, then I'll go back on Friday. I don't want you to spend Thanksgiving alone. Now, I really need the lady's room." She crossed to the bathroom and disappeared inside. The door to my room opened. Richard Korskin hurried in and pushed the door closed behind him. Did everyone ignore the "No Visitors" sign? He wore his white doctor's coat. With a doctor's coat on, very few people questioned where you went.

"Dr. Merchant, I heard you were awake. I know I'm not supposed to be here, but I had to speak with you as soon as I could. They said you were awake." He wore an expensively tailored suit with a red silk tie. He glanced around the room as if making sure no one was listening.

I rolled my eyes. "How did you 'hear' I was awake?"

Korskin smiled. "Let's just say I asked one of your nurses to let me know when you woke up. Don't tell anyone. Wouldn't want to get him fired."

"I'm going home this afternoon. You can call me on Friday."

"Well, it's kind of timely I talk to you now. I have been wanting to talk to you ever since Dr. Montana convinced Lamb not to go through with the PET scanner."

I pushed my way up in the bed. "Dr. Korskin, I'm in a hospital bed. I had a near fatal contrast reaction, and I'd rather not talk about this."

Korskin ignored my remarks. "There is a very large federal

grant the Institute can get if we install another PET scanner in town."

I closed my eyes and sighed. "Dr. Korskin."

"Please call me Dick." He smiled. Really?

"Look, Dick, you backed Lamb into a corner. You want the hospital to build you the facility but not get any of the revenue. You can't expect him to go for that."

Korskin's smile faded. "I have a new proposal. I'm willing to pay you to leave your practice and assume the head of the Fairmont PET Scanner. Your expertise is in nuclear medicine. You told me you already knew how to interpret PET scans. It would be an acceptable compromise."

For a second, the offer seemed very attractive. "Except for the fact I'm not leaving my group."

Korskin rubbed his temples and wore a pained expression. "At least think about it. Please." He reached into his coat pocket and took out an envelope. "Here is my proposal. Look at it and give me an answer no later than next Monday. I have special plans to make, and I need an answer soon." He started toward the door and paused. "Oh, and I'm glad you're better." His smile was strange, almost a leer. What was that about? He left the room.

I tossed the envelope in the trash can and looked across the room at the bathroom. Keri had the door cracked open. She looked out and her eyes were wide in shock. "Is he gone?"

"Yeah. What's wrong?"

She slowly left the bathroom, her eyes riveted to the door. "I recognized his voice, Jack. But he doesn't quite look like him."

"From before?"

Her eyes were wide with fear. "Yes. He was one of *them*, Jack. I know it. He was one of them!"

"You said you didn't recognize his face."

"I didn't have that good of a look at him then. But the voice, Jack. I'll never forget that voice." She shivered.

I sat up on the side of the bed. "That settles it. You're leaving now."

Keri shook her head and her lips trembled. "But he's still out there. Somewhere."

I stood shakily and held onto my IV pole. I started for the door.

"Where are you going?" Keri asked.

"To get you out of here. Bolaski said to walk, so I'm walking." I eased out into the hallway. I was on a circular wing, and I knew there was a corridor that led across the circle behind the nurse's station. When no one was looking, I started down the corridor, searching for the utility cart. It was just off the hallway and held all kinds of supplies. I grabbed some gauze and a hospital gown and robe. Dizziness gripped me, and I leaned against the wall.

"Dr. Merchant?" I almost fell. I tucked the supplies under my robe and turned. A nurse stood behind me.

"I thought I could walk around the circle but decided to cut across. But I don't think I can make it right now. Will you take me back to my room?"

She nodded. "Of course." She didn't want to have to write up an incident report if I passed out on her. She led me back to my room, and I closed the door behind me. Keri sat on my bed, and I handed her the gown.

"Put this on, then put your clothes in one of those plastic bags. Then we're going to wrap your face up like you've had brain surgery. If Korskin is still around, he won't give you a second look."

My strength returned when I sat down on the bed. Keri went back into the bathroom. She emerged dressed in a hospital gown and sat in the chair beside the bed. I took the bandages and wound them around her hair.

"Sorry to mess up your hair, but this is necessary."

"I'm so sorry, Jack. I did not know he would be here. It's been so long, but I'm sure of that voice. You are right. I never should have come."

I looked into her frightened eyes. "How could you have known he would be here? I will get you safely out of here." After I turned Keri into a mummy and she put the mask on, we walked down the hall to the elevator. Just two patients helping each other along. A man appeared from a connecting hallway. Korskin studied a small tablet in his hands and almost ran into me. He glanced up with a look of shock on his face. He tucked the tablet quickly behind him.

"Jack? Oh, good. You're up and about." He cleared his throat and averted his gaze. He held the tablet behind his back. "Don't forget to give that proposal a once over." Korskin patted me on the shoulder with a lame smile. He glanced once at Keri's face swathed in bandages. "Are you okay, ma'am?"

"She's a friend who had surgery. We're walking together to get our strength back." I said.

"Well, that's nice. He palmed the tablet and tucked it into the pocket of his white coat. He hesitated and nodded towards us once more before hurrying to the elevator. Keri's grip tightened on my arm. I held her motionless until Korskin disappeared into the elevator and doors closed.

"He keeps popping up!" Keri said. "You're right, Jack. I am more convinced than ever after hearing that voice close up. He changed his appearance, but it is him. Get me out of here before he shows up again."

I pointed to an exit sign, and we moved into a short hallway off the waiting room. "That's a stairway used only by employees. Korskin won't know about it. Head downstairs and get out of here. You need to make the call."

Keri paused as she unraveled the bandages. "That will be a problem. I'm not supposed to be here. You know what they will do to me if they find out."

I drew a deep breath. "Then you need to go back to Colorado. Tonight on the last flight out."

"Not until I'm sure you're going to be okay. What about Sanchez? Can you get her to look into Korskin? See if he is who we think he is?" Keri gripped my arm.

"Sanchez has tunnel vision." I said. "But there is my friend with the police department, Jerry. I could talk to him." I stepped closer and took her by the shoulders and looked into her eyes. "And you need to go back to Colorado until this is all over."

"What about tomorrow? It's Thanksgiving." She said.

"I'll be fine. I'll sleep all day, okay? Korskin might see you, so I can't take that risk. Go home. Please."

Keri frowned. "Okay, if you insist. But text me the minute you know something." She leaned closer to me and kissed me on the cheek. "Take care."

My heart sank within me. So many wasted years. So many missed opportunities. But I couldn't change the past. I gave her hand one squeeze, and she disappeared down the stairs. As I made my way back to my room, I tried to take my advice. Korskin was Janice's boss, and now, I knew he had a shady past. I couldn't change the past. Janice was gone. But I was convinced more than ever that Janice had been murdered. If I got out of the hospital tonight, I was going to pay Jerry Langley a visit on Friday.

SEVEN

Someone knocked on my door. I woke with a jerk and focused on the television. A football game was raging, and I had fallen asleep. I sat forward and glanced at the bowl of popcorn.

"Some Thanksgiving feast." I mumbled. I went to the door and glanced through my peephole. Could it be Keri? Had she stayed? For a moment, I hoped so.

Roger Montana and his wife Debra stood outside my apartment door. I jerked the door open. "What are you two doing here?"

Montana held a paper bag in each hand. "It was Debra's idea." He pushed past me into my apartment. Debra was tall and athletically thin, with a winsome smile and bushy salt and pepper hair. Before she met and married Montana, she had been in charge of the radiology department at Fairmont Central. She had left a stressful job behind. She leaned forward and kissed me on the cheek.

"Jack Merchant, you have gotten skinny since I last saw you." She took my arm and turned me back toward the living room.

"What is going on?" I managed.

"Well, Roger and I are on the way over to my son's house for Thanksgiving dinner and I told him we couldn't just let you starve on Thanksgiving Day." She moved into the kitchen and raised an eyebrow. Or two. "Well, is your dishwasher broken?"

I sat weakly on the couch. "No. I've been in the hospital."

Debra wore a long denim coat. She pulled it off and draped it on one of my two kitchen table chairs. "Well, the least I can do is load up your dishwasher. Roger, put the food on the table." She turned and studied my small kitchen table tucked into a tiny nook off the kitchen. "But clear it off first."

"Look, you two have better things to do." I said.

Montana sat the two bags on the coffee table and glanced at the television. "Like watching the Saints game!" He gave the back of Debra's head "the look".

"I saw that." Debra said brightly as she rinsed dishes and loaded the dishwasher. "Kitchen table. Clean. Now."

Debra Montana was the only person in the world who could tell Roger Montana what to do. She tossed a wet sponge over her shoulder, and he caught it. Montana cleared dirty dishes off the table and handed them to Debra and then sponged down the tabletop. I sat on the couch uncomfortable and, frankly, stunned.

"You didn't have to do this." I said.

Montana finished with the table and retrieved the bags. "I know. I should let you starve for a couple of days."

"What?" My face blanched.

"Roger!" Debra said over her shoulder.

Montana unloaded several containers of food. He was right. I had screwed up. My stomach rumbled. The fragrances of smoked meat and fresh bread made my stomach rumble. Montana brushed his hands and turned to study me with his impenetrable gaze. "I shot the pheasant myself. Marinated in my special sauce and baked with root vegetables. Debra made the rolls from scratch."

"And a small, sweet potato pie." She rinsed her hands and closed the dishwasher. She turned and smiled at me. "What Roger was trying to say a minute ago in his 'Roger' way is, Jack, you've got to get your act together." She moved over to the couch and sat beside me. "I know you lost everything to gambling. I know you're in a bad place, Jack. But do you remember what I told you when you joined the group right before I married Roger?"

I swallowed hard. "Yes." I looked into her intense brown eyes. "You said I was too good to pass up. An asset to the group. I wished that were still true."

"That's right. Roger," she motioned to him with her head, "didn't see it at first. He was going to let you go after the first year because the group was over staffed, but you proved your worth. You're a good radiologist, Jack."

I nodded and felt the tears in the back of my eyes. I had to keep them there. "It's been a year since Janice died. A rough year."

Montana crossed his arms and leaned against the table. "When I lost Barb to lymphoma, I had to start over, Jack. Debra helped me through it. She's smart. Too smart for the likes of us. I'd listen to her if I were you." His gaze fixed on me and for the first time, I saw something warm and caring in that gaze. "I've been where you are, Jack. I got through it and so will you. Find something else besides gambling to focus on beside your grief. Time will heal, but our group needs you at your best."

Debra reached across and slapped his arm. "That's not what you said you would tell him."

Montana flinched. "Okay, *I* need you in the group. You're too good of a radiologist. You're a hard worker. You were reliable."

"And I will be reliable again." I mumbled. Debra squeezed my arm.

"Okay, Roger, we got to get going." Debra stood and looked once at the television. "The Cowboys are going to win, you know."

"Nope!" Montana stood up. He started for the door.

Debra followed him. "How much did you bet?"

He paused at the door and glared at her. "More than you did."

I stood up and smiled. "And the two of you got onto me for gambling."

Debra raised an eyebrow. "I give my winnings to the church. And I will win! Happy Thanksgiving, Jack."

"Happy Thanksgiving. And thanks." I said.

Montana nodded toward me, and they closed the door behind them.

EIGHT

I ate the food from Roger and Debra and enjoyed every bite. Debra was right. The Cowboys won. More money for her church. I slept most of the afternoon and was in bed by eight. I never heard from Keri. Good! I hoped she had made it safely back to Colorado. Now I had to find Jerry and get him to investigate Korskin.

I still felt weak Friday morning, and a call to the police department led me to the medical examiner's office. Jerry was supposed to be there. And I wanted to talk to the coroner about exhuming my wife's body. Maybe that would satisfy Sanchez.

Francisco Labs occupied an old, renovated warehouse off Grim Drive not a mile from the casino district. Grim Drive was an apt name for the location of the medical examiner's office! I pulled into the parking lot in front of the drab exterior and stumbled as I got out of my car. A wave of vertigo made my head swim for a second. Orthostatic hypotension. Still dehydrated, maybe? I stood up too quickly. Maybe I should have stayed in for one more day. But the weekend was coming, and I was doubtful I could find Jerry over the weekend.

My breath steamed as I gasped and tried to steady my heart rate. The morning was chilly, with a hint of frost still covering the ground in the shadows of the ancient building. I drew a deep, strengthening breath and stopped in front of the glass doorway. Yes, the man looking back at me should have stayed at home.

I went in through the glass door into a waiting room with shag carpet and wood paneling. They may have renovated the exterior, but the interior was right out of the 1970s. A receptionist sat behind a counter talking into a Bluetooth earpiece, the only sign we were in the twenty-first century. She had short, dark hair and a pinched look on her face. She wore a pink sweater with Rudolph the red-nosed reindeer on the front. The red nose flashed.

"No, Alyssa, I told you I would not fight the Black Friday crowd. I do all my shopping online. Now, about that autopsy form you were supposed to fill out." She nattered on and I studied the office. A pink frosted Christmas tree stood in the office's corner and a matching pink wreath hung behind the reception desk. I stood in front of the counter until she could ignore me no longer. I resisted the urge to grip the edge of the faux marble top to keep from staggering back and falling into the shag carpet.

"May I help you?" She asked as she finally made eye contact.

"My name is Dr. Jack Merchant from Fairmont Medical Center. I was told Lt. Jerry Langley was here and I need to speak with him." I tried my best to sound authoritative. Instead, my voice was barely above a hoarse whisper.

The woman frowned. "I'm afraid he is here on official police business. You'll have to wait until Dr. Francisco is finished with him."

I leaned against the counter. "I need to speak with him, too."

Her eyes widened in shock. "Never let Dr. Francisco hear you say that. She is not a 'he.'" It was as if she were repeating something she heard daily. "And she is very precise about her pronouns."

"Fine. I need to talk with HER." Trying to keep track of all the new pronouns was like wandering through a maze on LSD.

"Do you have an appointment?"

I drew a deep breath, trying to keep my anger from getting the best of me, but a wave of dizziness passed over me again. The weakness was returning with a vengeance. I slumped against the counter and went down to my knees. My sight grew cloudy, and I broke out in a cold sweat. The receptionist was suddenly next to me, helping me to my feet.

"Look, if you're going to have a heart attack, I'll tell them both that you're here." She said as she helped me walk through an inner door and down a long hallway. She took me into a room with two couches, a couple of coffee pots, and a television. Some kind of break room.

"Lie down on the couch and I'll get some help." She helped me slump onto a couch. My vision cleared as I tried to focus on the local noonday news. A cheerful newscaster was beaming.

"And, in another of today's surprising developments, President Mitchell will soon pay a visit to Talako. The President will address a group of dignitaries at the Biotechnology Institute for the dedication of a new wing. Named after the late Dr. Janice Manning, the Manning Nanotechnology Development Center will be officially dedicated by the President."

I struggled upright. I blinked and tried to focus on the television again. "The Janice Manning wing is the brainchild of Dr. Richard Korskin, Director of the Biotechnology Institute. Here is what he had to say."

Korskin appeared on the screen, face beaming, bright teeth gleaming. "We are pleased to announce the acquisition of a $25 million grant to the Biotechnology Institute for developing nanotechnology. And to commemorate the opening of the Janice Manning Nanotechnology Wing, the President of the United States, Thomas Mitchell will be here to address local dignitaries, including our senators and governor. This promises to be an exciting development for the medical and scientific community of Talako."

They had named a wing after Janice? Why hadn't Korskin mentioned it to me before? More importantly, why wasn't I invited? The door opened and Jerry Langley hurried in, followed by a woman with deep red hair. She was short and a bit on the heavy side. Her skin was a light brown, covered with freckles. She wore a white pair of red cat-eye glasses. Her short, crimson hair framed a rotund face. A yellow antibacterial gown swathed her figure, and, for all the world, she looked like a giant lemon with legs. She stopped in between me and the television and pushed her glasses up into her hair. She regarded me with bright blue eyes.

"Are you OK?"

The dizziness was fading, and I was feeling stronger. I looked at Jerry. "I don't think I've recovered from my reaction this week. I left the hospital day before yesterday."

A pair of mirrored sunglasses sat atop Jerry's head, and he helped me to my feet. "You came to see me?" He wore a dark blue jacket and a turtleneck shirt. His badge hung from his belt and the jacket bulged over his pistol and holster.

"Yes, and Dr. Francisco." I glanced at the woman. "You must be Dr. Francisco."

She held out a delicate hand swathed in blue latex and formed a fist. "Sam Francisco. Sam is short for Samuela. My parents were strange. Fist bump, okay?" I started to return the fist bump, and she pulled her hand away. "Just joking. I've been digging through an open chest. And you are?"

"Dr. Jack Merchant. I'm a radiologist at Fairmont Medical Center."

Sam grinned and laughed. "Merchant? Your last name is Merchant?"

"Yes. Why is that so funny?"

"You're a radiologist. A shadow merchant."

I shook my head in puzzlement. "Shadow merchant?"

Sam stopped laughing and smiled. "That's what we called our radiologists when I was in the military. Shadow merchants. Those who ply the shadows of mystery, who delve in the dark recesses of the human body seeking disease." She delivered this last in a hushed, ghostly whisper. "Dr. Merchant, the shadow merchant. Wicked!"

She motioned to the inner door. "If you don't mind, I was showing Lt. Langley some lab results. You can walk back with us if you promise not to collapse into an open body cavity." We followed her out into the hall. Jerry placed his hand on my arm.

"You sure you're alright?"

"Yeah. I was stronger yesterday. Started feeling dizzy just now. I'm dehydrated, I think."

"You were in the hospital?"

I looked at him and sighed. "I had a reaction to some Xray contrast last week. Almost died."

Jerry's grip tightened. "I'm sorry to hear that. You should have called me. You still have my card?"

"Yes. I'll be fine, Jerry."

We had walked into a large, cinder block room with four stainless steel tables spread out away from us. On the nearest table, a shriveled body lay open to the world, entrails and lungs bursting through the incision. Sam picked up a sheaf of papers and handed them to Langley.

"Hypothermia. I'd say his death was from natural causes. You can mark him off your list."

Jerry nodded. "Good. We've got enough cases piling up without having to add one more homicide to the list."

I tried to pry my eyes away from the disturbing sight of the body. At one time, I had considered going into pathology until I attended my first and last autopsy. When the pathologist had peeled the scalp off the skull and rolled it down over the victim's face, I had fainted.

I glanced at the next table. A technician shrouded in a yellow gown, face mask and gloves worked on a nude body. The victim's clothes lay on a nearby table. I glanced at the shoes. They were military boots. A chill ran down my spine and I stepped closer, angling my head around the technician to see the man's face. The lower half of his face was missing, only the cloudy green eyes and the bald head remaining.

I pointed to the body. "I know that man."

"You know him?" Sam said.

"He works at Fairmont Central. In Radiology. He's one of our transport people. You know, the ones who go up to the floor and bring down patients for their tests."

Jerry stepped into my line of vision, eclipsing the grisly sight. "Are you sure?"

I glanced at Jerry. "I recognize his boots. And his face."

"What's his name?"

I stopped to think. I had never heard him say his name. "I don't know. He was new to me. You could call Murray Washington, radiology administrator at Fairmont Central and he can tell you. He's that man's boss. Well, he was his boss. What happened to him?"

"Don't tell him." A familiar voice sounded from behind me. I whirled to see Detective Sanchez storm into the room, followed by the hapless receptionist.

"I tried to stop her." The receptionist said. "I'm sorry, Dr. Francisco, but she insisted, and she pulled a gun on me."

"I only showed her my badge and my pistol. Didn't mean to scare her. The Fairmont Police Department returned a location from my BOLO on Merchant's car. Right outside." She grinned.

"Sanchez." I sighed. "You put a BOLO out on me?"

Sanchez's eyes blazed. She chewed on a toothpick. "I told you I would hunt you down if you didn't sign those papers. Your doctor threw me out of your room, day before yesterday, and we never finished our conversation. When I came by this morning at the hospital, they reluctantly told me you had gone home. So, where are the papers?"

I tried to think. "I was at the front desk and had them in my hands when I had a kidney stone attack. I don't know where they are."

"How convenient." Sanchez placed her hands on her hips.

"Who are you?" Jerry stepped up beside me.

"Lieutenant Sanchez, Homicide, Colorado Springs Police Department. Dr. Merchant here is a suspect in a crime." She lifted her badge into view.

"Why did you put a BOLO out on his vehicle?"

"He ignored a request for exhumation." Sanchez nodded toward me. "I need that body."

"What body?" Jerry looked at me.

"She thinks I killed Janice."

A puzzled look came over Jerry's face, and he glanced at Sanchez. "I thought her death was accidental."

"She was murdered." Sanchez fumed. "And I'm looking at the perp."

"Jerry, I think she was murdered, too. But it wasn't me. Sanchez has this wild idea I killed my wife." I said.

"For a half a mil in insurance." Sanchez spat the toothpick onto the floor.

"Hey." Sam insinuated herself between the two of us. "You pick that up. I keep a clean morgue."

Sanchez turned her wild eyes to Sam and seemed to calm down. "Dr. Francisco, I presume." She stooped down to retrieve the toothpick. At least she didn't put it back in her mouth. "Nice glasses. Love the maroon hair. This is the husband of the woman whose body I want exhumed."

Sam's mouth opened, and she was at a loss for words. She looked at me and then back at Sanchez. "My hair is Poinsettia Red, thank you very much. If you want the body exhumed, I need the release."

"Can I use your phone?" I motioned to the wall.

"Dial 9 to get out." Sam continued to stare at Sanchez.

I dialed Fairmont Central. "Lydia? This is Dr. Merchant. Did you find some papers at the front desk last week? You know, the day I had my kidney stone. You put them in my mailbox? Would you see if they're still there?" I waited, watching Jerry and Sanchez sizing each other up. Lydia came back on the phone. "Are you sure? Look around. They have to be there somewhere." I listened to her response and felt sweat trickle down my face. I hung up the phone.

"So, where are they? Your cat scan eat them?" Sanchez tossed the toothpick in a trashcan.

"They've disappeared. Lydia is our head administrative assistant. She can't find them. Claims she put them in my mailbox, but they're not there." I wiped sweat off my face and my hand trembled. My heart raced, and I felt loopy again. Maybe I should have stayed home. Or it could be my reaction to Sanchez!

Sanchez raised an eyebrow. "Now I've got to get back in touch with my office and have a new set drawn up! Merchant, you're looking more and more guilty as time goes by. Excuse me while I make a phone call." She pulled out her cell phone.

"Just a minute!" Sam said, and she grabbed Sanchez by the arm and pushed her cat-eye glasses up into her crimson hair. "First, sister, you don't come storming into my lab and you sure don't intimidate Missy."

"Missy?"

"My receptionist. I can have you thrown in jail for contempt of court. This is my lab, and you will not terrify my staff or harass my visitors." Sam motioned to the bodies. "Living or dead. Now you take you precious cell phone and your crusade and your happy butt out to the parking lot and take care of your business elsewhere." Sam leaned into her face. "And if you bypass Missy one more time, I'll have you thrown in jail."

Sanchez glared at her. "Take your hands off of me!"

Sam just smiled. "Nope, sister. Here, in this place, I am judge, jury, and executioner. You might say I am the queen, king, and prime minister, all wrapped in one. If you ever want to set foot in my lab again, you will do exactly as you are told. Got it?"

Sanchez's face turned red, and she jerked her arm out of Sam's grasp and put her hands on her hips. She pursed her lips and nodded. "I like you. Seems we got off on the wrong foot." Sanchez pocketed her cell phone and left the room.

Sam pushed her glasses back into her Poinsettia Red hair and pointed a chubby finger at me. "You're lucky you were sick, Dr. Merchant, or I would give you the same speech."

Jerry rubbed his face and looked at me. "Why does she think you murdered Janice? I thought they ruled it accidental."

"Money." I stated. "And I agree with her. At least that Janice was murdered." I couldn't tell him about my only alibi,

Keri. I had come here to ask him to check out Korskin without bringing Keri into the picture.

Sam nodded, glaring after Sanchez. She glanced back at me, and suspicion filled her eyes. "Well, once we get her body, I'll find some answers." Her gaze softened. "Are you OK with this?"

I felt myself tremble more. "No!" I looked back at the transport guy. "I almost died the other day right after he brought me some coffee."

Sam sniffed. "It wasn't the coffee that got him, that's for sure. Professional hit. They blew away his dental work and cut off his hands. No identifying body parts. Probably a drug deal gone sour."

I walked across the floor, my muscles trembling more. More sweat popped out on my face. I studied a bank of Xray monitors on a nearby console. The man's chest Xray was cloudy, the lungs filled with fluid. A ring like shadow lay over the heart.

"He had a heart valve. You can probably get the serial number off of it."

Sam moved up beside me and pointed to the technician working over the man's body. "Trenda is removing the valve now so we can get the number."

A wave of dizziness descended on me again and I slumped against the wall. Sam grabbed me.

"Dr. Merchant, what is wrong with you?"

"I'm dizzy again. I need to sit down." What was happening to me? I was suddenly dizzy and for a moment the world faded away.

NINE

Sam took my arm as I almost fainted. "Let's get you out of here. Langley, help me get him to my office."

They walked me out into the hall and ushered me into Sam's office. Piles of paperwork covered a nearby table. More folders sat on her desk. They eased me down onto a small sofa. Sam punched an intercom on her desk.

"Missy, bring me some water." She sat behind her desk and studied me with concern. "Maybe we should call your doctor."

Jerry stood guard beside me. "Why don't I take you to the ER?"

The receptionist came into the room and handed me a bottle of water. I gulped it down, suddenly aware of how warm I felt. I had a fever. The water tasted wonderful and instantly I felt cooler.

"Let me sit here a minute and let's see how I feel."

Jerry nodded and glanced at Sam. "I'm going to have a talk with my Colorado colleague. Putting a BOLO out on Jack when all she had to do was go to his address. As soon as you get the ID on the dead guy, call me." Jerry left the room.

"What other people are here but dead people?" Sam said and sighed. She tore the yellow gown off and stuffed it into a trashcan already too full of snack wrappers. I looked around at Sam's office and my eyes were inevitably drawn to two Xray monitors on a nearby console.

Once a radiologist, always a radiologist. Each monitor was the size of a Xray film and divided into four quadrants. In each "window" were ultrasound images. As I sipped more of the water, I focused on the images.

"Scrotal ultrasound? You do those on bodies?" I asked.

Sam sat behind her desk. "No. It's a study from an upcoming coroner's inquest." She took off her glasses and polished them with a cloth on her cluttered desk. "How are you feeling?"

"Better. Rehydrated. Someone die from testicular rupture?"

Sam froze and put her glasses back on. "What did you say?"

I motioned to the monitors. "Looks like the scrotum is full of blood. Trauma. Probably kicked in the groin."

Sam stood up and came around her desk. She motioned to the desk chair before the desk containing the monitors. "Would you mind giving me a curbside consult?"

I stood up shakily and sat in the chair. "Sure. What's the history?"

Sam pulled up another chair and sat beside me. "Technically, I can't tell you. But this one has me bumfuzzled." She studied me through her red glasses and nodded. "Okay, here goes. Twenty-two-year-old college junior home for the summer comes in with swollen testicles. No history of trauma. Has some other symptoms, but most notably chest pain. The ER doctor not only got the ultrasound of the scrotum, he ordered a CT of the lungs for pulmonary embolus, thinking the man had thrown blood clots to his lungs."

My forehead furrowed in thought. "That has nothing to do with trauma to the testicles."

"I know. In the ER report, the doctor denied the patient had any history of trauma. The young man codes and dies in the ER. My predecessor waived the autopsy. Sloppy. It's why he's gone. The family has been badgering my office for two years, wanting answers. I finally agreed to a coroner's inquest." Sam said. "Because there is no body."

"What?" I looked at her.

"The boy was cremated. All I have are the medical records. And it's a big mess. The ER was hopping that night at St. Alek. I don't know why the kid died, but there are some strange findings on his CT." She sat back and crossed her arms. "Care to see the images?"

"Yes." I scrolled through the ultrasound images using a mouse. "The testes are intact. No lacerations. Look, the Doppler images show normal blood flow. This is making no sense. With all this blood, the testicles should be ruptured." I closed the ultrasound images and went to a very familiar information page.

"I see you use the same PACS system I do."

"It's pretty standard."

I examined the list of the man's studies from the ER visit. I double clicked on the name of the CT of the lungs and images sprang onto the monitors. In one window were the axial images, slices through the chest like pieces of bread in a loaf. Next window showed the sagittal reconstructions which allowed me to look at the chest as if someone had sliced it from right to left across the chest. The third window showed the coronal image reconstructions as if the chest were sliced from front to back. By using all three planes, I could get a three-dimensional appreciation of the heart, lungs, chest wall, and upper abdomen. I hit a function key and the quality of the images changed.

"Let's optimize the images for bones. Because I see something very interesting." I started scrolling through all three sets and then pointed to the axial images.

"No pulmonary emboli, but there is some infiltrate in the left lung base." I pointed to the hazy of the lungs. "I would say it is a lung contusion."

Sam smiled. "Based on?"

"The rib fractures. See," I used the cursor to point at the three lower ribs on the left side where three obvious rib fractures near the rib articulation with the spine stood out. "And any good medical student should be able to tell you if you break the lower ribs on the left side, you might just fracture the spleen." I scrolled down through the lower chest into the upper abdomen where the normal spleen, instead of looking like a crescent-shaped organ, was a mishmash of tissue and fresh blood. "The kid had a ruptured spleen. He bled to death from a rupture spleen. Do you know how rare that is nowadays?" I gasped and smiled. "The blood in the scrotum! He was a weightlifter, wasn't he?"

Sam whistled. "You are good, Merchant. Why blood in the scrotum?"

"Probably had open inguinal canals, and the blood settled into his scrotum from his abdomen. Probably blew the canals open, straining down lifting weights. He would have had hernias eventually." I frowned. "But wait. That blood on the ultrasound didn't look acute. It looked old."

I sat back. Sam applauded. "Now you see the conundrum. No history of trauma, and yet he had three rib fractures. A ruptured spleen, and it takes time for the blood to settle into his scrotum. I looked and looked and even spoke to the ER doc. He was adamant the guy had no history of trauma. So how does a young man with no history of trauma get broken ribs?"

"Maybe he had too much to drink and fell and didn't remember it?"

"Possible."

"Okay, this is a typical detective story, Dr. Francisco. There are pieces missing and I bet they are here. These images came from St. Alex, right? Did he have any previous admissions?"

"None we could find."

I had a hunch. "Where did the kid live?"

"Over in Bayou City, close to the Bayou City Medical Center, south of town."

I nodded. "Do you have access to the PACS there?"

"I have access to all hospital systems in the area."

I closed the PACS and examined the desktop. An icon showed the PACS system for BCMC. "Bayou City Medical Center is an old, creaky hospital south of town. Only about 40 beds. We used to read their studies until the university took over the hospital. Did you check their ER for this patient?"

"No, I didn't."

"His full name is Eugene George Pennington, right?"

"Yeah, but his records insisted he went by the middle name." She pushed her crimson hair away from her face. "Who would want to go by Eugene?"

The information window opened for the BCMC PACS system and I typed the man's name into a search window, Eugene Pennington. I smiled and typed in George Pennington. "Aha! He was in their ER two days before his visit to St. Alex."

"Well, I'll be a suck egg mule." Sam said.

I glanced at her. "That's a new one on me."

"My grandfather used to say that. I have no idea what it means. So, this kid checked in under his middle name? Do the birthdays match?"

"Yes." I scrolled through the images listed and found a chest Xray. I opened the image and studied the lower left hand of the image. "There! Three rib fractures. See them?"

Sam peered through her glasses. "He was in the ER there with rib fractures two days before he died!"

I pointed to a window in the upper right-hand quadrant of the information page. "And look here. The technologist who performed the Xray did a good job. They asked the man what happened to him. Look what they put in the comment section. 'Kicked in back by fraternity brother.' You see, Dr. Francisco, good technologists will ask for more clinical information and put it in the comments."

"Which doesn't show up in the formal medical records." Sam whistled again. "His fraternity brother kicked hm in the back and the ER sent him home with back pain and never knew he had ruptured his spleen."

"And he came in two days later and died. The right hand didn't know what the left hand was going. I see this way too often. So much information out there and it's not shared properly. Hospitals are so concerned about security they are paranoid about sharing information unless specifically asked. And the ER is too busy to ask. This solves your mystery."

Sam nodded. "And I'll have to bring this to the district attorney's office. This could be involuntary manslaughter."

The water was helping. Or maybe it was doing what I was good at. It felt good to solve the mystery of what had killed this young man. It was also sad to know that we, as doctors, are only humans and human error can cause great harm. Especially when we so depend on impersonal technology. The human side of medicine gets lost in the digits.

Sam retrieved a legal pad from her desk and made some notes. It was only then I noticed she wore a brightly flowered blouse over bright green pants. The blouse had red, green, and gold poinsettia leaves.

"You like Christmas, I see."

She nodded. "Best time of the year. Love it." She looked up at me and squinted through her glasses. "Are you up to looking at another case that has me perplexed?"

I shrugged. "I'm feeling better."

Sam scooted me aside and tapped on the keyboard and brought up a set of Xrays. The two films filled each monitor and were of the abdomen. I studied the bowel gas pattern, and it was normal. Surgical clips in the right upper quadrant testified to the person's gallbladder removal. Calcification filled the walls of his aorta, the large artery that coursed down the middle of his abdomen. Bone spurs sprouted from the edges of his lumbar vertebral bodies. And visible at the lower end of the pelvic bones was a soft tissue shadow that testified this was a man. An old man. A man somewhere north of 80. In the center of his lower pelvis was an oddly shaped metallic body. I leaned forward. I pointed to it. "I've seen this before."

"You have?"

"Yeah. I'm trying to remember. Who is this?"

"One of my patients." She chuckled. I didn't laugh, and she grew suddenly quiet. "Sorry for the macabre humor. I owe them something. I must find out why they died."

"And this man?"

"How did you know it was a man?" She said smugly.

"I'm a radiologist. I observe everything in an image. Like his penile implant. What happened to him?"

"He had a massive intracranial hemorrhage and died at home." Sam said. She raised an eyebrow as Jerry came back into the room.

"What's going on?" Jerry asked.

"Your friend says he knows what this is." She pointed to the metal shadow.

He turned back to Sam. "Should we tell him?"

"I would consider him a consultant, an expert witness." Sam answered. I didn't like the sound of that. I had been on the witness stand before and I didn't like it. But the film was intriguing.

"Ever heard of Lancaster Williams?" Jerry asked

"Of Williams Petroleum? Wasn't he the founder?"

Sam nodded. "Died two years ago. Age 92. Should have left a multimillion dollar fortune to his three children. Problem is his kids' mother died two years before that. Lancaster outlived her. So, he remarried."

"Wait." I interrupted her. "I remember that part. She was 29."

"Exactly." Jerry said. "Now, the family is contesting the will that left everything to his young sweetheart. They suspect foul play."

Sam crossed her arms over her chest and sighed. "But my predecessor did a quick and dirty autopsy right before he resigned from office. Ruled it accidental. Just like the other case, the body was cremated. All I have are the Xrays taken at the hospital where he was pronounced DOA."

I studied the shadow. It was a metal disc about one and a half inches in diameter. Six triangular shaped holes were punched in a well-spaced pattern. Triangles? "I remember. One of the Xray techs had me check a chest film and this weird shadow was projected over the left lung."

Sam patted my arm and grinned. "Shadow merchant. See what I mean? Tell me Christmas is coming early!"

"Okay." I smiled. For the first time in a while, I smiled. "So, the tech was a bit stymied. I asked him if he had told the patient to take off his shirt. He hadn't. This thing was in his pocket. I had him get the patient back in and repeat the film with the man's shirt off." I was struggling to remember. Triangles? Tri-State? "It was a bottle. The triangles in the lid were holes for a shaker like a pepper shaker. But the shape was unusual until you looked at the name." I turned to Sam. "Tri-State Rat Poison. Their logo is a triangle. The patient said it was a rare poison he could only find around this area. You shake these little beads along the corners of your attic to kill mice."

"Rat poison?" Jerry stared at the film.

"Warfarin. It's an anticoagulant." Sam said.

"But how did it get down there?"

I looked at him. "With the top open, the poison would slowly seep out over hours, prolonging his blood clotting. All it would take is one blow to the head, one fall and he would bleed like stink. What you're looking at, Jerry, is a rat poison suppository."

Jerry looked at Sam, and she beamed. "Would you be willing to dictate your interpretation of these films for me?" She hurried to her desk and picked up a small handheld recorder.

"Sure." I said. I took the recorder and rendered my interpretation. Sam took the recorder out to Missy. I slumped back onto the couch. I was feeling weak again. The adrenaline from the excitement of solving these two deaths was fading. Maybe I needed to go home and get in the bed.

"Look, Jack. I've got to go. I need talk to the D.A. about this. We now have a case! Would you mind if I called and checked on you tonight?" Jerry said.

"Go ahead. If I don't answer the phone, I'm probably asleep. I feel like I could sleep for two days." I told him my cell phone number. He wrote it down on one of his cards and stared at the monitors. "I've got to get a warrant to search little Mrs. Williams' home. And her credit card records." He left as Sam came back into her office. She handed me a sheet of paper.

"Check it to make sure Missy got it right. Then sign it and I'll have Missy notarize it. Can I send your check to the hospital?"

I looked up from the paper. "My check?"

"Your consultation fee. Dr. Merchant, our neighboring parishes have joined to outsource their medical examining business after the debacle of the last coroner. They've given me a lot of leeway, including the funds to consult specialists and expert witnesses." She sat behind her desk. "In fact, I know you're not feeling well, but there are few other cases I would like to have you look at."

I signed the sheet and slowly stood up. My head was throbbing. I placed the report on her desk. "Hopefully, I'll feel better. When?"

"How about tomorrow?" She glanced at a planner open on her desk. "I'd let you take home the images on DVD, but there is the issue of a chain of evidence. How about at 11? Unless someone is killed tonight, I'll have an open hour."

"Tomorrow is Saturday. I didn't think you worked on Saturday."

"The dead don't punch a clock, Jack" She motioned to the file folders around her. "And the backlog is huge. I'll see you then." I started for the door and my vision swam again. But I wouldn't let Sam Francisco see me stumble. The last thing I wanted to do today was end up as one of her "patients". It was only then I realized I had never asked Jerry to look into Korskin.

TEN

I was hovering over my body. Montana pumped furiously on my chest while Jean squeezed a ventilator bag, breathing for me. My skin was deathly pale. Techs bustled about the room. The bald guy slipped in between two nurses and took my IV in his hand. He attached a syringe and injected the contents. Then he looked up at the ceiling and at me. The lower half of his face was missing. I screamed myself awake. I had soaked my tee shirt with sweat. My mouth tasted like dirty aquarium gravel. I glanced at my bedside clock. I had fallen asleep on the couch and had slept for fourteen hours!

I stumbled to the bathroom and studied my reflection in the mirror. My skin sagged in places where I had lost weight just in the last week. Dark rings surrounded my eyes, and my dark brown hair was plastered to my head in a "positive bed sign". I soaked in the shower until the hot water gave out and waited until the cold water made my face numb. The image of the transport guy kept surfacing. As did some other memories. A red shoe. The tunnel of light. They told me I had died on the table. Did I have a near death experience? And the dream from the other day of Janice speaking to me. Had that been heaven? I pushed it out of my mind.

I managed to get down a glass of orange juice and by 8 o'clock I felt stronger than the day before. The phone rang.

"Hello?"

"Dr. Merchant, this is Missy at Francisco Labs. Dr. Francisco wanted me to call and tell you she has a triple homicide to post. She wants to reschedule for next week."

I glanced at my calendar held to the refrigerator with a magnet from Pike's Peak. Janice had bought it on our honeymoon. "Uh, I'm at Fairmont East next week. Call me Monday morning and we'll set a time."

Saturday and I had no plans. What was new? I wasn't about to spend another day in my bed in this apartment so I fished Jerry's card out of the pocket of my unwashed shirt. Too many unwashed clothes surrounded me because I really needed to wash them. Where was Debra Montana when you needed her? Well, right where she belonged. I needed to unload the dishwasher. And I needed groceries. No way was I going to open the refrigerator. It wasn't because it would be empty but because it had food in there. Food I had purchased before I flew to Colorado Springs. Food that might grow the next generation of penicillin. Yes, I needed a housekeeper. But I couldn't afford one.

I dialed Jerry's cell phone. He answered after one ring.

"Langley."

"Jerry, it's Jack Merchant."

"Jack? Oh. Look, I'm sorry I didn't call last night. I was busy."

"Yeah. I heard about the triple homicide from Francisco. Can we get together sometime today? I have a favor to ask."

Wind whipped against his speaker. In the background, I heard a boat motor. "I'm awfully busy with this case. But I haven't had a bite to eat since midnight. How about we meet at Strong's Grill for breakfast?"

"Sounds good. I'll meet you there in fifteen minutes." I hung up the phone and studied the magnet of Pike's Peak. Janice's death was so tragic, and yet Jerry had been dealing with a plethora of homicides in the past two weeks. Maybe there was a murder virus on the loose. Something tickled my upper lip. I wiped at it and looked at the bright red blood plastered across my hand. I ran to the bathroom and looked in the mirror. Blood from my nose covered my entire lower face. So much for a good start to the day.

STRONG'S GRILL was an old Talako establishment situated across Queen's Highway from Continental College, one of the oldest colleges in the south. For the size of town it was, Talako had two universities and Choctaw Medical School, a private medical school. It was a small school with only fifty students per year. But, thanks to Dr. Fairmont having left behind a huge trust fund, the school was built and maintained as an exclusive medical school for the upper, upper echelon. Attaching the Institute to it had kept it alive and well.

Across Queen's Highway from the old, red brick buildings of Continental College, I found a parking spot and made my way into the crowded, old-fashioned diner in a one-story brick building that in its heyday had been a hardware store. Jerry sat at a table sipping coffee. They had never updated the interior of the diner since the 1950s. It was rumored Elvis Presley's first meal in Louisiana had been here at Strong's Diner. The Christmas garland draped around the periphery must have been left over from the 1950s too. An aluminum Christmas tree sat by the check-out counter.

"Jack, how do you feel today?" Jerry wore his police department uniform today and his mirrored sunglasses perched on top of his head. His eyes looked weary.

I sat down and pulled out a menu. "Better. Not so weak. I slept. A lot. I guess I needed it." No mention of the nosebleed.

Jerry ordered eggs and bacon and Strong's infamous hash browns. I had a short stack of pancakes.

"So, what did you want to talk to me about?" Jerry asked.

I glanced around the interior of the café. About twenty people were crowded in the room, but I doubted anyone would hear me above the commotion.

"I told you I thought Janice had been murdered. I couldn't put a finger on why I thought so. And then, Wednesday, some information surfaced that made me suspicious of Dr. Korskin."

Jerry's brow furrowed, and he leaned over the table. "The Institute guy?"

"Yeah." The server brought our breakfasts. I seemed to be breaking the fast with cops pretty often of late.

Jerry dug into his crispy reddish hash browns. "What kind of information?"

I ate one of the flaky, light pancakes. Syrup dripped down my chin and, for a horror-stricken moment, I thought my nose was bleeding again. I froze. I hadn't thought of that question and I hesitated. "Uh, I can't tell you. The source is confidential."

Jerry stopped chewing and studied me with flat green eyes. "Confidential?"

"Look, all I can tell you is that Korskin has some kind of illegal activity in his past. Look into it for me. Check him out. That's all I'm asking. After all, he was Janice's boss."

"Because you are convinced someone killed Janice?" Jerry said. "Jack, you're asking me to look into a well-known local doctor and community mover and shaker as if he were a common criminal and you can't give me any evidence to justify it?"

"Who is hosting the President of the United States!" I pointed out.

"And don't you think the Secret Service has already checked him out? Look, the police department is stretched to its limits with this upcoming presidential visit. And a rash of homicides, to boot. I don't have time to chase down a nebulous crime from one of the most respected men in this city based on a hunch. Without more than you're giving me, I could get into a lot of trouble."

Should I tell him about Keri? No, I couldn't reveal her secrets, not even to Jerry. "The confidential source is someone I trust who recognized him from the past. This person is convinced Dr. Korskin was involved in a horrific crime. If that is true, and I trust this person with my life, Korskin has a shady past."

"Who recognized him?"

My heart raced. "I can't tell you."

Jerry leaned back in his chair. "Even if Korskin has a 'shady' past, you haven't given me even the smallest idea of what his motive would be for killing your wife."

"Like I said, he was her boss."

"And he's naming a wing after her." He started eating his breakfast again. "Look, Jack, I am up to my chin in homicides. I haven't slept well in the past two nights. I don't have time to chase down some elusive nastiness in Korskin's past."

My heart sank. It was worth a try. "I'm sorry, Jerry. When you called this morning, I heard water in the background. I didn't know you were so busy. But please think about it." I ate some more of my pancakes. "Sounded like you were down by Choctaw River this morning."

"Yeah. Three guys were drinking at Veteran's park. One of them snapped and shot the other two, then killed himself."

"Murder suicide? Didn't you have another suicide? Guy who jumped off the bridge?"

Jerry glanced at me. "Now there's a strange one. He was a medical student. Third in his class. Happy girlfriend. No motive for suicide. We found his car parked at the head of the Texas Street bridge, still running, door open. Witnesses say he just walked to the middle of the bridge and threw himself in. No suicide note."

I finished my pancakes. Between Thanksgiving dinner and leftovers yesterday, I had eaten more in the past three days than in the past couple of weeks. "I've been there, Jerry. Medical school is stressful beyond belief. One day you're excited at learning how to cure pneumonia and the next your attending physician is reaming you out for not knowing the Kreb's cycle. And Choctaw Medical School is private. That means the cream of the cream of the crop. Very competitive. And, therefore, very stressful."

"Well, there seems to be something going on. The homeless guy, the jumper, your transport guy, and now three vagrants at Veteran's park. There's death in the air."

"Could it have something to do with the river?"

Jerry scraped the last of his eggs off his plate with a piece of toast. "Probably just the holidays. Always bad at this time of year. Depression, stress, anxiety, anger, money problems. You name it. Don't try to be a detective, Jack."

"Oh, but I am. That's what a radiologist is. We look at diagnostic images all day long and try to piece together the puzzle of what is going on. It's like one long murder investigation. We pull together bits and pieces of evidence and give the physician the most likely diagnosis. We're medical detectives. It's the way we think." I sipped some coffee.

"Jerry, when I look at an imaging study, whatever the type, sometimes I feel like I'm missing something. I look at the images and there is this, well, itch in the back of my eyes. It's like there is something wrong but I can't see it. But in the interest of time I go ahead and render an interpretation. But that itch stays there for hours, sometimes days. I can't tell you how many times I wake up and remember a finding on that study and I kick myself. I go back and pull up the study and there it is, an obvious abnormality that I just couldn't see at the time."

Jerry nodded. "I know the feeling. It can be the same way with a murder case. All the pieces are there and sometimes it's my subconscious mind that works in the background putting the pieces together."

"Exactly!" I said. "That is why I am convinced Janice was murdered. The pieces don't fit together around the circumstances of her death. Something strange happened in that hotel room and I can't figure out what it was. It's the itch that I can't scratch!"

Jerry motioned to the server for more coffee. "So you think like a detective. I never realized that. OK, why would there be a connection with the river? Something in the water?"

I shook my head. "Forget it. I was just trying to help. When you put the pieces in front of me, I can't help but try to solve it. It's the way my mind works."

"Like the rat poison yesterday?"

"Yeah. Once I saw the film, I couldn't let it go. I had to figure out what it was."

"And so, you hear a little snippet of gossip about Korskin and you see murder." Jerry sipped his fresh cup of coffee.

I sighed. "Jerry, please help me. You said you would do anything for me. Can't you just run a background check? Maybe check with Secret Service or the FBI?"

"Like I said, they probably already have, and he's fine or the President wouldn't be coming."

I leaned back in the chair and stared out the window of the café. Reddish brown leaves were swirling in the cool air. "Maybe I'm just paranoid."

"Maybe you just want answers where there aren't any. You think someone murdered Janice and you can't give me any good reasons, so you look for murder in the eyes of the people you trust the least. Did you have a run in with Korskin lately?"

I glared at Jerry. "I hate it when you're right. He's making a move on my radiology practice."

Jerry smiled. "There you go. Look, Jack, you've been sick lately. It's been a year since Janice died. And that was a pretty big bender you went on last week. You're probably tired and you can't think well when you're tired. I should know."

I looked back at him. "Even though I slept well last night, I had some weird dreams." I paused. Jerry and I had been through a lot while in college. He had been my best friend. But time, ever the enemy of relationships, had sent us along diverging pathways. Even so, I trusted the man. "Jerry, do you believe in near-death experiences?"

Jerry raised an eyebrow. "I didn't see that question coming."

I rubbed my chin. "I remembered things while I was, uh, dead. You know, the tunnel of light, the out-of-body experience. And Janice." My gaze met his.

Jerry blinked. "Yeah, I've heard of people having NDEs. I don't know what I believe about them. Did you see Jesus?"

I swallowed. The image of the bearded man flitted across my mind. "I don't know."

"Jack, you need to talk to someone. Do you know anyone who has had an NDE?"

I thought for a second. There was one person at the hospital I had overheard at lunch one day. I smiled. "Tell you what, Jerry. If you carefully check on Korskin for me, I'll talk to someone. Today."

Jerry wadded his napkin and tossed it on his plate. "OK. I give in. I'll check into Korskin." He stood up. "But quietly."

I rose and pushed my chair under the table. "And, while you're at it, check and see if your victims have anything in common. I can see one thing that might tie them together."

"What's that?"

"The transport guy worked at Fairmont. The medical student at the medical school. Maybe there is some kind of tie in with the medical establishment." I paused, a grin on my face. "Maybe they all knew Korskin."

Jerry shoved my shoulder and slid his sunglasses over his eyes. "Nice try. Jack, you're stretching it real thin. I got to go to work."

ELEVEN

The woman amazed me. She sat at the slot machine slumped back on a stool. Her skin was as gray as the gathering storm clouds outside and she had an oxygen tube snaked beneath her nose. In her left hand, she held an unfiltered cigarette she had lit from the one she had just finished. In her right hand she held an oxygen mask pressed to her face. She would gasp for air, sucking in the life-sustaining oxygen flowing from her tank tucked beneath the stool. Then she would let the mask dangle from her neck and inhale a lung full of the cigarette smoke and while holding it in pull on the slot machine handle with her right hand. When the cylinders stopped rolling, she would exhale the smoke and descend into a coughing fit that stirred the red garland draped around the machine. Then she would wipe tears from her eyes, drop another penny into the penny slot machine, and start the cycle over again.

Was this where I would end up in thirty years? Broken, shrunken, dried up failure of a man reduced to smoking and playing the penny slots? For a moment, I thought I was looking at a good example of what hell could be like. In fact, the woman was so close to death I wonder if she had a near death experience every time the slots stopped rolling.

After mentioning my possible near-death experience to Jerry, I recalled one of our radiology engineers talking about having a near-death experience. The engineers were the miracle workers of the starship Fairmont, keeping the aging equipment running with hair pens and duct tape. The hospital listed Virgil Brown on the call sheet for engineering emergencies. Believe it or not, machine breakdowns happened more often than they should. It all went back to those hair pins and duct tape "repairs". Brown wasn't on call this weekend, so I called him at home. His wife informed me he was spending the day at Neptune's Lagoon. So, breaking my promise to Jerry and to myself, I had found myself at a casino at ten thirty in the morning.

Neptune's Lagoon was much seedier and run down than the more upscale Paradise Cay. The clientele was older. There were more penny slot machines. Their Christmas decorations were limpid and dusty.

I left the emphysematous woman to her slot machine and looked for Virgil Brown. He was a six and a half foot tall African American with short, black wiry hair shot through with gray. He was hard to miss and tipped the scales at over three hundred pounds. And all those pounds were muscle! Rumor was, he had been on track for the NFL when he was a linebacker at LSU until he blew out his knee. I spied him sitting at a blackjack table. I walked up behind him, and he glanced over my shoulder.

"Well, hey doc. If the CAT scan is on the fritz, I'm afraid I can't help you. It's my day off. Hit me." The dealer slid a card in front of him. "I'll hold."

"No, I came here to talk to you."

He glanced over his shoulder, puzzlement on his face. "Talk to me? About what?"

"A tunnel of light."

His eyes brightened, and he mumbled something to the dealer, raking his winnings into a cup. "I was wondering when you would look me up. Come on, let's get a beer."

He started for the bar and I shivered. The muscle tremors were coming back on a smaller scale. I tried to ignore them and hurried after Virgil's receding figure. "Don't you think it's a little early for a beer?"

Virgil stopped and turned to study me. "It's not for me. I just assumed you would want one. I hear you really put them away not long ago."

Was everyone aware of my business? Of course, they were. Gossip was the lifeblood of the medical community. "Look, why don't we just have coffee?" I noticed a door leading outside. "On the balcony."

"Suits me fine." He asked the barkeep for two coffees, and we went out onto the deck overlooking Choctaw River. Scattered tables were empty of patrons and an icy wind was blowing in from the west. The clouds continued to churn above us. We would have rain before afternoon. Virgil motioned to a table and sat down.

"What's up?"

I sat down. "Virgil, I don't know where to start."

"Hold it!" He put up a hand. "My grandmother calls me Virgil. My mother called me by names I'd rather not repeat, God rest her vile soul. Please, call me Gill." He leaned forward, a twinkle in his eye. "You rearrange the letters in vile and what do you get?"

"Uh, live?"

Gill frowned. "Wrong! Evil."

I swallowed. I had heard this man was strange. "So, your mother was evil?"

"Probably demon possessed." He sipped some coffee. "I tried to exorcise her when I was eleven. She set me on fire." He pulled up his tee shirt and revealed his chest covered with scar tissue, looking like dark, wrinkled leather. "Fourteen skin grafts. She went to jail and died from AIDS."

I blinked. "I'm so sorry."

"Don't be. All of that made me who I am today. So, what's up with you?"

"I had an, uh, episode last week. I had a contrast reaction."

"Doc, you died." He stated flatly, his eyes wide and filled with mirth.

"OK, so I died. And I saw some things. I overheard you telling your buddies at lunch that you did the same thing."

"I did." He stared at me.

"So, what should I do?"

Gill shrugged. "Beats the heck out of me."

I sighed. This was getting me nowhere. "Look, I think I had the wrong idea. I'll be going."

"Sit down, Doc." He put a huge hand on my shoulder. "Tell me what happened."

I sipped my coffee and felt another wave of rigors pass over me. "I was floating over my body. And then I was outside the hospital, I think. There was this red shoe. And then there was this tunnel. And," I tried to slow my breathing. "I can't remember everything."

"You don't right off. It comes to you in bits and pieces. Did you see Jesus?" His eyes widened expectantly.

"Well, I saw this man with a beard."

"And what impressed you about him?"

"Well, uh, he was in charge. He was, wise."

"Sounds like Jesus to me. Yep, thank God for Jesus!" Gill

snapped and chugged down his coffee. "There's many people who see this man and they call him Jesus. Even when they've never heard of Jesus."

"Well, Gill, I'm not a very religious man."

"Neither am I." At that moment an elderly man passed by me and paused, gazed fixed on Gill

"Minister Brown? How are you doing today?"

"Just great, Benny. Coming to the park tomorrow?"

"Wouldn't miss it. You gonna have donuts and coffee?" The man licked his lips.

"Yep."

"Nine o'clock?"

"Sharp."

The man seemed to notice me for the first time. "You ought to come, too. He's a right smart man." He patted Gill on the shoulder and walked on down the deck.

"You're a minister?" I asked.

"If you are a child of God, you are, too." He leaned forward, and the table creaked under his weight. "I'm not a preacher, although I have the gift of prophecy."

"You can tell the future?"

Gill laughed. "See, you need to do more than just read your Bible. The gift of prophecy means you always seek after Truth and tell Truth to those around you. Gets you into a lot of trouble. Which is why I'm not a preacher. I'd tell the church members a lot of Truth they can't handle. So, I minister in the name of Christ."

"If you don't preach, what do you do on Sunday?" I watched the man disappear around the bend of the riverboat balcony.

"Oh, I bring coffee and donuts down to Veteran's Park. About thirty people show up. I talk to them, and we sing a little." He sipped more coffee.

"Sounds like a preacher to me."

Gill's features clouded. "No. I told you I am not a religious man. I just try and tell the truth." He leaned forward and his eyes twinkled. "And listen. Actively listen. No preaching."

"Got it. You were just talking about Jesus and all."

Gill pointed a large finger at me. "Jesus spoke out against the religious leaders of the day. That's what got him killed. Now, back to your little trip."

I shook my head in amazement. This guy was something. "I saw my wife."

"Dr. Manning?"

"You knew her?"

Gill relaxed into his chair. "Now and then, some engineers at the Institute would ask me to come over and help them troubleshoot a problem. I met your wife over there in her nanotechnology lab. She had some neat toys."

"I've never seen the lab." I realized. Janice had kept her laboratory a secret to me and just about anybody else not closely associated with the Institute. She seldom spoke about her work.

Gill cocked his head at me and grinned. "You know, the other day I was thinking while I was sitting on the throne."

"What?"

"Oh, I do my best thinking while I'm going to the bathroom." Virgil's eyes widened. "Sorry. That was a TMI."

"TMI?" I asked.

"Too much information. Anyway, as I was saying, I had this thought just about the time I flushed the commode."

"That's a TMI with an FBS." I interrupted him.

"FBS?"

"Full body shudder." I smiled, and it felt good. I laughed. It felt better.

Gill's eyes suddenly filled with life, and he slapped the

table, laughing so hard tears came to his eyes. He gasped for breath. "Good one, Doc."

"So, what was your thought?" I pushed away my cold coffee.

"When you can't remember something, go looking for it."

"What?"

"Where did you see this red shoe?"

I searched my memory. "I was kind of floating up through the floors of the hospital. Maybe around the third floor?" I looked at him and raised my eyebrows. "This is crazy, Gill,"

"Sure it is. Let's go find your red shoe." He stood up.

"Now?" I looked up at the giant of a man.

"You got other plans?"

I shook my head. "No. But if you let me go to the bathroom, I might think of something."

TWELVE

By the time Gill and I arrived at Fairmont Central, rain was drizzling from a leaden sky. I had parked in the parking garage and Gill followed me in his truck. I couldn't believe the man was willing to go back into the hospital on Saturday to look for a red shoe. The room I passed through during my NDE had hanging plastic sheets and the bed sat in the corner.

"What are we going to do?" I asked as we entered the building.

"Go to 3 West and see if we can find a shoe." He said. "3 West sounds like your description. It's closed for renovation."

Gill ignored the workers rewiring the nurses' station, and we moved through hanging sheets of plastic down the short corridor to the eight rooms that comprised 3 West. Four rooms looked out over the central complex of old and new buildings at the heart of the hospital. Gill opened a door at the end of the corridor, and we exited out onto the roof. The rain was coming harder, but I still searched the rooftop outside the inner four rooms. No red shoe. My glasses were fogged by the cold rain.

"Let's look outside the other four rooms." Gill pointed back to the door.

We went back inside and stepped into one room on the opposite side of the corridor from the roof side rooms. I crossed to the windows and peered out. The wall of the hospital fell away three floors to the street below. Running the length of the building was a slatted ledge about two feet wide. It provided shade from the setting sun on the set of windows below it. Six metal vanes angled away from me, held together by metal braces. The old windows swiveled inward at an angle. I pulled one of them open and squeezed my head and neck out.

The shaded ledge above stopped some of the rain falling down the side of the building, but allowed huge, fat drops of cold water to drip down my shirt. I had one of those full body shudders. I looked up and down the ledge. No shoe. If I looked upward, the angle of the slats was just right for me to see through the ledges above me. No shoe.

I pulled back inside, wiping water from my face. Blood covered my hand.

"Doc, you OK?" Gill's eyes widened at the sight of the blood.

"Just a nosebleed. I don't see the shoe, Gill."

Gill studied the ledge and nodded. "It could be wedged in the slats on the ledge below us. See, the slats are angled away from us, and you can't tell what's between them."

I found an old towel in the bathroom and wiped blood from my face. "How would I have seen it?"

Gill pointed out over the street. "From out there."

I sat on the bare hospital bed and held the towel against my nose. With time, more and more of the NDE was coming back to me. I recalled passing through the ceiling of the floors below me. During the experience, I passed through this room with the bed pushed into the corner and my body went out through the wall and out over the street.

"Yes, I was out there looking back. Gill, if what I experienced was real and not some drug induced hallucination, not some last dying flare of neurons, then the shoe is right out there wedged in between the slats. The only way I could have seen it was from a vantage point out there floating in the air!" Across the street, an elementary school covered the entire block, no part of it any higher than one story. "There is no other vantage point this high, Gill."

Gill was still as he watched the rainfall from the sky. He glanced at me and smiled. "Everybody thought I was crazy, too. Said I had a bad drug trip."

My nose had stopped bleeding, and I felt a cold shiver pass over my body. I sat on the bed and wrapped the towel around my shoulders. "What happened, Gill?"

He turned his dark brown eyes in my direction. "You don't remember, do you?"

I had something to do with his NDE? "I guess not."

Gill pulled a tarp off a chair and sat down. "It's been two years. I was out at Fairmont East working on the CAT scanner. Lucy Stone came and got you."

Lucy was the head tech at East. I felt the tickle of familiarity. "Wait. I'm remembering. You had coughed up blood. "

"Yep. Right in the middle of the CAT scan room. I took you to the bathroom and showed you the blood in the sink."

"That's right! I called your doctor at Central and talked you into going to the hospital because you were going to go home."

Gill nodded. "You know what happened next?"

"No. I think I went out of town that evening. I was on a cruise for two weeks. That's right. And, when I came back, I was out at Fairmont Central for a while. I didn't see you for several weeks."

"That night when I started coughing up blood, the doctors told me I had a Rasmussen aneurysm. Know what that is?"

I nodded. "You must have had some type of pulmonary infection when you were young. We see it in patients who have tuberculosis. One of the cavitary lesions eats into a pulmonary artery and you bleed from the lungs."

"I never had TB. But I had a rip-roaring case of fungal infection when I was a kid. They planned to stick that garden hose down my throat to cauterize the bleeding. They were putting me in a wheelchair to take me down when I passed out. Fell right out onto the floor of my room."

Gill grew silent, wiping his hand across his face, his eyes focused on something I could not see. "I floated just like you did. Went through walls and ceilings. Found that tunnel. But at the end there was this barrier, this soft curtain or something. I pressed my face against it and if felt like fur or feathers. I don't know. But on the other side of it, I could hear something." He looked at me, his voice soft in contrast to his enormous frame. "The most beautiful music you've ever heard. It was something not anywhere close to human. You could feel it, you could taste it. I tried to get through the barrier, and I heard this voice. It told me if I saw what was on the other side of that wing, I wouldn't want to go back."

"Wing?"

"It was an angel with his wings wrapped around me to keep me from going farther. Because, you see, Doc, it wasn't over for me, yet. I heard my wife's voice calling me. She was saying how much she loved me, and I made a choice. I came back."

An eerie silence filled the room. Gill moved over to the bed and sat beside me. It groaned under his weight. "I had dropped out of church for a while. Got hurt by some things going on. Funny thing is, I don't even remember what hurt me so much. Sometimes we shoot our wounded."

"That doesn't just happen in the church." I said, thinking of people like Sanchez. Or myself!

"Well, I was furious for a couple of years at God for what that church did to me. Realized I had made the choices not to go back. So, I looked for some way to justify my return trip from what must have been heaven. Why had God sent me back? I felt like God wanted me to go where no one else cares to go. I go to the boats and the bars and the places you'll never find a preacher. And I try to be a friend to those people and sometimes they come and listen to me talk. No preaching, just talking and listening. Know what I told them just last week?"

I studied his face, his shiny eyes. "What?"

"When bad things happen, we don't need to ask 'Why?' we need to ask 'What?'."

"I don't get it."

"Doc, what are you going to learn from this experience? If you dwell on the 'why' you fail. But, if you look beyond the reasons and try to discover what you can learn from it, so it won't happen again, then you redeem it. You make it worthwhile."

I pulled the towel from my shoulders and studied the blood stains left by my nosebleed. "So, I shouldn't question why my wife died?"

"That's not what I'm saying. Don't ask God why she died. Ask yourself, 'What can I learn from her death?'"

I looked out the rain-stained window as some broken pieces of my puzzle of a life fell into place. "If you had never gotten hurt and never walked away from church, would you be where you are now, talking to the people who need you most?"

Gill smiled. "Now, you're getting it. Sometimes God must let us slip and fall into our own mess to make us look up to Him. Maybe that's what you need to do. What's eating you the most right now?"

"I think someone murdered my wife."

Silence filled the room, interrupted by Gill's heavy breathing. The bed creaked under his weight. "Sorry, Doc. That's some heavy stuff to carry around. Maybe that's the question you should focus on. I bet you've spent the last year wallowing in self-pity, blaming God or yourself for her death. If you think someone killed her, go find those answers. Channel all this pity into action."

"I guess you're right, Gill."

"I know I'm right." He stood up and said, "I always am. Yep, thought of all that while I was in the bathroom."

I smiled. "You have a smart bladder. See if you can get it to help us find my red shoe."

"Oh, I know where it is. Wedged in one of those slats right outside this window. And I have just the tool downstairs to get it." Without a word, he left the room.

Back at the window, I studied the slats running along the ledge just below me. Rain had beaded the surface, and it was raining even harder. There! Was that a small, white string? A shoestring?

With effort, I pulled the cantilevered window open a few more inches, and I could squeeze my head and shoulders through. I reached down toward the shoestring and almost reached it. If I could squeeze another inch or two of my body out the window, I could snare it with my fingers.

Something snapped and the struts holding the window broke, allowing the window to swing fully in toward the room. But my weight was directed outward and instead of falling back into the room, I slid out through the open window. I tried to catch at the old brickwork beneath the window but could find no purchase for my grasp. I slammed onto the ledge, the heavy metal support pole catching me in the middle of my back. The slats bent underneath my weight, and I started sliding out toward the three-story drop to the busy street below.

Wedging my forearm between two slats, I stopped sliding. Closer to the support beam, the slats were less malleable, and I wrapped both arms through the slats and around the support beam as the rest of my body slid out into air. My body hung from the sagging slats and my arms were wedged painfully around the support beam.

Back toward the window, I noticed something red. Barely a foot to my left was a red tennis shoe wedge between two bent slats visible only from my perspective. I had been right. I had seen the shoe. Tightening the grip of my right hand on the support beam, I slid my left arm out to snag the shoe. I pulled it loose and hugged it to my chest. Now that I had my answer to the reality of my NDE, I was probably going to experience another one. But, in that moment I wasn't afraid, knew no regret. I found a quiet peace.

The sudden bending of the support beam shattered the peace. The ledge lurched downward, and I slid outward, held in place only by my right arm, wedged painfully between the vise like grips of two slats. Maybe if I said a little prayer. Maybe if I agreed to go to church. Maybe there was a God after all.

Someone grabbed my shirt collar, and I looked up into the face of Gill Brown. Close enough, God, I said.

MY HANDS SHOOK SO BADLY, coffee sloshed out onto the table in the hospital cafeteria. Gill took the cup from me and sat it next to the red shoe.

"You OK?"

"No. I'm not OK. Do you realize what this shoe means?"

"Someone's walking around barefoot?" Gill said as he sipped at his own coffee.

My hands shook some more. "No! It means that my entire world is turning upside down. There is more to life than just biology! It means I had an out-of-body experience. It means I've got a soul. It means I'm really screwed up." The words spilled out of me in a rush.

"And you didn't know all this before?" Gill was far too calm.

"Yes, and no. I knew some of this could be, but I just didn't want to believe it." I studied his calm, passive face. He rubbed his nose and sniffed.

"Look, we don't want to believe there is a God. If God exists, then we are answerable to God for all our choices. It's better to think it's all just a throw of the dice. Then, no matter what we decide, it's okay because there's not somebody taking notes on our lives. But, like it or not, there is something to this world past our senses. You know it in your gut. Just cause you don't like it, don't change the truth. So, deal with it." He sipped his coffee and smiled. "Have a nice day."

"I'm going home and lie down. I don't feel so good." I said, taking the shoe and hugging it to my chest.

"Doc, take care." Gill said. "Go home and think a little bit about all that's happened."

"I've got a lot to think about." I hugged the shoe tighter.

THIRTEEN

By dusk, sweat soaked my hair, and I felt feverish again. After taking some pain medicine, I wrapped up in my bed covers, trying to screen out the dark cold coming night and the fear that gripped my heart. I drifted on the waves of near slumber.

"GIVE ME THE DEFIBRILLATOR!" A man in a white coat yelled. I was above him, not over two feet away from his head. He had a balding spot. His voice was familiar. He was one of the ER doctors. White coats and scrubs huddled around a body on a table. The ER doctor grabbed two defibrillator pads and shoved down on the body's chest.

"Clear!" He shouted, and the body convulsed with the shock. I looked at the face, slack with unconsciousness. It was me. There was no particular surprise at this. It seemed perfectly natural. In fact, I felt no fear. A peace I had only dreamed of had come over my hovering body. Near the edge of the circle of nurses and doctors, Baldy stepped into the room. He looked

around as if he were trying not to be noticed and pulled a small syringe out of his pocket. He stepped deftly between the dodging, weaving bodies working on me and reached for an intravenous line. Without hesitation, he stabbed the needle of the syringe into a port and injected a black liquid into the IV line. The liquid moved quickly down the transparent line until it disappeared into my arm. Baldy nodded and slid quietly out the door.

I SAT bolt upright in my bed; my body drenched in sweat. The dream had come again, only this time, much more realistic than before. Gasping for breath, I patted my bare chest with my hands. I was here in my bedroom. I was real, and I was alive.

Blinking in confusion, I tried to adjust my vision to the dark room around me. The clock showed two AM. I got out of the bed and made my way to the tiny den of my apartment and grabbed a cold beer from the refrigerator. I slumped into my recliner, my hands shaking from the recent memory. The bottle lip clattered against my teeth. The bottle slipped from my hand and rolled down my body and across the floor, trailing beer and suds on the carpet.

What had I seen? More memories of my near-death experience? The red shoe sat on the coffee table not three feet away and I looked at it like it was a cobra about to strike. If all I had seen had truly happened, then what had the bald man injected into my IV?

The memory of the experience was now as clear as the red shoe sitting on my coffee table. I had told Gill this changed everything for me. Did it? Where did God fit into this scenario? Jesus?

Standing shakily, I made my way to the closet. On the top shelf, I spied the old wooden box. My aunt had given the box to me when I was a young boy. She collected antiques, and the box fascinated me when I first saw it on the huge mantle of her garage sized fireplace. As a small child, the fireplace seemed that large at the time. Aunt Myrtis had given me the box for my birthday and since the age of ten, I had put all kinds of memorabilia in it.

I placed the box on the table next to the red shoe and opened it slowly. The odor of old paper and cedar wood wafted over me. I gently took out the upper tray filled with odds and ends from my childhood to access the lower section of the box. Ah, there it was. A Bible. At least, a New Testament. It had a dark blue leather cover and was the size of a paperback. My mother had my name etched in silver in the lower corner.

Inside, I studied the dedication page. "To Jack from Mom and Dad on the occasion of your baptism." I had been ten years old when I "walked the aisle" and "gave my life to Jesus". Funny, but I had not thought about that day in years. My finger traced the cursive writing of my mother. She had a bouffant hair-do and cat eye glasses. In fact, Dr. Francisco reminded me of my mother. But my mother and father were long gone. They had died in a car wreck on the way back from Branson, Missouri, when I was a senior in medical school. I had lied to Bolaski to protect Keri. My parents were deliriously happy.

I picked up the Bible and held it to my nose and inhaled the fragrance of old leather and, yes, a hint of my mother's favorite perfume. I hadn't thought about Jesus in years. Medical school and residency had taken up all my time. Not to mention, Janice. And then, my job with the radiology group at Fairmont demanded ten-hour days. And, then the real problems began. The unwanted memory suddenly returned.

"JACK, TELL ME SOMETHING GOOD." Janice reached for my hand. The ultrasound technologist moved the probe across Janice's lower pelvis. I squinted at the screen and felt a flicker of excitement.

"I see a fetal pole!"

For a second, the tiny bean shaped object sprang into view on the ultrasound machine monitor, the small forming body of our child. As the technologist typed on her keyboard and moved cursors around on the screen, my hopes ebbed.

"What is it?" Janice whispered. "Why are you frowning?"

"An early fetus, darling. Let's see how far along you are." My voice shook with fear.

Janice's lips creased into a tight line, and a tear ran from her eye. "There's something wrong, isn't there? I can tell from you face."

"Just give us a second." The technologist had put the Doppler part of the ultrasound field in the center of the fetal pole. She was looking for a heartbeat. There was none! She tried three more times, each time changing her angle.

"It's dead, isn't it?" Janice said hoarsely. "Just like the other two!"

"It just may be too early." I tried to sound reassuring. Janice glared at me.

"It's the radiation, isn't it?" She said. "You're a radiologist and it's the radiation. Genetic malformations from the radiation. Right?" Tears were pouring down her cheeks. She reached down and grabbed the probe out of the tech's hands and tossed it aside. The tech barely caught it before it hit the floor. Janice whirled out of the bed, pulling up her running pants and smearing the ultrasound gel over her abdomen.

I tried to grab her arm, and she shoved me aside. "Don't touch me."

My heart sank. "Janice! Please!"

Janice threw aside the paper blanket and shoved her finger in my face. "I'm done, Jack! I'm done with trying to have us a child. It's obvious we will never have a baby. Got it? God doesn't want another one of us walking the face of this earth." She sobbed and dashed out of the room. I tried to follow her but by the time I got to the waiting room, she was gone.

Back at work, I tried calling her phone. It went to voicemail until the mailbox was full. Ron Charles sat at the other reading station at Central.

"Hey, Jack, seen the latest Marvel movie? Man, that thing was impressive." He held the microphone up to his lips. "Susan McNeil, two view chest Xray. The heart is within normal limits for size. The aorta demonstrates uncoiling most likely because of atherosclerotic disease or long-standing hypertension. There is a two centimeter, spiculated mass projected over the right lung base that was not present on the previous film from one year ago. This must be considered neoplastic in origin until proven other-wise. I recommend CT of the lung with contrast for further evaluation."

Ron pointed to the screen. "What do you think, Jack? Pretty obvious cancer, right?"

I glanced listlessly over my shoulder. "Sure, Ron."

Ron fell silent and placed his microphone on the desk. "You okay?"

I sighed and looked back at my own monitors. "We just did an ultrasound on Janice. Looks like fetal demise."

His chair squeaked, and I felt him loom over me. He put a hand on my shoulder. "Jack, I'm sorry. I know the two of you have been trying for a while. Maybe you need to go to genetic counseling."

My anger surged. "It's me, right? We work hard every day taking care of all these patients and we stand in that room while doing procedures and our bodies just soak up the radiation! Why do we do this, Ron? Now, there is something wrong with me. I'm the reason we can't have a baby."

Ron stepped back and put up his hands. "Hey, calm down, Jack. You know the amount of radiation we receive is negligible. We wear our lead aprons. Unless you're Rolly or Dog and spend hours in the angio suite, you've got nothing to worry about."

"I'm sorry. I'm just upset. Janice stormed out and I can't get her on the phone."

Ron glanced at his watch. "Hey, you've only got an hour left in this rotation. Take off and find her. I can handle the rest of the reading for the afternoon. I try to imagine what I would want if I were in your place. It's not that complicated. Now, go! Find Janice. She needs you."

IT WAS EARLY OCTOBER, *and I knew exactly where Janice might be. Along the Talako River in October, the city held its Autumn Festival, complete with crafts, food, art, and entertainment. This is where I first met Janice. I parked along the city street overlooking the broad expanse of grass and open space leading up to the river. White canopied booths covered the grounds. The Texas Street bridge crossed just above me. Passing booths of art, crafts and food, I walked toward the nearest bridge pylon. Janice was sitting on a bench, head cradled in her arms, her blonde hair draped over her face.*

I quietly sat beside her. "I figured you'd be here."

She looked up at me and then at the pylon. "I'm sorry, Jack. Disappointment is like a knife in my heart."

A mural covered the huge concrete pylon before us. It rocked and vibrated with passing cars on the bridge above us. "You remember when we met here?"

Janice nodded. "Of course, I do. I was sad."

"Depressed. Suicidal."

She looked at me. "I wasn't that bad. Mike had broken up with me. He wanted a token wife. Not someone smarter than he was."

Chuckling, I said. "Then you should be grateful, or you would never have met me."

Janice almost smiled. She poked me. I walked toward the pylon and paused before the scene. Mary and Joseph sat in the manger surrounded by animals. The stark, multicolored broken tiles merged into a touching image. Cradled in Mary's arms, shards of light surrounded a small child's head. At that Festival an artist had drawn scenes on each pylon and then allow people to fill in the image with tiles. I had first seen Janice standing before this incomplete image of the Nativity.

"You were putting the final touches around Jesus' face." I reached out and touched the image of the Christ child.

Janice moved up beside me, her arms hugged tightly across her chest. "I filled in the light radiating from his face. He brought light into the darkness."

I slowly reached over and pulled her against me. "You brought light into my darkness after," I paused. "She died." The lie came easily to my lips, and I wished I could tell her more.

Janice stiffened at my touch but soon melted into my side. "We both lost someone. Oh, Jack, what are we going to do?"

"What we always do. Press on." I turned her to face me. "I have a surprise for you."

Janice's red-rimmed eyes focused on me. "I hate surprises."

"We are going to Colorado Springs for our tenth anniversary. Let's make it a time just for us. Let's reboot, redo, re-up our vows, whatever you call it."

Janice finally smiled and wiped a tear from her cheek. "I'll lose the baby first."

"You'll be fine by then. We can take our time and think about what we want to do next. There are still some options."

Janice nodded and put her hands on my face. "Jack Merchant, now I know why I love you so much. You are eternally optimistic, but you're a terrible liar."

"Okay, so maybe I just now thought of going for our anniversary. We can stay at the cheesy motel where we spent our honeymoon." I smiled, and she followed suit. Her smile lit up my world.

"Okay, I'm in."

I leaned in and kissed her. "I love you, Janice."

She pulled back and tears dripped from her lips. "Ditto."

ETERNALLY OPTIMISTIC? My optimism had died in the fiery tempest with Janice. And now, unasked and undesired, God had burst into my life at the end of a tunnel of light and holding a red shoe. I opened the New Testament at random and looked at the center of the right-hand page. A passage was highlighted in yellow with my mother's initials next to it.

"Brothers and sisters, we do not want you to be uninformed about those who sleep in death, so that you do not grieve like the rest of mankind, who have no hope. For we believe that Jesus died and rose again, and so we believe that God will bring with Jesus those who have fallen asleep in him."

The verse was from 1 Thessalonians chapter 4. Something

was scribbled in the margin next to my mother's initials. I squinted in the pale light of my bedside lamp.

"Our hope lies beyond the grave!" Was it true? My gaze shifted to the red shoe. God had shown me there was more to me than just a brain. There was more to me than neurochemicals. This red shoe represented something transcendent, something undefinable in my world of science. I closed the Bible and placed it next to the shoe and touched the shoelaces, still moist from the rain.

If this was real, then I had a lot of thinking to do. And, perhaps, praying too.

FOURTEEN

After falling back into a restless sleep, I woke up Sunday morning and spent the rest of the day in the recliner, drinking juice and popping pills, trying to get rid of the headaches and the fevers and chills. Probably a cold from being out in the rain. And almost dying a second time in less than a week. The growing headache was so intense, I couldn't think any more about the shoe. Or the Bible. By evening, I was feeling better, and the chills suddenly stopped. I found some sleeping pills tucked away in the back of my medicine chest. They were over two years old. They had been for Janice. I took them anyway, so I would sleep through any more resurfacing memories.

"DUDE, YOU LOOK LIKE CRAP." Moondog said as he came through the door to the reading room at Fairmont East. Our reading room gleamed with white walls and carpet. Paintings hung along the walls outside our office. East was pristine and new, a bright and gleaming place of modern healing. It made Central look like something out of a horror movie. I sat in front of the other PACS system monitor.

"Good morning to you, too." I mumbled as I cycled through the last of the exams for reading. Dog sat at the other station and logged in.

"Bro, Roger said you haven't been feeling well."

"Probably just a cold."

Dog turned toward me, raising his scrub shirt to cover his mouth. "Don't breathe in my direction."

I laughed and shook my head. "I'll go get a mask."

Dog chuckled. "Jack, you had a contrast reaction and almost died. You have every reason to feel bad. You sure you can work?"

"I'm tired of lying in the bed." I said. 'Remembering my death,' I wanted to say.

"Hey guys, how's it going?" Doctor Reese walked into the room, trailed by his ever-present nurse, Molly. Reese was a tall, heavy-set man who always wore his blue jeans and a denim shirt. He sported a huge handlebar mustache and one of the busiest internal medicine practices in the city.

"Morning Bill." I said. "What can I do for you?"

"I need to see a CAT scan on Dorothy Mercedes."

I pulled up the search menu and typed in the first three letters of the woman's last name. A list appeared, and I gasped. There, just two names below Dorothy's, was Janice Merchant. Bill, sensing my unease, leaned over to squint at the screen.

"Why don't I get Dog to look at it with me?" He whispered.

My hands were shaking, and I leaned back in my chair. "OK." I managed.

Reese drifted over to Moondog's station, and they lost themselves in conversation over Dorothy Mercedes' CAT scan. I looked at the name floating in front of me. In this list were the ultrasounds of our children who never lived. My finger twitched as I held it over the mouse button. One click on her name and our entire journey would show up in dates and times of regrets. I closed my eyes and clicked the mouse button.

When I opened my eyes, it shocked me to see the topmost exam was an MRI two days before we left for Colorado. November 18, Mickey Mouse's birthday! Janice's love of all things Disney came back to me. She had told me to remember Mickey's birthday in my NDE. Or was it a dream?

I felt a chill and clicked on the MRI. Images appeared on the other monitor. An MRI of her pelvis popped up, several imaging sequences in a four paneled window. My heart skipped a beat, and I felt the tears fill my eyes. She had gone ahead with the plan we had never agreed on!

"HEY, babe, I heard you went to see Mary today." I said.

Janice picked at her kale salad and kept her gaze on the plate. "Who told you that?"

We had cooked dinner and stayed in for the weekend. I had planned a delightful meal and then a walk in the park. I could feel the heft of the ring in my pants pocket. "Her partner, Fred. Are you feeling okay? I thought everything went well after." I glanced at her, and she still avoided my look. "Losing the baby."

"That went fine." She said tersely. She picked at her salad. The silence was deafening.

I placed my fork on my plate and drew a deep breath. Nothing could ruin this day. Nothing! "Is there something else going on?"

Janice paused and dropped her fork. She looked up at me and her eyes filled with tears. "I don't want to go through this again."

"Through what?"

"*Getting pregnant and losing a baby.*"

I was silent for a moment, trying my best to read the moment. "So, what are you thinking?"

"Hysterectomy." She said. "I've had bleeding off and on after every pregnancy. Mary thinks I have endometriosis and multiple fibroids. It's only going to get worse for me."

My face warmed with anger. Now was not the time for this argument. I had planned on asking her to marry me again. A new ring. A new ceremony in Colorado Springs in a week. A new beginning. As calmly as possible, I said. "What about a surrogate?"

Janice wiped away the tears. Her cheeks reddened. "I'm done, Jack. I don't want to do this anymore with you. I don't want to have a baby. I don't want a family, okay?"

My heart raced, and it came out before I could stop it. "So, what you're saying is I'm not the reason we can't have a child. It's you!"

Janice froze and blanched.

"I'm sorry. I didn't mean that."

She stood up slowly and nodded. "I guess the truth is finally out. You just decided for me. I'll call Mary tomorrow. I'm going to bed. To sleep. Alone. Don't bother waking me up for the rest of the day. I suggest you go somewhere for the evening. Maybe even for the night." She said these words calmly, but her lips were trembling, and her hand was shaking as she turned and went to our bedroom, slammed the door and locked it.

THE MEMORY WAS ALL TOO real and far too painful. After a couple of days, I talked her into going to Colorado after all. The reason we had gone away for a week became not for a renewal of our vows, but so I could convince her to cancel the hysterectomy. I got my money back on the ring. Now, I realized without my knowledge, she had come here to East to have an MRI of her pelvis. Why? Most likely, it was a pre-operative study to assess anatomy before the surgery. Or maybe she did it to prove to me she needed the surgery? After all, I was a radiologist. What better proof could she give me than a radiology study?

I ran my cursor over the first set of images and scrolled through them. Instead of the crystal-clear image of all the organs in her pelvis, the image was filled with a multitude of black spots. We called them "black holes"; artifacts produced by some type of ferromagnetic substance in the body. The metal interfered with the magnetic field and produced a loss of signal to the MRI receptors. But these were scattered, tiny black holes all over her pelvic region. I pulled up the next sequence. More black holes. All the pulse sequences had black holes. It made no sense. Janice had never had surgery, so there should not have been any metal such as surgery clips in her pelvis. She had never been shot, so there shouldn't be any kind of metal shrapnel present. It had to be a glitch in the machine, not metal fragments in my wife's pelvis!

I went back to the information page and looked for the initials of the MRI operator. JG. Jose Garcia, the chief MRI tech. Hurrying out of the office, I almost ran down the hallway past bewildered Xray techs and into the MRI suite. Jose huddled over the keyboard, watching a sequence of MRI images appear on the monitor. Through the window above his desk, I saw a patient stuck head first into the huge donut of the MRI machine.

"Jose, why didn't you tell me you did an MRI on my wife?"

Jose, a short, squat man, turned fiery eyes on me. "What?"

"I just found an MRI on my wife done two days before she died. It had your initials on it."

Jose's eyes narrowed, and he frowned. "Oh, yeah. I remember that. We tried to do an MRI of her pelvis, but we got artifacts. I thought she told you."

"No, she didn't tell me. Why was she getting an MRI?"

Jose shrugged. "I don't know, Doctor Merchant. She had an order from her gynecologist. But it was weird. No matter what we tried, we got these metal artifacts throughout her pelvis. She even went back to Xray and had them Xray her pelvis. No metal."

I calmed down and slumped into the chair beside him. "Do you think it was the machine?"

Jose shrugged. "I don't know. It didn't happen again that day. I even had Gill look at it."

"Can you pull her images up and make me a data disk?"

Jose's expression soured, and he held back his protest. "Sure, Doc." Jose liked nothing to interfere with his imaging.

I walked back to the reading room and dialed up Gill. "Gill?"

"Had any good memories lately?" His voice was slow and laconic.

"As a matter of fact, I did. But I'm calling you about an MRI done on my wife over a year ago."

"Sorry, Doc. I don't read MRI's."

"You came over and looked at some kind of artifact."

"Oh, you're at East. I didn't catch that. Yeah, I remember that. Couldn't figure how those black holes appeared. I checked out the coils and the pulse sequences. Everything was copacetic. No problems."

I hung up the phone after thanking Gill. Having the MRI without my knowledge hurt me. And I never had the chance to repair that broken relationship because she died! It seemed our relationship was full of black holes, sinking beneath the weight of our differences. My attention returned to her MRI. What could have caused the artifacts?

Connie, the chief secretary for the department, walked up behind me and handed me a note. "Dr. Francisco called and said to remind you to meet her in her office this evening."

I looked at the note like it was in a foreign language. I had forgotten about our meeting. "Thanks, Connie."

Connie patted me on the shoulder. "She said something about a body they had exhumed. Said you would be interested."

An icy chill ran down my back. Had they exhumed Janice's body?

FIFTEEN

Dr. Sam Francisco held a blender cup filled with a dark green liquid. She sipped at it and grimaced. "I hate this stuff. But it keeps me healthy. Offsets the radicals in my bloodstream from lack of sleep." She glared at the cup and placed it on her desk. She still wore the red cat-eye glasses that almost matched the red of her hair. Christmas music by Frank Sinatra played quietly in the background. "It's almost 6 P.M. and I still have a day of work before I go home. Now, Dr. Merchant--" She crossed her hands on the desk.

"Jack." I said, trying to hide my irritation. "I never signed a paper for Janice's exhumation."

"Jack, they found the original notification and sent it to me. The other day you said would agree to it. So, I proceeded." She frowned. "I'm sorry. I thought it would spare you more grief. Plus, I've been a bit busy." She retrieved the form from a folder and slid across the desk. "So, if you would be so kind as to make all of this legal. Unless you want Sanchez to show up again."

A Santa shaped mug held several pens. I grabbed one and signed the form. "Now, it's all legal. So?"

"We exhumed her body this morning. It's in one of the coolers. I plan on doing another post tomorrow." Sam put the form in the folder.

I felt nauseated at the smell of the vile green swill in the cup. For some reason, I could smell it strongly and it sent a sweet, sickly wave down the back of my throat, almost eliciting a gag. What was happening?

"I ran across an MRI she had the day before she died. There were some strange artifacts produced by the MRI. We call them 'black holes'. Usually, some kind of metal in the tissue, but Janice didn't have any reason for metal to be there. Maybe you could look at the pelvic region. See if you find anything odd." I wiped sweat from my forehead and couldn't believe what I was saying. Was I so callous and, yes, casually talking about the autopsy results on my wife's pelvis?

"Could have been some kind of injection. Some medications can contain metals. But the metal would be in such small quantities, I doubt it would mess up an MRI. Maybe your machine malfunctioned." She reached for the cup, and I put up a restraining hand.

"Sorry, could you wait before taking another swig? I'm a little nauseated."

Sam paused and put her hands back on the desk. "Sure. This must be hard for you."

"Look, about malfunction, I thought of that. Our engineer assures me the MRI was working just fine." The room swam with an onslaught of dizziness, and I slumped back in my chair. "I brought a copy of the MRI for correlation." I placed the disc on her desk.

"You know, I wouldn't know much about what I'm looking at. That's why I have you as a consultant." She grimaced. "Jack, you don't look so well."

"Have you found out any more about Baldy?" I ignored her comment.

"Yes, I did." She leaned back in her chair. "Problem is, I don't know how much to tell you."

"I'm on the payroll now."

"As a consultant." She pursed her lips. "That's what I wanted to talk to you about. I'd like to keep you on a more permanent basis. I won't need you all the time, but if you would look at occasional cases with me, I would pay you a small stipend."

I wiped at my forehead. "Would it mean going to court to testify?"

"Rarely. You don't like lawyers, do you?"

"No. I almost had a heart attack in my first deposition. I ended up in the ER on heart monitoring. My blood pressure was high enough to qualify me for the intensive care unit."

Sam shrugged and adjusted her red cat-eye glasses. "Jack, it's the nature of the beast. If you get put on the stand, you'll be the expert. You'll know more about these imaging procedures than anyone else in the room. It won't be about you. It'll be about the evidence. Circumstances will be different."

Few doctors liked the idea of working with lawyers. Lawyers were our adversaries, their whole reason for being to accuse doctors of purposefully hurting the very patients they had taken an oath to heal. "If I agree, will you tell me what you found out about Baldy?"

Sam raised an eyebrow. "If that's your price, I will. You sign a confidentiality statement and a nondisclosure agreement with this department, and I'll tell you anything you need to know about the cases I consulted you on."

"Where do I sign?"

Sam shuffled through papers on her desk and pulled out a folder with my name on it. "I had these ready in case you agreed." She handed a pile of papers to me. I squinted as more dizziness hit me and shuffled through each paper until I had signed them all. "Now, what did you find out?"

"You paid little attention to the fine print." Sam said,

"I trust you, Dr. Francisco. After all, you trusted me enough to make me your newest consultant."

She placed the papers back in the folder. "Okay, his heart valve had a serial number. We were able to trace down the date and time of his surgery. Turns out he had the surgery in Switzerland. His name is Wilhelm Klause."

Sam's door opened and Jerry Langley stepped in. He took one look at me and frowned. "Jack, what are you doing here? I have an appointment."

"I do, too. Besides, I'm now an official consultant with the coroner's office. Several trees died to document that fact." I patted the folder before me.

Jerry's face clouded, and he glanced at Sam. "Is that such a good idea?"

"He picked up the poison bottle. I can use all the help I can get. I was just giving him the skinny on Baldy." Sam said.

"Baldy?" Jerry raised an eyebrow.

"Sorry, I named him that." I said.

"What did you find out?" Sam said.

Jerry sat beside me. "What about Jack?"

"He's on the payroll now. Just signed an NDA."

Jerry frowned and opened the folder he carried. "Well, Jack's orderly is not exactly in the medical profession. Turns out he is a known mercenary. He's implicated in several third world country rebellions and is suspected in over a dozen assassinations."

"An assassin working in one of our local hospitals?" Sam said as she stood up from behind her desk. "That's strange, isn't it?"

"Well, not necessarily, considering the president of the United States will visit here next week." Jerry closed the folder.

I felt my heart racing, and I began gasping for breath. An assassin had injected something into my veins during my code the week before? "Sam, I had a near death experience last week." I blurted out.

Sam froze. "An NDE? What does that have to do with anything?"

I was breathing harder. "I recalled something from the NDE. A red shoe caught in one of the hospital's ledges on the third floor. There's no way I could have seen it from the ground or the roof. I found it on Saturday. It was there just as I had seen it."

Sam sat down and regarded me with skepticism. "Are you sure you didn't see it or overhear a patient talking about it?"

"I'm sure, Dr. Francisco. And there's more. The other night I had another memory from the experience. During my code, this Klause guy came in and injected some kind of black liquid into one of my IV lines."

Sam looked at Jerry. Jerry sighed. "Jack, you've been sick lately. Maybe you were hallucinating. Maybe it was the medicine you've been taking."

"No!" I slapped the desk in front of me. "It was real. It happened. And now, you're telling me this man who injected something into me was an assassin? And he turns up dead the next day in what looks like a professional hit. None of that is a hallucination. It is real."

Sam reached over the desk and patted my hand. "Now, Jack, calm down."

"I've been sick ever since the code. What if he injected some kind of virus or something? I could be on my way to a painful death, and I could infect half the city."

Sam quickly pulled back her hand. "Then let's do some

tests. I can have your blood drawn right here and we'll run it through our lab."

LATER, I winced as Trenda stuck the needle into my arm. She smiled. "Sorry, my patients usually don't feel anything."

I looked away at Jerry leaning against the wall. He was tapping the folder against his leg, studying me with a quizzical look.

"What?"

"I checked on Korskin like you asked. Brilliant physician. Lots of accolades and published papers. But there is one thing kind of strange. All his records are rather pristine for the last five years and then they get murky."

"What do you mean by murky?"

Jerry pushed away from the wall and walked across the lab room while Trenda continued to extract large quantities of blood from my arm. "Call it an intuition. I've seen this kind of thing before. It's as if someone purposefully filled the records with lots of details in case someone looks at them. But only back to a certain point. As if whoever put them together tired of the details and wasn't worried about anyone digging any deeper than the past five years." Jerry stopped and looked at me, his eyes filled with weariness. "Jack, the president is coming to town. If there was anything seriously wrong with Korskin, the secret service would turn it up."

Trenda pulled the needle out of my arm and left the room, carrying too many vials of blood. I pressed the cotton swab on the puncture site. "You don't sound too confident. Maybe they won't have that 'funny feeling' like you do. I know there's something there, Jerry."

"Your source told you, right? If you would tell me more about your source."

"Out of the question." My cell phone rang. I took the phone out of my pocket and bent my arm over the cotton swab. "Hello?"

"Dr. Merchant, this is Dick Korskin. Did I catch you at a bad time?"

I looked at Jerry and frowned. I mouthed "It's Korskin." Once again, the man's timing was spooky. I stood up, suddenly dizzy. "Uh, no, Dick. I was just having some blood drawn. I've been feeling under the weather lately."

"I'm sorry to hear that. After a good night's sleep, you'll feel back to normal. Look, I know we didn't part on a friendly note the other day, but I was hoping you could come to a private reception tomorrow evening at the Institute. A few of your wife's friends want to get together to tour the new wing before the public gets to see it later in the week. I thought you might like to attend."

I wiped at my sweaty brow and leaned back in the chair. The thought of raising more memories of Janice was painful. But the chance to find out what she was doing was too good to pass up. "I'd be honored. What time?"

"Oh, around seven ish? I'll see you then. And bring that proposal with you."

I pocketed my phone and looked at Jerry. "I'm going to a reception for Janice's new wing tomorrow evening."

Jerry shook his head. "Oh, no you don't. Jack, don't go snooping around on me. If Korskin has a shady past, as you claim, you could be in danger."

"Now you're worried about the man being dangerous? I'm already in danger. A known assassin squirted something in my veins. What could be worse?" I pushed past him and headed for home.

SIXTEEN

"Welcome, Jack. You look better than the last time I saw you."
Dr. Korskin shook my hand as I stepped through the glass doors
into the vast atrium of the Biotechnology Institute. His hair, as
usual, was perfectly combed and his suit fit him like a glove. My
scrubs, on the other hand, hung on me like clothes on a skele-
ton. I couldn't put on the suit I had bought when I had asked
Janice to marry me again. I pushed my glasses back on my nose
and tried to look "healthy".

"Your advice seemed to have worked. I slept better than I
have in weeks and my fever and chills seem to have gone. I
might be over things." I lied.

"Good." Korskin smiled and motioned me toward the elevator. "Janice's co-workers are waiting. We plan to have the President and members of his cabinet on Friday when we will
officially dedicate Janice's wing." Korskin led me into the
elevator and pressed the button for the ninth floor. We soared
up through the tall, open Institute atrium, the glass windows
giving an excellent view of the cool night. Beyond the atrium

windows, the skyline of Talako appeared, huge spotlights of the casinos sweeping the sky, beckoning gamblers to their paradise.

"I don't know what got into me. I forgot to invite you to the Presidential reception, so I thought I could give you a private tour tonight." Korskin said.

The doors to the elevator opened, and we walked down an empty hallway toward a wing of the X shaped building. A lump formed in my throat as the doors to one wing came into sight. "Janice Manning Nanotechnology Division" gleamed in metallic letters above the door. Korskin opened the doors, and we walked into a modest reception area filled with a dozen people.

The next few minutes were a blur to me. I remembered most of the people, but their recollections of Janice brought tears to my eyes and filled me with unbelievable sorrow. Korskin finally came to my rescue, handing me a fluted glass of champagne.

"Let me show you the lab area, Jack. I think you might need a break from all these people." He led me past the reception desk and into a long, well-lit hallway.

"This would have been Janice's lab." He motioned to a door, and we pushed into a vast area filled with biological equipment and computer screens. "We have the latest computer technology and the latest nano-equipment."

"What was Janice working on just before she died?" I left the champagne on the counter. The thought of drinking it made me nauseous.

Korskin motioned to a computer monitor, and his hands danced over a keyboard. The screen came to life with spinning, floating shiny globules. "She called them nannomemes. A building block for artificial cells. Imagine being able to replace lost blood cells with artificial cells that have a much longer life than red blood cells. Or imagine replacing dead muscle tissue in the heart with a nannomeme that functions as cardiac muscle. Of course, we're no where close to that level. These are only computer models Janice developed. But we're hoping that within five years, we will have the first prototypes. Microscopic, no, molecular level machines utilizing genetic engineering."

I watched the globules spin across the screen. "That's amazing. Janice never told me about this."

"She kept her work a secret. Publish or perish. She wanted the credit when the papers were published." Korskin said.

"Funny you should say perish." I whispered.

Korskin paled. "I'm sorry. I didn't mean that, Jack. It's just a figure of speech."

"I'd like to see her office."

Korskin tensed for a moment. "We left it just like it was. I know it's been a year, but we kept everything in her office until after we dedicated the wing. Then we're going to go through her office and archive her belongings."

"There might be something in there I'd like to have. You know, some mementos. Would you mind showing me?"

Korskin looked away and then nodded. "Okay, sure. This way."

He led me down the long corridor to the end of the wing and pulled out a key to unlock the door in front of me. He opened the door and the stale odor of a space long closed wafted over us. I turned on the light.

Janice had never been a tidy person. Stacks of papers covered her desk. On the wall above her desk, she had hung pictures. One showed us at the Garden of the Gods in Colorado Springs on our honeymoon. The tall, red stone pillars towered around us as we stood arm in arm.

"Our honeymoon." I pointed to the picture, and suddenly the weight of loss hit me like a ton of bricks. Korskin grabbed me as I stumbled and guided me into her chair. He backed away and just looked at me. Korskin didn't know what to do. He stood in the doorway and then motioned outside. "I'll go get you some tissues."

The door closed behind him, and I fought for control. I had only a few seconds to snoop around. I knew Janice kept her private stash of snacks in a drawer on the side of the desk. It was an odd desk we had found at an antique store. The back, right-hand corner of the desk boasted a secret drawer. I leaned over the desk and felt for the small indentation. We had learned how to push the latch and the drawer would pop open.

The drawer snapped open, and I shoved my fingers into the empty space. Outside, I heard Korskin's footsteps coming my way. My fingers brushed aside candy wrappers and empty boxes of cigarettes until they touched something hard and cold. My fingers closed on a small computer tablet. I pulled the tablet from the drawer and without looking at it, slid it into my scrubs pant pocket and closed the drawer. I slumped back into the chair just as Korskin came through the door carrying a box of tissues.

"Here, Jack. I know this has been so hard on you." He pushed the box in my direction.

I took a handful of tissues and blew my nose. Blood gushed across my hand and splattered on the papers on Janice's desk. More blood poured down my face onto my scrubs.

"Oh, my God." Korskin said. I lurched up out of her chair and the dizziness hit me and I fell over the chair onto Janice's desk, pulling all the papers and all her untidy life down onto me into darkness.

SEVENTEEN

I blinked at the bright lights glaring down into my eyes and tried to sit up. A hand pushed me back, and I looked up into the face of Dr. Elon Goodman, one of the ER physicians at Fairmont Central.

"Lie back, Jack. You're OK." He said.

I returned to my prone condition with little persuasion. "What happened?"

"You had quite a nosebleed. I'd say you lost a unit of blood before we could get it cauterized. Fortunately, you were out most of the time." Goodman said. "Jack, I'm afraid I've got some bad news."

I looked at him, his eyes filled with that sadness all doctors get when they must tell their patients they're going to die. "What?"

"Dr. Sam Francisco tracked you down and faxed me your lab work. You've got leukemia."

Someone kicked me in the gut! I gasped and aspirated blood gurgling in my throat. "Leukemia?"

"Acute Myelogenous Leukemia. I've put in a consult to Linda

Krale, the oncologist. We're going to put you in the hospital over at the Cancer Treatment Center and start chemotherapy tomorrow."

I shook my head. This was coming too fast. "Tomorrow?"

"Jack, you know you must move quickly with leukemia. I'm sure Linda will want to do a bone marrow in the morning to stage it and get some more blood for smears. Do you have any preference for a surgeon to place you port?"

The port would be an indwelling venous catheter inserted beneath my collar bone through which to infuse chemotherapy. I tried to answer, but my mouth wouldn't work. "I don't care. We can place those in radiology now. Call Rolly. He's the best interventional radiologist in the group." The "port" would have a subcutaneous "well" just under the skin in my upper chest with a catheter threaded through the subclavian vein into the right atrial chamber of my heart. Medication could be given without the worry of scarring down a peripheral vein.

"Look, you've got some visitors outside. I would not let them in, but you look like a deer caught in the headlights. Why don't you talk to them while I arrange transport to the Cancer Treatment Center and then we'll talk some more afterwards?"

I nodded, my mind whirling with confusion. Goodman opened the door and Keri rushed in. She came to me, throwing her arms around my neck, tears dashing down her cheeks.

"Why are you here?" I whispered.

"I heard you were in trouble. I'm sorry, Jack. I never left town. I had to make sure you were going to be OK." She pulled back. Tears streaked her face. "I'm sorry."

"You're placing your life in danger. We found out Korskin has a dirty past and if he finds out you're here, he'll kill you."

Keri glanced over her shoulder at the door to my ER exam room. "She is out there! I think I'll be safe with a cop by my side."

"Sanchez?" I groaned.

"You called?" Sanchez walked in. I swore as Sanchez stepped up to my bed, hands on her hips.

"Sanchez, what are you doing here?"

"Following all leads, Jack. And the biggest lead is standing across from me." She pointed at Keri.

"Leave her out of this, Sanchez."

"She's not some long-lost relative, Jacky baby. And, your parents never divorced. The newspaper archive told me about the wreck."

I shook my head. "I just found out I have leukemia, Sanchez. Chances are I'm going to be dead in a few weeks, so you've got your killer. Are you happy? Now go back to Colorado and leave us alone."

Keri winced beside me at the word, "leukemia". Her hand gripped my arm.

Sanchez shook her head. "Not that easy. I want answers. And from you, not your buddy on the police force."

"Jerry?"

Jerry peeked into the room and walked into the room. "Hey, Jack. I tried to stop her from bugging you." He glared at Sanchez. "Evidently they don't believe in professional courtesy in Colorado Springs." Sanchez glared back and Jerry ignored her and came up on the opposite side of the bed from Keri and Sanchez. "Jack, what's happening?"

"I've got leukemia, Jerry. I'm going to die."

We were all quiet for a moment except for the sound of Sanchez tapping her foot. Sanchez finally huffed away and sat in a chair. "When you get through singing 'Kum Ba Yah', let me know."

Jerry ignored her and nodded. "We're here to help you, Jack. You're not in this alone." He studied Keri and sighed.

"Look, I heard from Sam, and I can't share anything else until you tell me who Keri really is."

I tensed. "What do you mean who she 'really is'?"

Jerry gave me a look I recalled from our days in college. It was the look he often gave me when I used some lame excuse for why I blew a test. It wasn't because of the flu. It was always a party.

Keri looked at me. "Jack, we've got to tell them. Between jaguar over there and your good friend, they'll eventually find out."

"But your life will be in danger." I drew a shuddering breath. "You'll have to change your identity again."

Keri smiled. "I'm pretty good at it." She looked at Jerry. "Jerry, that's your name, right?"

Jerry nodded. Keri crossed to the door to the hospital room and glanced outside. "Okay, I think we have some privacy for a few minutes." She said as she turned back to the room. "I'll tell our story. It began with a vaccine. Before COVID became a pandemic, the federal government was stockpiling preventative equipment in case of a new SARS outbreak."

"I seem to remember reading about that." Sanchez said. "A scandal. Funds had been diverted that were intended for the preparation. The government claims that's one reason we were so unprepared for COVID."

"Right. Only the funds were not diverted. Money had been spent on vaccine development from gain of function research on possibly emerging viral agents. Problem is, the vaccine was defective." Keri said. "A well-known pharmaceutical company claimed to have already perfected the next vaccine. But the vaccine was faulty. Over 100 million doses had to be destroyed. At least that is the official story."

Sanchez shook her head. "Don't remember that."

"The media downplayed that story." Keri said. "Would have embarrassed the government."

"They sold those vaccines to the U. S. Government for 20 dollars a dose." I said. "They would have been worth 2 billion dollars to the pharmaceutical company. But it turns out the truth was worse than a defective vaccine. The vaccine wasn't defective. Want to know who blew the whistle?"

"Who?"

I pointed to Keri. "She did."

Sanchez sat back. "What?"

"Go ahead. Tell her the story." I nodded toward Keri.

Keri cleared her throat. "Detective Sanchez, if you share any of this with anyone, it will cost me my life. Swear on your badge, you will tell no one."

Sanchez pursed her lips and crossed her arms. "Okay, I'll buy. I swear."

"My former name was Dr. Theresa Douglas." Keri drew a deep breath and told her story.

EIGHTEEN

Houston, Texas

DR. THERESA DOUGLAS rubbed her eyes and tried to focus one more time on the computer screen. Her laptop sat in its own pool of wan light in the dark office. She glanced up at the clock on her desk.

"It's ten o'clock!" She said. Where had the time gone? She yawned and then reached out and touched the clock shaped like the extraterrestrial character Stitch. It was her favorite Disney character. Mainly because she was adopted just like Stitch. And it had been given to her by the love of her life, Dr. Jack Merchant. She glanced at her cell phone and noticed the text that had come through about an hour before. She swore quietly and picked up the phone.

"Where are you? We were supposed to have pizza." It read.

Theresa shook her head and typed. "Sorry! You know me. I was checking out the latest test runs on this new vaccine."

"As part of your grant, right?"

"I have to get money from somewhere. Have you eaten yet?"

"No. Wish we could go out but I'm on call. Just finishing up an embolization."

Theresa smiled and typed some more. "I'd much rather spend time isolated with you. I'll be downstairs in an hour. Get some delivery pizza." She typed. Her boyfriend was a fellow in radiology and was working furiously in the adjacent medical center while she kept late hours in the medical school laboratory.

Theresa glanced once more at the laptop and frowned. Something was definitely off and she couldn't for the life of her figure out what. The image of the vaccine RNA sequence spun in an image window on the laptop screen. She rubbed her tired eyes and saved everything in the sequencing program and sent it off to the cloud. Then, an uneasy feeling came over her. She blinked and looked at the laptop one more time. Something had been itching at the back of her mind. But, what? She took a flash drive from her desk drawer and backed up all her data onto the flash drive.

"You're being paranoid." She said quietly. She took the flash drive and tucked it into her pocket. She hung her lab coat on the rack by the door to her office and decided to make one quick run to the restroom before leaving.

After taking care of her business, she looked at her reflection in the mirror. Dark circles under her eyes were testimony to the long hours she had been working to verify the effectiveness of the vaccine for SARS as soon as possible. Who knew when the next epidemic might come? She pinched her cheeks and ran a hand through her unruly hair. She wore a Stitch tee shirt and jeans and she glanced down at the character.

"What do you think, Stitch? Will we make it?"

Stitch was silent. As she studied the image of the animated

alien, the creature's row of perfect teeth reminded her of something. She swore out loud and put a hand over her mouth.

"That sequence I was worried about! Base pairs lined up in a perfect array. Too perfect?" She blinked as she recalled the memory of the images from her laptop. Possibly genetically engineered? If this was true, then the vaccine reflected RNA not from a possible viral mutation but from a genetically engineered virus! She turned away from her reflection and put a hand to her mouth. No! It couldn't be. What had she discovered? The vaccine was meant to combat a virus that was NOT natural! The implications of her discovery almost drove her to her knees. From her almost perfect memory of the vaccine sequence, the pieces fell into place like a perfectly finished jigsaw puzzle. If what she suspected was true, that meant that somewhere, a virus would be loosed on the world that was genetically engineered!

Nausea gripped her. Could it be? Was a huge pharmaceutical company manufacturing a vaccine for a virus that was manufactured? And if so, by who?

She stood up shakily. Surely not the vaccine manufacturer. Wait, could THEY unleash the virus on the world? Gain of function research was meant to force a virus from an animal vector into mutating to the extent it might infect humans. Then that virus could be the source of new vaccines in case the virus ever did just that, break through to humans. Was this virus already there? Was it the source of a new epidemic that only this vaccine could stop?

What had she read somewhere about the new vaccine? The government was purchasing it for over two billion dollars! If this engineered virus broke out, how much more would a company make? Would someone actually release such a virus on purpose? The idea smacked of the latest biological thriller novel. She had to go back and verify all of her conclusions on the information on her laptop.

Voices came from outside the restroom door. Who could be here this time of night? Janitor, maybe? Her boyfriend? Panic gripped her along with the surging paranoia.

"This is crazy!" She whispered. She went to the door of the restroom and put an ear to the door. More than one voice. Something again tickled at the back of her brain and she turned the light off and cracked the door.

Four men stood outside her office quietly talking among themselves. She did not recognize any of them. One man with his back to her wore a suit coat and his blonde hair was cut short. Two others wore green surgical scrubs, face masks and surgical caps. The fourth man wore a white lab coat and had red hair and a pale face. His eyes glistened in the meager light from the empty office.

"I know she's here." He said. "She hasn't checked out of the building yet."

One of the scrub wearing men looked at the other. "You didn't have to kill the security guard." The man said. His voice shook.

"Losing your nerve?" The man in the suit said and he stepped back into the shadows. "This will be worth billions unless she blows the whistle on things. We have a tight schedule to meet. We must move tonight. And she will be a problem." He motioned to the red-haired man. "Go get her laptop and any notes from her desk. The only reason I am here is to see if she has cracked the coding. That last upload to the cloud seemed far too suspicious."

The red-haired man nodded and went into her office. The man in the shadows pointed to the men in scrubs. "Go check out the break room and then the other offices. She has to be somewhere on this floor."

The red-haired man returned and handed over her laptop. "I put the virus on the server. It will erase everything." He said.

"Check the restrooms." The Shadow Man said.

The red-haired man shook his head. "I'm a scientist, not a mercenary."

"You sold your soul to the devil when you signed on for this." The Shadow Man said. "Just go find her."

Theresa backed into the restroom and tried to ease her breathing. What could she do? She had left her purse in her office with the pepper spray on her key ring. She searched her pockets and found only the flash drive. A green exit sign above the door gave enough light to look around the restroom. Three stalls on one wall with a counter with three sinks on the opposite. The back of the restroom had a door leading into a janitor's closet.

Theresa hurried over to the closet and opened the door and slid inside. The smell of disinfectant tickled her nose and she prayed she wouldn't sneeze. The lights came on in the restroom and spilled through the crack at the base of the door. She looked around her. On the back wall was a narrow metal door about five feet tall and almost two feet wide. She pulled on a metal tab and the door swung in toward her. Beyond was an access hallway filled with pipes and electrical conduits. There was barely enough room for her in that hallway.

She heard the man open a stall door and she shoved her hand against her mouth to keep from screaming. She stepped over the threshold of the utility doorway and started sliding sideways. The button on her jeans caught on the door and she was stuck! She silently swore and tugged at the button. The second stall door opened, and the man's shadow now eclipsed the bottom of the closet door. The third stall door opened.

She jerked and jerked and felt the button tear from the denim and pop forward into the closet. She gasped as the button tumbled toward the concrete floor. Instead of clattering on the concrete, it fell into the mop sitting in the mop bucket. She slid into the utility closet and pulled the door closed just as the man rattled the closet door. The lights came on in the closet and spilled around the edge of the utility door.

Theresa pushed herself back into the wet pipes and felt power cables tangle around her feet. Something brushed the back of her neck, and a spider ran across the front of her neck and up onto her face. She shoved her hand in her mouth and swiped the spider away with the other hand. She pushed herself further down the narrow tunnel into the narrow space between two pipes.

The door to the utility closet opened and light gushed down the narrow hallway. The man's shadow fell across the floor just an inch from the tip of her shoes. She heard his breathing. She smelled the odor of his sweat.

Then, he closed the door, and she heard his footsteps move away from the closet until she heard the restroom door close. Now what to do? If they didn't find her, they would come back! She had to get out of here! Her cell phone was in the office with her purse. She moved deeper into the utility hallway's interior. Another spider scurried across her face and into her hair and she fought the need to scream.

Theresa reached the far end of the narrow hallway and found another door. Where did it lead? If it led into another bathroom, then the man could be waiting! She quietly opened the door and looked out into a dimly lit stairway. It was the stairs at the back of her floor but on the other side of the building from her hallway. If she hurried, she could get down the stairs before they came for her.

Theresa climbed out through the access door onto a stairway landing and brushed cobwebs from her hair. Someone was coming down the stairs above her! Another was coming up the stairs from below! Voices!

"She's not down this way." The red-haired man's voice came from the landing below just out of sight.

"She's not up here." One of the scrubs said.

Theresa grabbed the handle to the door to the wing opposite hers and slowly opened it and stepped through. She was on the far hallway opposite her side of the building. It was another biology lab. The odor of agar and biological wastes filled the air. She hurried down the wall of the long lab following the meager light from the exit sign. She paused as the door to the lab opened and yellow light spilled into the room. The red-haired man stepped through. Behind her, the door to the other set of stairs opened and the two scrubs stepped through. Where was the fourth man, the man in charge?

She pressed herself against the wall and tried not to move. But, if they turned on the light, they would see her. On the wall beside her was a red square. The fire alarm! She grabbed the handle and pulled it down with all her might.

Strobe lights flashed in the ceiling and an alarm sounded. She put her hands against her ears and ran across the lab away from the wall and into the depths of the lab counters. She brushed against a metal cylinder on the counter, and it tumbled off. The end broke off and gas began to spew into the air. Theresa heard the three men come after her. What to do? She squatted behind a counter with her hands pressed over her ears while the strobe lights painted the lab in bizarre moving shadows. On the counter above her was a Bunsen burner lighter. She grabbed it and clicked it several times, holding it toward the tank.

The explosion knocked her back underneath the counter. Flames filled the air and she saw the red-haired man running away from her. One of the scrubs lay on the floor, flames engulfing his clothes. She backed away and her hand trailed through blood. She turned. The other scrub wearing man lay on the floor. A shard of the oxygen tank protruded from his left temple. His chest was moving. He was still alive. Where was the shadow man?

The next few minutes were a blur as first responders hurried through the door into the lab. A fireman picked her up and carried her out of the lab and down the hall. He propped her next to the stairway and she coughed. The door to the stairway opened and, in the shadows, she saw the red-haired man in his white coat. His eyes reflected light as he glanced at her. He made his hand into a "pistol" and pointed it at her. The door closed before she could say anything, and she descended into a bout of coughing until she passed out.

NINETEEN

Theresa paced back and forth in the small room. A knock came from the door, and it opened. A face appeared, a man with gold rimmed glasses and a shock of unruly dark hair. Theresa rushed across the room as Dr. Jack Merchant slipped through the door and closed it behind him.

She threw herself into his arms and he hugged her tightly. They stood like that for what seemed an eternity until she pushed herself away and looked through tear-stained eyes at his face.

"How did you get in here?"

Merchant took off his glasses and wiped his eyes. "I called in a favor. I read a mammogram on one of the guard's wives and diagnosed her breast cancer last year. I saw him in the hallway outside the closed courtroom."

"I'm supposed to be sequestered like the jury." Theresa said.

"I know. Why?"

"There's still two men out there who know my identity. The FBI is keeping me under protective custody."

"Which is why I haven't been able to talk to you since this all began. They're moving very quickly." Merchant held her hand.

"I know. It's been a blur. With the government involved, the case is going before a judge only. No jury. And this impacts 'national security' according to Ross."

"Ross?"

"FBI Special Agent Franklin Ross. I gave him the flash drive with the evidence the vaccine was from an engineered virus." Theresa said. She came back to him and nestled her head against his chest. "Oh, you didn't ask for this, Jack."

"That doesn't matter. I've loved you since the day we met."

Theresa looked up at him. "Over a cadaver, of all things."

Merchant smiled. "It was a special case."

"Very sad." She said. While working on her Ph.D. in genetics, Theresa had been involved in the evaluation of a case with bizarre genetic anomalies. She shuddered at the memory of the deformed fetus. "But I understood why you wanted to get Xrays for documentation."

"You're asked to do a lot of things in your fellowship you wouldn't normally do in private practice." He shook his head. "Lord keep me from becoming an 'interesting case'."

"Like me?"

"I'm talking medically. Not legally. What will happen now?"

Theresa rested her head against him again. "If the one survivor talks and they find the other two surviving men, it's over."

"And if he doesn't?"

Theresa buried her face deeper into his chest. "I don't know. He had same damage to his skull but his mind wasn't affected. Ross won't say. I'm the only one who can identify the other two men who escaped."

A knock sounded on the door. Theresa clung to his chest as the door cracked and she heard the guard's voice. "Sorry, but time is up Dr. Merchant."

Merchant gently pushed her away and kissed her on the forehead. "I'll see you when this is over. Love you."

Theresa clung to his arms as he pulled away and he threw her a kiss. The guard closed the door as Merchant exited and Theresa gave in to the sobbing. She backed slowly across the room to the far wall where one frosted window let wan sunlight in. She was leaning against the window when the explosion shook the building and shoved her out into the morning air.

EVERY MUSCLE in Theresa's body ached as she tried to sit up on the gurney. Her face felt taut with numerous steri-strips. She looked around the small hospital room and reached for the nurse's call button. Her hand shook and she looked down at bulky bandages covering both hands. Her last memory was of the explosion and being thrust through the window.

The door to the hospital room opened and a man in a tan overcoat stepped in. He wore a wrinkled red tie over a rumpled white shirt. His eyes were hidden behind sunglasses. As he neared her hospital bed, the odor of cigarettes wafted over her.

"Where am I? What happened?" She managed through swollen lips.

FBI Special Agent Ross pulled off his sunglasses. "In a hospital room. There was an explosion. Louis Esposito, the surviving man from your quartet of perps, is dead along with two guards. The explosion sent you through the window and you fell two stories into a construction dumpster filled with boxes or you would be dead."

Theresa looked at her hands. "Jack?"

"Your boyfriend? The one who bribed a guard to see you? Probably saved your life. He's fine. Other than he thinks you're dead." Ross ran a hand through his hair and sighed.

Theresa tried to turn and get out of the bed and pain lanced down her back. "I have to see him."

Ross stepped in front of her and put out a hand. "I'm afraid that is impossible. The world thinks you are dead. We need to keep it that way."

"What?" Theresa said. "No! I want to see Jack! Now!"

Ross pulled up a chair and sat by the bed. "Listen to me. This organization is bigger than we thought. It has huge international ties. Politicians. Criminal cabals. All trying to capitalize on a future pandemic crisis. Security is tighter but there are lots of holes opening up in that security around the world. Big things don't get through. But small things, money, cryptocurrency, drugs are finding new ways to slip under the radar. Like international assassins. We have some leads thanks to you, but they are few and far between. And, when we find them, you can identify them." Ross reached out and patted her bandaged hand. "But if you surface now, you will be targeted. You will be assassinated."

Theresa jerked her hand away. "What are you saying?"

Ross' dark eyes burned. "Do you love your boyfriend?"

"Yes."

"Do you want him to die?"

"No!"

"If they find out you are still alive, they will target him to find you. The only way to protect him, to keep him alive, is for the world to continue to believe you are dead." Ross said.

Theresa collapsed back into the bed and moaned. "No! This can't be happening."

"Your only hope is to disappear. Take on a new identity." Ross said. He stood up slowly and rubbed his mouth. "I need a smoke. A U. S. Marshal will be by today to start the process of putting you into the witness protection program. From this moment on, you are officially dead. And gone." He paused at the door and looked back at her. "I'm sorry." He left the hospital room as Theresa fell into hysterical sobs.

TWENTY

Jerry sighed. "That's quite a story. Theresa, right?"

"Yes." she said quietly

Sanchez sat forward in her chair. "And just when and where did you find out Theresa was still alive?"

"I'll tell you." I said.

I SQUINTED *into the bright sunlight as I examined the squatty, squarish red stone perched precariously on the tip of the rock beneath it. The brochure came from the display at the main entrance to the "Garden of the Gods" and explained the significance of this rock.*

"Janice, this is amazing."

Janice put a hand on my arm. "So precariously balanced."

"That is why it is called Balanced Rock." I tapped the brochure and turned to kiss her on the lips. She looked away.

"Problem?" I said.

"No." she said, pushing her blonde hair out of her face. "Just wish we were just as balanced."

Our marriage was far from balanced and there were problems. I had hoped a return to the location of our honeymoon would rekindle the fire.

"I need a smoke." She stepped away and disappeared around a nearby boulder. I saw the smoke plume above the rock. If only our relationship had as much fire.

I circled the huge rock, trying to focus on the brochure. "Balanced Rock is composed of the Fountain Formation. This is a combination of coarse sand, gravel, silica and hematite. The hematite gives the rock its red hue." Who cared, I thought. Janice sure didn't. As I reached the far side something clattered behind me and whirled.

The woman sat on a nearby flat stone. An easel stood before her, and her palette and brushes lay at the base of the rock. A hairband held her bushy dark hair away from her face and her mouth opened in a perfect "O".

I felt my world tilt and slide sideways and dropped the brochure. This couldn't be possible.

"Theresa?"

The woman glanced at me, and her eyes widened in shock. She put a hand to her mouth and slid off the other side of the stone. She ran down a path deeper into the towering rocks. How could this be? I hurried down the path after her, weaving and dodging between rocks. "Wait? I just want to talk to you." I shouted.

The sun burned into my neck, and I heard stones clatter around the bend in the walkway. The woman cursed. I came around the rock and the woman sat on the ground, holding her ankle. She looked up at me and tears had streamed through the red dust on her face.

"Theresa?"

"No! You can't be here! You can't see me." She shouted.

"Jack?" I whirled. Janice was coming toward us on the path. "Why are you running?"

The woman stood shakily to her feet and leaned against a rock. "He heard me fall and cry out." She said.

I turned to Theresa and her eyes burned with fire. "Thanks for coming to my aid."

I blinked in surprise and held my tongue. Maybe I was mistaken. Theresa was dead, killed in an assassination in the courthouse seven years before. Janice passed me.

"Here, let me help you. I'm Dr. Merchant."

"I'm Keri Holt." She said.

Janice took 'Keri's' arm and slung it around her shoulder. She paused and glared at me.

"Well, don't just stand there, Jack. Take her other arm. We'll help her back to the car and take her to first aid."

I looked into Keri's eyes as I took her hand and pulled her arm around my shoulder. Her hair smelled the same. Her eyes still had those small punctate points of green and gold. She still wore the same deodorant! We walked her back to our car and helped her into the passenger seat.

As we drove, I glanced at 'Keri' in the front seat of our car. Janice spoke from the back seat, telling Keri all about our first trip to Colorado Springs for our honeymoon and this trip to celebrate our fifth wedding anniversary. Keri was tense in the front seat with her hands gripped into fists. I kept quiet until we pulled into the main station. We helped Keri out and took her into the first aid station. The attendant motioned us down a hallway to a small room and Keri settled onto an examination table. The attendant looked at her ankle.

"Looks like just a sprain. I'll get some ice and a wrap." He said. "You might want to go to the ER and get it Xrayed. Just in case there is a fracture."

Janice smiled at Keri. "Jack can look at it. He's a radiologist."

"Really?" Keri managed and looked down at her ankle.

I motioned to the hallway. "Maybe we should get her some water."

Janice nodded. "Good idea. Don't want to get dehydrated."

When she left the room, I sat in the chair before her. "Theresa? Is it you?"

Tears trickled down her cheek. "Yes."

"But you died. They told me you were dead." I managed. My heart raced at the implications.

"Jack, I had to disappear. To protect you." She reached out and touched my cheek and I jerked away.

"You didn't want me to go with you?" Was all I could think of saying.

"You already had a job lined up after your fellowship. You can't be a practicing doctor with a new identity." She pulled back her hand. "I'm so sorry. I've missed you so much. And now you're married."

I stood up and my face burned with anger. "You should have told me."

"They took me away right after the explosion. Immediately. I never had a chance. Even if I wanted to." Keri said as she wiped tears from her face.

"Everything okay?" Janice reappeared with a cup of water.

"Yes." Keri said and she reached for the cup of water. "I was just telling Jack how grateful I am he showed up at just the right time."

"Yeah. Just the right time." I said tersely and I turned and walked out of the small room. Pacing the waiting room, my heart and my head warred against each other. Theresa had been everything to me and then she was gone. True, I had met Janice and she became the love of my life. Now all my old feelings for

Theresa came rushing back. I felt a hand on my shoulder and turned to Janice.

"Honey, she wants to thank you for helping. I'm going to drive back and get her painting equipment and bring it here. Why don't you stay and make sure she gets that wrap on properly." She glanced over her shoulder at the young attendant. "I think all he has is rudimentary first aid."

Janice walked out of the first aid station. I turned and looked back down the long hallway. Oh, how I desperately wanted to take Theresa in my arms. She was lost to me and now she was back! She was alive! I rubbed my face as the attendant appeared bedside me.

"Dude, I heard you're a doctor. Maybe you should wrap her ankle." He held out the brown bandage.

"You'll do just fine." I said as I walked out the door into the bright sunlight. Now I felt like the Balanced Rock, precariously perched on the pinnacle of indecision. I couldn't just walk away from my marriage no matter how troubled because I loved Janice no matter what problems we were having. But Theresa was alive! Which way would I lean? Which way would I go? I sat on a bench in front of the first aid station and my mind raced. Janice pulled up in our rental car and parked next to the bench. She got out of the car and sat beside me.

"How is Keri?"

"The attendant is wrapping her ankle, I guess."

I felt her gaze fixated on my face. "What? Why didn't you do it?"

"Just being around her made me very uncomfortable. Janice, I thought she was someone from my past." I said hoarsely. "She reminded me of someone I once cared about who passed away."

Janice put an arm around me and pulled me to her and the sudden warmth was comforting. How I had missed it. And it took a shock from the past to make me see what I had right before me.

"I'm so sorry. Grief can do strange things especially when you least expect it." She leaned in and kissed my cheek. "You need some time?"

"Yes."

She got up and went back to the car and gathered the painting equipment and took it inside. Theresa had been a promising biologist with a Ph.D. in genetics. Now, 'Keri' was an artist? How does one walk away from the chosen lifestyle and choose something much less? It had to be painful for her. She almost died, I reminded myself. She was fortunate to be alive and she had a new life. I needed to leave that to her. The cold air conditioner blew on my hot face as I slid behind the steering wheel. Janice appeared from the clinic and sat in our car's passenger seat.

"The attendant is going to take her back to her car. She says she can drive home. Want to say goodbye?"

I put the car in gear and backed out of the driveway. "I already have."

TWENTY-ONE

Two years later

"WHAT ARE YOU DOING?" *Janice said over the cell phone speaker.*

I sat on the rock and put my hand over my eyes to squint into the setting sun. "Taking a break."

"It's awfully quiet." Janice said.

"I'm outside."

"How did your presentation go? Meet anyone you know at the seminar?"

"It went just fine."

"You're not very talkative."

"I'm remembering."

Silence. Then, "Remembering what?"

"How good it was to be here a couple of years ago for our fifth anniversary. Things started out bad and then they were good. But that was before." I searched the rocks. Would 'Keri' be

here? Would she be painting the rocks in the setting sun? That was too much to ask for.

"I'm sorry about what happened." Janice said.

"I know."

"I just needed some time. Things at work, you know." She mumbled.

"Time to run off to Europe for a supposed seminar only to hang out with who?" I said through grit teeth.

"I told you nothing happened." Her voice was strained.

"Then why did he answer your phone?"

Silence again. I stood up as I saw movement in the far rocks. She was here! Keri walked toward me along the same path where she had turned her ankle two years before. She had not seen me yet.

"I told you we were having a few drinks in my room. Six of us. Nothing happened, Jack." Janice said. "Is this really about the miscarriage?"

"I should be asking you that." I said hotly. "I got to go."

"Please don't." Janice pleaded.

I ended the call. Keri had heard me talking and had paused along the pathway. She looked at me, her head tilted slightly. She dropped her easel and messenger bag.

"No!" she said.

I hurried down the dusty path toward her, and she put up her hands to ward me off. "No, Jack! You can't do this!"

"Theresa, I had to come find you."

She shook her head. "I knew you were here. I saw your name on the seminar list."

"You still follow medicine?"

She put her hands down and hugged herself. "Yes. I miss it. But I've found a new career in art. You can't be here."

"It's been years since that night. The latest pandemic is over.

The case is dormant. I checked with Ross." I took a few steps toward her. "Don't worry. I didn't say I had seen you."

Keri picked up her easel and messenger bag. "You've been doing your research. You know they are still out there. The red-haired man and the Shadow Man. They are still a danger to me. No, Jack. I have a new life. You have a new life."

"My life is no longer new."

Keri flinched, and the warm red sunlight of the setting sun painted her face from the side. A tear trickled down her cheek. "I will not be the death of your marriage, Jack. What we had was wonderful, but it is over."

"My marriage is on the rocks." I said as I drew closer.

Keri squinted at me. "You've been drinking."

I looked away. "Too much lately. And gambling too." I looked back at her. "Ever since I found out you were alive, Theresa."

Keri dropped her easel again and marched toward me. "My name is Keri. No! You will NOT blame this on me! You will not destroy your marriage because of me! I will not be the cause of this."

She was close to me now, the tiny flecks of greenish gold flaring in her eyes. I reached out and grabbed her by the shoulders and tried to kiss her. She fought me and pushed me away. "No, Jack! This is not you!"

"No, I haven't been 'me' since I found out the woman I loved wasn't really dead!" I shouted. "Not since I found out you ran off to a new life and left me behind standing before an empty coffin!"

Keri's lips trembled, and she put a hand to her forehead as she paced before him. "Jack, you have a life! You have a wonderful wife with a promising career. Wake up! I can't come back. If I did, I would be dead! Do you understand? I'm already *dead to you. And if I come back, you would be dead, too! They would find you and use you to get to me, then kill us both!"*

My groaning screams echoed off the rocks. She rolled her eyes and then put her arms around me. She rested her head against my chest, just like she had that last day in the holding room. I let my tears come and felt them run down my cheeks to drip into her hair. Her sobs shook along with mine.

"I'm sorry, Theresa. So sorry."

"For what?"

"For not being there to protect you that night in the lab."

She pushed back from me, and her tear-stained eyes gleamed in the fading sunlight. "Jack, you don't have to protect me anymore. I'm safe. I was doing my job. I'm happy here without you. We can never have what we had. It's over and we will never have it again." She wiped the tears from my face. "Your wife needs you. Don't push her away. Don't wander into the minefields with me. You have a life, Jack. Live it. Love it. Enjoy the life I never had. Fight for it!" She stepped back from me, her hands resting gently on my chest until she let them drop beside her. "You and I both know there is more going on here than just finding me. Whatever is going on in your marriage, I am not the answer." She stepped farther away and hugged herself. "Jack, you have a life. Don't throw it away. This is my life. That is yours. The most we can ever be is friends, and we can't even be that in real time."

Keri reached into her jeans pocket and pulled out something shiny that caught the last rays of the setting sun. "My engagement ring. I take it off when I paint." She held it out for me to see. "His name is Jason. He's a good man. Please don't endanger your life or ours. I have thought long and hard about loving again and the danger I would place them in."

My heart almost stopped at the sight of the ring. "Does he know?"

"No." She put the ring back in her pocket. "It's best he doesn't."

I gasped for breath like a dying man and fought back the pain. "Can you call me if you ever need me? If you ever need to talk? Give me that one string to connect us?"

Keri blinked away tears and nodded. "Yes."

I fished in my pocket for the business cards I had brought with me for the seminar and handed one to her. "That's my cell phone number. If you ever need me, if anything happens to you, please call me. Even if all you want to do is just talk. I'll listen and I won't say a word. No one will know, uh, Keri. No one."

She nodded and picked up her equipment. In the gathering dark, she moved past me and I desperately wanted to reach out and take her in my arms. I fought the desire and closed my eyes as she walked out of my life. Again.

TWENTY-TWO

Fruit spun on the slot machine screen in front of me. Bells went off and lights flashed. Oh, joy, I had won a thousand dollars. I sipped at my drink again and placed my card in the slot to accept my win. An attendant ran up to the machine and excitedly proclaimed, "We have a winner!"

I waved him off and stumbled off into the smoky interior of the riverboat casino before the man could snap my photo for the winner's circle. The man tried to follow him, but I slipped between two rows of machines and out onto the deck. The river rolled beneath me, churning around the stationary riverboat. Tied down and not allowed to do what it was meant to do, cruise the river. Trapped, and I understood that feeling. I tossed back my drink and threw the glass into the river. The lights of downtown glittered on the water.

"A penny for your thoughts?"

I whirled. Janice sat down at one of the unoccupied tables. "I see you won the jackpot, Jack."

Dizziness threatened my balance. Maybe I would be lucky enough to fall into the river. "What are you doing?"

"Checking up on you. I got home from work, and you were gone. Again. I knew where to find you." She pulled a cigarette out of her purse and lit it with a silver lighter. "I know this is the only place you can still smoke indoors, and it is the only place you can hide."

"I'm not hiding." My voice reeked of weakness, not the bravado I had intended.

Janice inhaled the cigarette, and the red glow lit up her face. Tears trickled down her cheeks. "Jack, I don't know what is going on with us, but I have a good idea what is going on with you."

"Really?" I stumbled over to the table and sat across from her. "Why don't you illuminate me?"

"I know about Keri." She said.

An icy wave washed over my face. Nausea gripped me. "How?"

"After we met that woman in Colorado Springs three years ago, I did some research. Theresa Douglas died in an explosion during the trial of the Vaccine Bandits. She had a boyfriend, but they never mentioned his name. You told me in Colorado Keri reminded you of someone you had lost." She stood up, blowing smoke into the cool air. "That must have been painful seeing that woman who reminded you of Theresa. It brought up so many painful memories, didn't it?"

Should I tell her the truth? "Yes. She died, and I was left behind." Pain blossomed in my chest, and I leaned against the table. "I loved her so much, Janice. Then she was gone. Just gone. And then I saw her again!"

Janice looked out over the river and drew another lungful of smoke. The red tip of her cigarette cast her eyes in a ruddy light. "I know what is like to lose someone." She looked back at me. "So do you. You could have told me about this a long time ago. Instead, you have carried this pain since you saw Keri. Theresa's gone, Jack. It's time to let the past be the past. I'm here. Now. I love you and I will always love you. I cannot replace this woman from your past. First loves are always the hardest to get over."

I looked up into her face, filled with sympathy. If she thought Theresa was dead, I wouldn't tell her anything differently. A pang of guilt grabbed my gut. Why was I perpetuating a lie? Was it because I hoped beyond hope Theresa would one day take me back? Was our marriage that much of a sham? Janice stood before me, alive, vital, loving me! I was drunk at the casino instead of being with this wonderful woman who had stayed beside me through the tough times. "I loved her so much, but you are right. She's gone. Forever. I can never have her back in my life."

Janice tossed her cigarette over the railing and stood up. She sauntered over behind me and put her arms around my shoulders. She buried her face in my hair and mumbled into my ear. "I'm in your life forever, Jack. If you let me stay there. We've been fighting a lot, but we are still here. Together. We still have a love deep down for each other. I don't want any other man. I don't love anybody else but you. Do you understand?"

I felt the tears pour from my eyes. It was over. Truly over. Theresa, dead or alive, was gone. Janice was in my life, and she wasn't going anywhere! I stood up and embraced Janice, pulling her into an embrace, drowning in her warmth and love. "I'm so sorry for doubting you. Theresa is gone and you are here for me, for us."

"Forever!" she whispered in my ear.

TWENTY-THREE

Jerry massaged his face and nodded. "The two of you have been through a lot."

"I thought it was over, but Theresa called me a few times after that." I said.

"You met her the day your wife died? She was the person in the car with you, wasn't she?" Sanchez said. She had pulled the chair over beside my bed.

I glanced at Keri and nodded. "Yes."

***

ONE YEAR AGO

"I HAVE LITTLE TIME." I said as I hunched over the coffee shop table and cradled my cup. The sound of the hissing espresso machine filled the surrounding air. Keri sat stiffly on the other side of the table. It had shocked me to find her standing by my

car when I had gone out to get Janice some snacks. "I told Janice I would run to the convenience store."

Keri stared off into space while her coffee cup steamed in front of her. Her face was pale, and her eyes rimmed in black. "I called your office. They said you were out of town. It's the week of your anniversary and I thought you might be at the motel. With her."

"You mean my wife? Yes, I would spend my anniversary with my wife." Especially after what we have been through in the past few months, I thought. But Keri didn't need to know that. In contrast to her usual perky demeanor, she sounded so different, so dreadful.

"He died." She whispered.

"What?"

"Jason. In Afghanistan."

"When?" Was that the only thing I could think to say?

"A month ago. Jack, he's dead."

I reached over and placed my hand over hers. It felt like a cold, dead fish. "I'm so sorry, Keri."

Keri blinked and turned her gaze on me. Her eyes focused on me for the first time. "Now I know how you felt on the day you thought I had died." She pulled her hand from beneath mine and put both hands over her face. She sobbed and tears trickled over her fingers. "I'm so sorry, Jack." She gasped.

I drank some more coffee and struggled for words. "Look, Keri, I'm very sorry for your loss. But as you told me to, I moved on. I'm working on my marriage with Janice. This trip is supposed to make things better."

Keri just looked at me, dabbing at her nose with her napkin. "Of course. I didn't mean to mess things up with you and Janice. I want you to be happy. After all, you kept your life, and I lost mine. And now I've lost both you and Jason."

I glanced at my watch again. "It takes time to get over the loss, Keri. It won't be easy."

Her bright, wet eyes focused on me. "Am I keeping you from something?"

"Janice doesn't know. I mean, she thought I was just going to the convenience store."

Keri's eyes opened, and she dropped her hands into her lap. "I'm sorry to have inconvenienced you, Jack." She stood up and woodenly walked toward the door.

"Wait, Keri. I didn't mean it."

Keri ignored me and walked out the door and directly into the parking lot. A car screeched to a halt and the sound of its horn barely registered with her. I hurried out the door and grabbed her by the shoulders, pulling her back away from the car as it moved into the drive-through lane.

"Keri, please. I didn't mean to be so insensitive. Let me take you back to the motel to your car."

Keri jerked out of my grasp. "I can walk."

I looked around at the busy parking lot and the nearby road as traffic whizzed through the crowded streets. "It's too dangerous in your condition."

She turned and glared at me. "Just what is my condition, Jack? Huh? You do not know what my life is like. I have a doctorate. I was on task of becoming the chief researcher at the medical school. I had plans and visions for my future and now I'm here, eking out a living as an artist while you have the life I should have shared." She balled her fists and pummeled my chest. Her bushy, dark hair tangled around her face. I backed away, pulling her gently against me until I stood by the passenger side of my rental car.

"Theresa, stop!" I tried to catch my breath. She wasn't hitting me hard enough to hurt me and slowly, her frenzied bashing against my chest subsided and she fell into me, pressing *her head into my chest. For a moment, I was back in the holding room at the courthouse.*

"I know how you feel. Theresa, I lost you. I not only lost you physically, but when I found you were alive, I lost you again to someone named Keri." I whispered in her ear.

She slid her arms around my chest. "I lost you, too, Jack. I wanted you to come with me, but I couldn't ask that of you."

"I would have come with you." I said quietly. "I would have given up the life I have to be with you." Pushing her back gently, I looked into her red-rimmed eyes. "But I found someone else who I have loved now for ten years. It has not been easy, but I refuse to give up on my wife. I had to let you go, and it wasn't easy. I had to let you go twice."

She nodded and rubbed at her eyes. "I know. I found someone, too. I will have to find a way to live now that Jason is gone. I loved him." She looked into my eyes. "Not as much as I loved you, but I loved him. Oh, Jack, what are we going to do?"

"You said it before. Those conspirators are still out there plotting new ways to make billions. If you come forward now, they will have you killed. They will not take a chance you might recognize them. It is not safe for you to come back to the life you left. You told me that two years ago. I almost left Janice to come be with you." I said. The image from the last ultrasound surfaced from my tortured memory. Could I have had a family with Theresa? No! I couldn't go there!

"I know that now. I have relived the past two encounters over and over. Jack, if I had not have found Jason, I would have asked you to leave Janice for me." She put a hand on my cheek. "But I love you too much to ask you to do that now. I would never want Janice to feel the way I feel now. This is our lives now. We have to accept it." She stepped away and hugged herself. "I just had to see you, talk to you, about Jason."

I turned quietly and opened the car door. "Let me take you back to your car."

She nodded and slid into the passenger seat. I climbed behind the wheel, and we drove through the take out lane to get Janice a coffee and a pastry. The ride back to the motel was quiet. I pulled up across from her parked car and got out. She held up the bag with the coffee and pastry.

"Don't forget this for your wife. I'm sorry I was so upset."

I walked around the car and took the bag from her. We stood apart. "You'll work through this, Theresa. So will I. We have no choice. Your life depends on it."

Keri looked at me one last time. "Sometimes I don't know if I want to go on living."

I didn't like the sound of that. "Look, why don't you meet me later at a restaurant? Janice wants to go shopping at the outlet mall and she told me I could go to the bookstore. Instead, we can meet. We can talk. I'm sorry I seem so distracted. Things are better, but we still have issues we're working through. That is why I brought Janice back here for our anniversary."

Keri put her hands over her eyes. "He won't be here for our next anniversary. And neither will you."

"I understand. When I thought you died, it took me months to recover. I know what you're going through. And we can talk about that later. Okay?"

She handed me the cup of coffee. "Take your snack to your wife."

I glanced at my watch and then up at our room as I took the cup. It was time for me to confront Janice. I wanted the truth. She had mentioned having a hysterectomy. Was she going through with it? Would we be able to work through this? Would our marriage survive this crisis? Or would I soon be alone like Keri?

Before I could say anything else, Keri walked away and got

into her car. It was while I was turning to go back to the rental car to park it in a slot that the explosion came out of nowhere. Heat and broken glass surrounded me, and I ducked. I looked up as flames gushed out of a motel room. Our motel room! I dropped the coffee and pastry and ran up the stairs into an inferno.

TWENTY-FOUR

"She was the person in the car." I said to Sanchez. "But if I told you, her life would have been in danger."

"I told Jack I would talk to you, but he wouldn't let me." Keri rubbed my hand.

Sanchez nibbled at a toothpick. "Still doesn't change the fact you might have killed your wife."

"I think Korskin had something to do with it." I managed through clenched teeth. "Keri, tell them."

Keri sighed. "When I saw Korskin in Jack's room last week, I recognized his voice. I will never forget the other two men, and Korskin is one of them. I'm certain of it. He was the red-haired man. If he saw me and recognized me, he would have me killed."

Sanchez pulled the toothpick from her mouth. "You buying this, Langley?"

"I've done some background checks on Korskin. His past is solid. A little too solid." He studied me and then Keri. "The man could have dyed his hair. I believe you."

"Now you know." I looked at Sanchez. "Leave her out of all of this. Don't endanger her life again."

Jerry placed a hand on Keri's arm. "Even though I believe you, I need more evidence. If I bring this to the secret service now, they will bury me. They would never admit they are letting a fugitive criminal mastermind slip through their hands."

"What can I do?"

"I need more details on the case you testified in."

Keri put a hand to her mouth. "The case is sealed. I was told if I ever revealed information from the trial, I would be arrested."

Jerry frowned. "I expected as much."

"Okay." Sanchez stood up and came over to my bed. "Looks like we got an impasse."

My nurse came through the door and looked at us. "Uh, I must get Dr. Merchant ready for his bone marrow aspiration. I would like for you to leave."

"If Korskin is guilty and we uncover it, the FBI would be very grateful, Keri. I think they would waive any charges against you. But I understand. Just don't waste time. We're on the clock." Langley said.

Keri wiped away tears. "Let me think and pray about it. Jack is on the clock, too." She said and her voice broke with emotion.

"THIS IS GOING TO HURT, isn't it?" I looked over my shoulder at the doctor hovering over my backside.

Dr. Linda Krale looked at me from the foot of my bed. "Just a little bit."

"Let me guess, a little bee sting and then pressure." I said.

"Is that what you tell your patients before you shove an 18-gauge needle into their liver?" She smiled at me.

"Yeah." I cringed as she infiltrated the skin over my iliac crest with lidocaine. "Crap! That's more like a red wasp than a bee."

"You ain't felt nothing yet." Linda continued.

The diameter of the metal cannula for a bone marrow aspiration was three times larger than the needle I used for CAT scan guided biopsies. And it had to be screwed down through the bone to the marrow. Did I say that correctly? Screwed down as in manually shoved through the hard calcified cortex of the surface of a bone! And then, when the marrow was aspirated, there was this great sucking pain. I know. I had done them under CAT scan guidance, as some oncologists preferred the radiologist to do the procedure. I guess that way the patient wouldn't hate them as much. After all, most patients only saw a radiologist once in a hospital visit and it is easier to hate a stranger!

Tears streamed down my face when she drilled the cannula through the cortex of the bone on my upper pelvic bone. I bit the pillow when she aspirated the marrow and cried with relief when she pulled the needle out of me. I would never think about a biopsy casually again. From now on, I would never complain about having to do a bone marrow biopsy under CAT scan guidance. Because we gave the patient sedation and pain medicine!

"There, all done." She said cheerily.

"What are my chances, Linda?" I asked as I turned over and tried to relax in the bed.

Linda's face darkened. "Mixed, at best. It depends on how much infiltration of the marrow there is and the degree of poor differentiation of the cells. You may need a bone marrow transplant."

"When will you know something?" How many times had my patients asked me that question?

"I'm taking this sample to pathology right now, so it doesn't get lost. Bruce Wiggins said he would process it before lunch. He's the best pathologist at bone marrow analysis and I hope to know something by this afternoon. I promise I'll come and tell you what we've found. Some of this will have to be sent off for immunoassay and genetic tests. But the basic staging of the disease will be set in stone by this afternoon."

"When will you start the chemo?"

"As soon as we talk this afternoon. You'll need a port for infusion. I'm thinking about a PICC line to begin with. Now, we have some certified nurses that can put it in. Or you can get one of your colleagues to do it until we get your port in."

A PICC line was a long IV that was inserted into a vein just above the elbow and threaded to the level of the heart. It was useful for long-term infusions.

"I think Rolly is working today. I'll get him to put one in."

"Good. So, I'll see you in a few hours." Linda patted my arm and left the room.

I thought back on the near-death experience. The pain had been caused by a kidney stone. But, if I had a kidney stone, why hadn't I passed it? Maybe I did and never knew it. After all, I had received lots of IVs during the code and afterwards. The more I thought about it, the more I realized all my recent problems dated back to that one incident when Baldy had injected something into my I.V. What if it was some kind of radioactive poison that produced leukemia? But my hair hadn't fallen out. At least not yet.

The old pity took me then, dragging me down into the mire and muck of depression. Janice was dead. Keri was here and had placed herself in danger. A rabid detective was convinced I had murdered my wife. I had almost died and now, if things did not change, I would be dead within weeks. I groaned under the weight of it all and tears filled my eyes.

Gill would have told me to straighten up. Maybe he would have told me to trust God. Truth was, I hadn't thought about God in a long time. At least since I had gotten furious with him for letting Janice die. He could have saved her. Why did he let her die? And why was he letting these things happen to me now? I wanted to shake my fist at God, but the truth hurt that I was responsible for so much of my sorrow. I had started gambling after Janice died. She had smoked in bed and, if she hadn't been murdered, then she had brought on her own death. Just how much did God have to do with all my misery? How much did I?

"Penny for your thoughts?"

I realized I had closed my eyes, and I jerked them open when I heard the voice. Gill stood by my bed. "Gill?"

"Heard you were dying. Thought you might want some company. It's not like we haven't died before." He pulled up a chair and sat next to the bed.

"I was just feeling sorry for myself, and you had to interrupt me."

Gill crossed his arms over his chest. "By all means, continue. I can even throw a few insults your way, if it'll make you feel worse. Hey, I can tell you what the techs say behind your back. That would do it."

I raised an eyebrow. "What?"

Gill grinned. "Other than you're a jerk and you have a gambling addiction, they mostly like you. Seems like you are a good radiologist. At least, you used to be."

That made me sit up. "What do you mean 'used to be'?"

Gill stroked his beard. "Well, Doc, you aren't the same stellar rad you were when you first came here. You used to be kind to all the techs. Now, they say you have a fuse shorter than Montana's." He leaned toward me. "And that is saying a lot."

I slumped back into the bed. "I guess I haven't been myself since Janice died."

"That's understandable. She completed you. Now, you're only half here." Gill sat forward and put his hands on his knees. "Doc, you gotta find all of you before this leukemia kills you. Do you know where you're gonna spend eternity?"

I rolled my eyes. "Is this the 'dying man' conversion attempt?"

"Yep." Gill sat back. I glared at him. He smiled at me. "So, what'll be, Doc. Heaven, hell, or oblivion?"

My face warmed, and I looked away. "I just don't get it. Why would a loving God send someone to hell for eternity for just a lifetime of sin?"

Gill chuckled. "Here we go. Heard that one before. Let me guess. Why does God allow bad things to happen to good people?"

"Yeah. Why?"

Gill shrugged. "I don't know about you, but I ain't a good person. Never have been. Never will be."

I blinked and looked away again. "You just said some techs said I'm a good radiologist."

"All the time?" Gill said. "Are you good all the time? Hey, are you good most of the time?"

"Not really. You know that."

"Don't matter what I know. Matters what you know. Now, here's the real question. If you don't like God. I mean, if you don't believe in God, why would you want to spend eternity with him? Seems like *that* would be hell."

I slowly turned my gaze back to him. "What?"

"Heaven. Hell. Sometimes, you gotta look at them as choices. Hell is where God ain't. Heaven is where God is. You don't want to believe in God, or you don't like God, or you even hate God, then it would be punishment to stay with him forever. So, you made a choice. Be with the God you hate or be apart from God. You're not with God then, by definition, you would have to be in hell. Simple." He sat back and crossed his arms again.

I shook my head. "Hell is a punishment, though."

"And if you're an atheist, going to heaven would be a punishment." He rubbed his beard. "Look, Doc, it's simple. We are either here by chance or we're here by design. Now, if we are here by chance and you believe in God and you become a Christian who respects people and helps people and takes care of widows and orphans and you die and God doesn't exist, what have you lost? You spent an entire life trying to do good because you are representing Christ. You spend a lifetime trying your best to show love to everyone around you. But, if you reject God and you live that 'bad' life we talked about full of self-centeredness and taking advantage of people and hurting others and you die and there is a God, you miss out on everything. You've had a purposeless life and now, you get to sit around in some gray, dull hospital room in hell wishing you had believed."

"Where do you get this stuff?"

"C. S. Lewis' book, 'The Great Divorce'. And it ain't about marriage. You ought to read it sometime." He nodded. "Oh, and the Bible, of course. You ever read the Bible from start to finish?"

"Hardly. But I did Bible drill when I was a kid."

"It's a really interesting set of books. You might want to try it sometime. It has a scary beginning, a tedious middle filled with human defiance, but a happy ending. Right now, you need a happy ending, Doc. Just pray about this whole situation." He stood up and nodded his head. "Yep, pray about this whole situation and make your choices before it's too late. If I'm not mistaken, you saw something when you died. Something you can't explain. Something that still beckons you. Want to know why?"

"Why?"

"Because God has put eternity in the hearts of all men. That's in the Bible. We long for it. We live for it. We look for it. But most of the time, we accept a counterfeit version that we think we can control." He headed toward the door and paused. "Sorry, brother. We can't control anything." He walked out.

I didn't want to think about it anymore. Gill was right about experiencing something otherworldly. When I gazed at the ceiling tiles, I remembered the tablet I had found inside Janice's desk. Getting out of bed, I rolled the IV pole ahead of me and went to the small closet in the corner. My scrubs from the night before were still in their plastic bag crusted with the blood from my nosebleed. I hoped no one had found the tablet. My hand snagged something cold and metallic in one pocket and I pulled out the tablet. The door opened behind me, and I tucked the tablet under the meager protection of my open backed hospital gown.

"Jack? Nice cheeks." Sanchez stood in the doorway. She wore a brown leather jacket over her shirt and jeans. She had tucked her hair beneath a knit cap. I pulled my gown closed behind me and hurried to my bed, sliding the tablet under my pillow.

"What are you doing here?" I asked as I slid back into the bed, wincing when my sore hip touched the mattress. "The nurse asked you to leave.

"Just making sure you didn't leave town."

"I wouldn't get too far in this garb." I said.

"It's cold as a well digger's feet out there. I thought

Colorado was cold." She pulled off the knit cap and shook out her hair.

"It's the humidity." I said. "Nothing worse than a wet cold. Except for maybe a visit from you."

Sanchez walked over and opened my water pitcher. She pulled open the drawer on my bed-side table. "You got any food in here?"

"I had some gelatinous glob for lunch, but I didn't eat it. It's right outside on the food cart if you're still hungry."

Sanchez smiled and laughed. "Look, I came by to tell you what Dr. Francisco found on the post of your wife."

I held my breath and then exhaled. "What did she find?"

"Nothing. Nada. No explanation for her death. In fact, she tested for chemical accelerants. Nothing there."

"Are you saying you don't believe I did it?"

Sanchez stopped smiling and looked out my window. "As much as I hate to admit it, I believe you, Dr. Merchant. If someone murdered your wife, it wasn't you, and I can't figure out how they did it."

I sighed and pulled the sheets up to my chin. I was suddenly cold. "Something happened in that room, Sanchez. I still believe she was murdered."

Sanchez nodded and looked back at me. "Your story about the insurance checks out. I talked to your agent. Your wife took out the policy and never let you know."

I studied her face. "You think this was suicide? Don't you realize I've thought of that, too? If she had set herself on fire, there would be accelerants."

"I know. Doesn't make sense."

Sanchez sat in the chair beside my bed. "Hey, I'm sorry about the leukemia. That sucks."

"You're about as sympathetic as an ice cube." I said.

Sanchez's features softened, and she nodded. "Look, Doc,

I'm just doing my job. You and I both think your wife was murdered. It's my job to figure that out. You have a special relationship with your patient, don't you?"

"Yes."

"I take that same responsibility toward my victims. They deserve everything I've got. So, if I've been a witch about it, sorry. It comes with the territory." She pulled a toothpick out of her jacket pocket and stuck it in her mouth. "Keri is in the clear. You're in the clear. So, I guess that means I need to think about your wife's relationships with her co-workers." She glanced at me. "Korskin, for example."

"It's about time you sank your jaguar claws into him." I said.

Sanchez's eyes lit up with anger, and her face reddened. "Who said anything about a jaguar?"

"The waitress at the coffee shop in Colorado."

Sanchez swore. "That's the last time I give her a tip." She got up and walked out of the room.

TWENTY-FIVE

Once Sanchez was out the door, I pulled the iPad mini from beneath my pillow. I powered it on, and it asked for Janice's fingerprint. I pressed my finger on the reader and it failed, of course. It then asked for a password. Fortunately, I knew her password for her Apple account and I typed in the letters even as my eyes blurred with tears. "JackNJill4Ever". I took my glasses off and cleaned away the moisture. The memory came back.

11 YEARS AGO

"YOU REALLY ARE A KLUTZ, *aren't you?" Janice stared down the steep stairway at me. We were at the Seven Falls in Colorado Springs. The metal stairway wound its way up hundreds of feet to the top of a massive waterfall cascading through seven different levels.*

"I told you I don't like heights." I gripped the wet, slippery stair rail with trembling hands. We were almost to the top, and I tried not to look out over the turbulent water chugging down the mountainside to my right. Two children ran past me and knocked me toward the railing. I grabbed the metal rail and swore.

"Jack, it's just a set of stairs. You will not fall. We're almost to the top." She turned and sprinted up the rest of the stairs.

Slowly and painfully, I made my way up toward the top platform. The setting sun disappeared behind the mountains and colored lights came on, painting the falls in a stunning display of rainbow hues. I finally reached the top level and reached for Janice's hand.

She gripped my hand and pulled me up beside her. I grabbed her and hugged her close. "I know this is just our honeymoon, but you have to be patient with me. I've never been much of a risk taker." I mumbled into her left ear.

Janice pushed me gently away and smiled. Her eyes sparkled and she kissed me. I tasted the nicotine on her lips and felt the warmth of her arms around me. She pulled away and her gaze locked onto mine. "Jack Merchant, I will never let you fall. We aren't Jack and Jill! If you fall and break your crown, I promise not to come tumbling after. Instead, I will take care of you."

HOW THINGS HAD CHANGED since then! Blinking tears from my eyes, I studied the tablet. There were the usual icons of Apple apps on the home screen and one mysterious looking icon shaped like a hexagonal gem. Underneath the gem was one word, "NMemes". I was about to press the icon when there was a knock on my door. I slid the tablet out of sight and Dr. Korskin stepped into the room. How did the man know how to make such dramatic appearances? He crossed quickly to my bedside, his face filled with concern.

"Jack, Jack, Jack! I just heard you were diagnosed with leukemia. I am so sorry."

He wore a white coat with the Institute name tag. He grabbed the bed rail and sighed. "If there is anything I can do, let me know. The Institute is at your disposal."

I smiled weakly. "Thank you, sir. I just had my bone marrow test, and we will soon know how bad it is."

Korskin crossed his arms. "I am so sorry. First, you get accused of murdering your own wife and now this."

I froze and slowly looked up at him. "How did you know about that?"

He tensed for a second and then frowned. "Well, I saw that detective out in the hallway the other day. I'm sorry, but I had to ask around. I thought Janice's death was an accident."

I studied his eyes and his face for any hint of malice. He had a good poker face if he was involved in Janice's death. I looked away. "Well, you can relax, Dr. Korskin. Dr. Francisco did a post on my wife's body and concluded there was no evidence of a homicide." I looked back into his eyes. "Detective Sanchez has changed her mind. She no longer considers me a murderer." I did not mention Sanchez would be looking into Korskin's past.

Korskin straightened and a hint of a smile crossed his lips. He relaxed his crossed arms and nodded. "That is wonderful news! Good news! Great, Jack." He leaned over me, and his eyes filled with mischief. That was the only way I could describe how I felt at what he said next. "Now, you need to stop thinking about the past. We have to live out Dr. Manning's legacy with this new wing and her research finally seeing the light of day. Jack, put this behind you. You have so much to live for! Find something to live for!"

I sat back from his curious speech. "But I have leukemia. I don't have but maybe a few weeks to live."

Korskin opened his mouth and straightened. His hand touched something in the pocket of his white coat. He looked down at his pocket then back at me. "Well, about that. Miracles can happen, Jack. Miracles can happen." He grinned once more and walked out of the room.

Before I could mull over what he had just said, Dr. Krale came into the room. She frowned at me. "Uh, Jack, I have bad news."

My heart froze. "You got the results already?"

"No! That's just it. The lab can't find your bone marrow samples. I took them a little over two hours ago and walked the samples to the lab myself." She turned as a nurse pushed a table into my room with a sterile tray on it. "I'm sorry, but we have to do another bone marrow test."

TWENTY-SIX

The dinner tray was a tasteless repast, and I pushed the rolling table away without taking a bite. Both of my hip bones hurt after the second bone marrow. And they had drawn more blood to go with the bone marrow tests. It seemed as if an endless parade of people had come in and out of the room in the last few hours since Korskin had left. I had hidden the tablet away in the table's drawer beside my bed, wrapped in a pair of my underwear. I figured no one would go digging through my underwear.

The sun was setting beyond the windows of my room when Dr. Montana strode in. His lanky, languorous stride always amazed me. The man never seemed to be stressed or in a hurry. He pulled up a chair and sat by my bed.

"Jack?"

"Montana?"

"Well, I got good news and bad news."

I studied his piercing eyes. They must have gotten the bone marrow results back which meant someone had fast tracked it. "How long do I have left?"

He shrugged. "Beats me. That's the bad news. You'll have to come back to work tomorrow."

My mouth fell open. "Look, I know I have missed some days working lately. Everyone has covered for me, and I plan on paying them back. But the leukemia?"

Montana did something I had rarely seen. He smiled. "That's the good news. Your bone marrow is normal. The last blood work they drew was normal. You don't have leukemia."

I sat up abruptly. "What?"

"Can't explain it. Maybe getting you lab drawn at the coroner's office is not the best procedure! Possibly they got your previous blood work mixed up with a dead person."

"But the nosebleed." I mumbled.

"Look, Jack, don't look a gift horse in the mouth. Every marker in your blood and bone marrow is totally normal. Wiggins said something about some contaminant on the slides probably from a bad staining reagent, but he double and triple checked. You have a clean bill of health." Montana stood up. "I wanted to tell you myself."

I blinked as a sudden wave of emotion came over me. "I don't know what to say."

Montana looked away and for a moment, seemed to have something in his eyes. He looked back at me. "Jack, you've been through the wringer the past year. When we hired you, everyone was amazed at your acumen. You are one of the best radiologists I have ever worked with."

I heard the 'but' coming. "But?"

"I know you've been down and out since Janice died. I hated that for you. But I need you to get on with your life. I've been covering for you and making excuses with the medical staff. Some of your work has lagged. But in the past few months you've seemed to get back on your feet."

"Until I went back to Colorado Springs." I said.

"Yeah, I guess being accused of murdering your own wife might mess with your mind. And nearly dying during a radiology test."

"And being told I have leukemia."

Montana nodded. He crossed his arms. "You know I'm not a very religious man. Doesn't mean I don't believe in God. I think God may be trying to get your attention. Maybe trying to get you to move on with your life." His stoic and steely demeanor returned. "Just don't take too much longer. Believe it or not, we need you in the group. Okay?"

I sat up and nodded. "Yes, sir."

Montana laughed. "Sir? I'm not your father. You're going home tonight. They're letting you leave this place. Tomorrow, take the home rotation and read from your home station. I got everyone to switch around." He started toward the door. He paused and turned back to glanced at me. "If I was a more religious man, I'd say this was divine intervention. Maybe even a miracle." He shook his head. "But, I'm not, so I won't say that. But take it as luck or take it as a miracle, Jack. See you soon."

TWENTY-SEVEN

The coffee was hot and strong. I sat on the small balcony of my apartment the next morning breathing in the cool November air. The sky was leaden and wept a fine, cold rainy drizzle that did nothing to dampen my spirits. I was alive! I did not have leukemia!

I tasted the sweet, strong notes of the coffee and sat back in the half-broken chair I had thrown out onto a balcony I seldom used. Wind blew the misty cold rain into my face, but I didn't care. I had slept for twelve hours after coming home the night before. The only downside was the ache in my hip bones from the bone marrow tests.

Now, just after seven in the morning, I was enjoying feeling more alive and feeling better than I had in weeks. No, months. In fact, I was almost giddy. I wanted to hop over the balcony of my second-story apartment and run for miles and miles. Of course, that would be a stupid thing to do; to break my legs less than twenty-four hours after leaving the hospital.

My cell phone rang, and I glanced at the caller ID. Sam.

"Hello." I answered the call.

"Jack?" Sam said over the speaker. "I heard you're going to live."

"That's right. I don't know what happened with your lab results, but I do not have leukemia."

"Yeah, I'm looking into that. Errors like that cost my predecessor his job. I hate to bother you at home, but if you have some time today, could you run by the office?"

I looked down at my pajamas. "That would mean taking a shower and putting on real clothes."

Sam laughed. "You're having a gown day?"

My heart sank. Janice had used that same term for any day she didn't have to leave the house and could wear her pajamas all day. "Yeah, something like that." I said hoarsely. "I'm working a shift from home today and I should be done by three."

"Working from home? You radiologists have it made." She said.

"That's one way to look at it." I said. "But the other way to think about it is I can never get far enough away from the 'office', even at home."

Sam chuckled. "Well, I wanted to review your wife's autopsy results. You said you wanted to talk about it and Sanchez jumped the gun and talked to you before I could. She may have given you a broad picture, but I can go into specifics."

"Sanchez told me the preliminary results were negative for homicide." I sat forward.

"That's true. Now the final results are in. And I found something strange."

I tensed and some of my coffee slopped onto my hand, burning my skin. "What?"

"I'd rather not say over the phone."

Did I detect a note of paranoia in her voice? "Well, in that case, I'll be there right after three."

"Good. See you then."

I stared at the blank face of my cell phone. What had she found? Something strange? I hurried back inside my apartment to my home station. A tower sat on the floor and three monitors were spread out on a folding table in the corner of my living room. I brushed aside napkins and desiccated pizza from the keyboard and logged in.

The familiar work lists filled my information monitor. I tried to log in and had to type in my user name three times. My hands were shaking. Not from feeling bad. I felt great. Shaking from what Sam had said. What had she found? Fortunately for me, the home reading rotation was nothing but plain Xrays. Nothing complicated, like CAT scans or MRIs. I could almost read them in my sleep.

A steady stream of patients kept me busy for most of the morning. I took a lunch break at noon and tried to find something worth eating in my refrigerator. The milk had not expired, and I found some stale cereal. I ate a bowl and spied Janice's tablet on the kitchen table where I had left it the night before.

The tablet was dead. I looked around my living room at the piles of dirty clothes. I really needed to clean up the place. I found the white, plastic bag the nurses had stuffed my belongings into when I left the hospital. I dug through the blood crusted scrubs looking for the charger. Wait! I had found the tablet in Janice's office then passed out. I had not found her charger. She had one at our old house, the one I had lost.

I started digging through trash on the couch and on the small kitchen table. My phone had a different charger than the tablet. I hurried into the bedroom and stood in front of the closet. My heart sank as I realized what I had to do.

I opened the door and reached into the back corner. I pulled out the large, black suitcase. I placed the suitcase on the rumpled bed and fought the feeling of panic and fear. Inside this suitcase was all that I had kept of Janice's things. When I had lost all the money; when the bank had repossessed our house; I had only a couple of hours to grab what I could to take with me. The bank got everything else.

I unzipped the suitcase and slowly laid back the upper lid. The fragrance hit me like a blow to my gut. Janice's favorite cologne wafted into the air. It knocked me back into the wall and I slumped to the floor. I couldn't do this, couldn't dig through her things to find the charger. There had to be one at her office. Or maybe Sam would have one.

Somehow, I managed to close the suitcase and zip it closed. I stumbled back to the work station and tried to lose myself in work.

"WELL, you look a lot better than the last time I saw you." Sam said as she sipped her green concoction. Her hair today was a matching green along with shiny green cat-eye glasses.

"Green hair?" I said.

"They call me Ms. Christmas." She opened her white lab coat to a green sweater covered with bright sequins in the shape of a Christmas tree. She touched the star at the top of the tree and colored lights blinked. "What do you think?"

"I'm glad I don't have migraines."

Sam chuckled and turned the lights off. She slid piles of paper around on her desk and found a black remote control. "Will this bother you today?" She tilted her head toward the glass.

"Not as much as the sweater." I said quietly, my mind still back in the bedroom; still focused on the suitcase.

"Too bad." She sipped some more and grimaced. "I could

use a good excuse to bypass today's dose of good health." She turned in her chair behind her desk and motioned to a large monitor on the wall. She clicked the remote and moved through menus and windows until she came to a header page with "Janice Merchant Manning" written in bold letters across the image. She glanced at me. "Are you sure you're up to this, Jack?"

I nodded numbly. "Just don't show me her, uh, body. You sounded paranoid on the phone."

Sam thought for a moment. "Let's just say I shouldn't be discussing the results with you. Conflict of interest if this ever goes to a trial. Now, I was going to go straight for the slides. You asked me to take a look at her pelvic tissue. I managed to take some samples and here is what I found."

The screen filled with an abstract mosaic of pink, white and blue. I recognized desiccated cells with their purple nuclei. The clear globules of fat tissue were interspersed between the thousands of deformed cells. "Obviously the tissue is markedly malformed from the passage of time, but I managed to rehydrate the tissue enough to get good stains. Now, here is the puzzling finding I didn't want to talk about over the phone."

Sam moved the remote around pointing it at the monitor. An arrow followed her motion and came to rest beside a small, black lobulated spot. "Notice there are several of these in the field. They're lobulated and completely black. At first, I thought they were some kind of contaminant. But here is the interesting finding."

Sam moved the image aside through several windows and came to rest on another slide. The tissue was markedly different from the first sample. The cells were scant and scattered through the strands of dark connective tissue were black crystalline structures. "Carbon from the fire." Sam said quietly.

I felt the heat on my face. Heard the explosion of glass and my heart raced.

Sam glanced at me. "Want me to go on?"

I managed to nod. Sam pointed to the black crystals. "Notice the difference in shape. These black crystalline structures came from the fire. Soot from other things burning in the room." She clicked the remote and the image enlarged. "But here is the strange thing. Look at this one small area of preserved tissue." Sam pointed to a tiny area of tissue that still had some pink and white globs. Imbedded in the center of the image was another of the black globules. Only, this globule had a serrated edge and a tiny, thin line extending from the serrated edge. "See that straight, thin protrusion?"

"What is it?"

Sam turned to me. "I don't know. These globules are not from the fire. And, Jack, that straight line? Nothing in the biological realm can form an exact straight line."

My forehead furrowed and I stood up and crossed to the monitor. "What are you saying?"

"I think this thing, whatever it is, is fabricated."

I glanced at Sam. "You mean, man-made?"

"Yes." Sam clicked the remote and the screen went dark. She looked around her office and raised her voice. "My conclusion is this is some kind of fabricated contaminant from the fire."

I started to speak, and she put finger to her lips. She stood up slowly and motioned to the door. "Let's get some coffee. Follow me."

I hesitated for a moment and Sam glanced over her shoulder. "Don't worry. We're not viewing any bodies." She took my cell phone from my pocket and placed it on her desk. Sam led me out into the hallway and out the front door. The air was chilly with a cold front moving in. More cold rain! She motioned to a minivan with a red nose on the grill and brown antlers from the side windows. "Rudolph." She smiled. "Get in."

I climbed into the passenger side of the van and Sam started the engine. She turned up the heater full force. "Where are we going?"

Sam turned on the radio and jazz music filled the air. "Nowhere, Jack. I just needed to get away from the office for a moment." Sam tapped the pockets of her white coat and glanced into the back seat. "We need some total privacy. Jack, I don't know what is going on, but those globules?"

"Yes."

"I've found them in several other tissue samples. I had to go back and look for them, but they are there." Her face paled and she licked her lips. "We are into something deep and dangerous, Jack."

"What do you mean?"

Sam looked back at me, and behind the green glasses, her eyes were clouded with fear. "Those suicides I posted in the past few days. They all have these globules in their tissue. Not only that, but two of the homicides in the past three weeks showed the globules."

I blinked and looked away. "I don't understand? Are we looking at some kind of virus? Some kind of chemical? Something that is changing people's behavior?"

Sam was quiet as jazz played around us. "I don't know right now. But the fact that something that appears manmade may be present in the bodies of all these victims and your wife from over a year ago speaks to an enterprise that is long in execution and with wide reach. Who could have that kind of influence? What is this all about?"

"I don't know, Sam. But the more I dig into Janice's past,

the more I might be able to find out. This could be why she was murdered. What about Baldy?"

"I hadn't thought of him. I'll check his tissue." Sam nodded as "Jingle Bell Rock" filled the van. She patted my arm. "Be careful, Jack. You just survived a leukemia scare."

"I don't have a choice, Sam. I must get the answers. Do me a favor. Get my bone marrow samples and take a look at them."

"Why?"

"Montana mentioned Dr. Wiggins saw some kind of contaminant in my bone marrow."

Sam's eyes widened behind her glasses. "Oh my! Looks like there's a Scrooge loose somewhere."

TWENTY-EIGHT

After leaving Sam's, it was close to 4:30 P.M. by the time I found the courage to enter the front doors of the Institute. The sky had grown even darker and the fine, misty rain had changed over to a steady, cold downpour. Thunder rattled the windows of the glass entrance as I walked in. Before I went to see Sam, I had put on my scrubs and my white coat with my name monogrammed above the pocket. I looked official. And hopefully intimidating. Two security guards stood by the entryway into the large open atrium.

"Sir, would you walk through the metal detector, please?" The guard directed me to a metal detector. "Remove all the metal items from your pockets, please." He pushed a plastic bowl across the metal table. I placed my phone, car keys, and the iPad in the bowl. He motioned me through the metal detector and the lights blinked green.

"Why all the security?" I asked as I put away my things.

"The president will be here later this week." The guard said. "Check in with the reception desk."

I nodded and made my way to the reception desk. Another

security guard sat beside a small, diminutive woman. She glanced at the guard nervously. "May I help you?"

"I'm Dr. Jack Merchant. Dr. Janice Manning's husband. I wanted to retrieve some items from her office, please."

The receptionist nodded and held out her hand. "I.D. please."

I took my driver's license out of my wallet and placed it in her hand. She glanced at it and then at me and turned her back to make a phone call. I couldn't make out her conversation. Finally, she turned back to me and handed me back my license.

"Dr. Korskin's secretary said to come on up, but they cannot let you into the office without Dr. Korskin's permission. He is currently in a meeting, but you can wait in the reception room. Tenth floor."

Ah, the penthouse suite. Of course, that is where Korskin would reside. The security guard behind the desk escorted me to the elevator and even waited until I got on to use a card to activate the ride to the tenth floor. "Don't get off at any other level." He growled. I nodded.

Korskin's reception room was more ornately decorated than the building foyer, with festive Christmas trees and green and red garland along the walls. Windows behind the receptionist looked out over the city and the river. A young man looked up at me. "Dr. Merchant? Please have a seat."

"Do you have a restroom?"

The young man's lip wrinkled in annoyance. He pointed to a hallway. "Down the hall to your left."

I headed off down the hallway toward the restroom. But my goal was not the bathroom. I was determined to see Korskin no matter what. And, if I could catch him off guard, the more the better. Passing the restroom, I paused before double doors. A placard beside the doors showed Korskin's name in huge letters. I was reaching for the handle when the door opened.

The man standing before me was huge. Although his hair was salt and pepper, his bulging biceps and large chest defied his age. I looked into the face of someone I had seen on the movie screen many times.

The man paused and glanced over his shoulder. "Dick, I think you have a visitor."

Korskin appeared beside the man and his face paled at the sight of me. "Jack?"

"Uh, sorry, I was heading to the restroom. They made me come up here to get permission to get some photos from Janice's office."

Korskin seemed to relax. He smiled thinly. "Dr. Jack Merchant, David Boone."

The big man took my hand and shook it. "Ah, Dr. Manning's husband."

David Boone stood before me in the flesh. Once a professional wrestler, he had moved on to Hollywood and made a fortune in movies about aliens and combat mercenaries. All the while, he had invested in several companies and over the past ten years had formed Boone Media Network, a conglomerate of various technology companies. He was worth billions. And he knew Janice?

"It's a pleasure to meet you, Mr. Boone."

"David, call me David." He smiled and his facial bones bore the slight deformity of years of steroid use. "Dr. Korskin and I are old friends."

Korskin nodded nervously. "Uh, David has donated millions to the Institute. He is one of our biggest supporters."

Boone studied me and I felt like a butterfly pinned to a dissection board. "I am sorry to hear about your loss, Dr. Merchant. Dr. Manning was a talented individual."

"I guess you are here for a movie?" Talako had added some

smaller movie studios after Katrina forced movie production from New Orleans to northern Louisiana.

"Oh, no!" He smiled. "I am here to greet the president." He turned and clapped Korskin on the back and Korskin almost fell. "Dick has agreed to let me sit on the stage. After all, that is where I belong." He lifted an eyebrow and slid past me. "I'm heading to New Orleans to visit a movie set and then I'll be back at the end of the week. See you then, Dick. Give my regards to your daughter."

Korskin flinched at that remark and looked away. I watched the man recede down the hall and the look on Korskin's face was a mixture of relief and fear. What was going on here? He finally looked back at me, and his features hardened. "What do you want from Janice's office?"

I swallowed and tried to hide my nervousness. "Now that I know her office was preserved, I would like some photographs she has of us." I looked down with my best sorrowful look. "I'm not proud of the fact I lost our house, and the bank took everything. I don't have many mementos of our time together."

"Of course." Korskin said, and fidgeted with something in his pocket. He pulled out a key ring. "I'll take you down there now."

I RUMMAGED around Janice's office but couldn't really look for much. Korskin stood in the door and watched my every move. In one of the drawers, I found the charge cable. "Ah, this I can use. I lost the charger for my phone." I tucked it in my coat pocket before Korskin could say anything. Framed photos sat on her desk, and I took them all. In the office's corner, I found Janice's Vera Bradley backpack we often took on trips.

She had accidentally left it behind in Talako when we went to Colorado a year before.

When I picked it up, Korskin stepped into the office and stuck out his hand. "If you don't mind, Jack. I need to check the backpack for any proprietary information. You understand, don't you?"

He took the backpack, and I bit my tongue. I wanted to lash out at the man. Korskin dumped the contents of the backpack on the desk. Various cosmetic items rolled around. A pack of cigarettes. A lighter. Korskin nodded. "Looks fine." He put the items back in the backpack and placed the picture frames inside. A small sculpture caught my attention, and I gasped. "Oh, my!"

Korskin stiffened. "What?"

I pointed to the awkwardly fashioned turtle. "One of Janice's attempts at art. She took a sculpture class once when we were at Perdido Key. It was supposed to be a sea turtle. But it looks more like a cow patty."

Korskin actually smiled. "I was wondering what that was supposed to be."

The sculpture was as big as a toy flying disc, and I slid it into the backpack. "It may be ugly, but it was something Janice valued." I felt tears in my eyes, and I drew a deep, shuddering breath. "I think that's all I can do right now, Dr. Korskin."

Korskin actually released his breath. Had he been holding his breath? If so, why? "Very good, Jack." He reached into his pocket and pulled out a glossy piece of stiff paper. "I have a few of these left, and I was saving one for you. It's a ticket to the Presidential reception. I would have saved you a place on the stage. After all, you are Dr. Manning's husband. But, well, David Boone insisted."

I nodded and took the ticket. "I understand. Money talks."

Korskin laughed nervously. "Sometimes it shouts!" He

motioned for me to leave and then paused. "Oh, by the way. Congratulations on NOT having leukemia. I told you things would turn out just fine. Don't forget that!"

I squinted at him. What a strange thing to say. "I'm thankful for miracles." I fought the desire to run down the hall and I made my way out of the building.

TWENTY-NINE

Dr. Francisco's paranoia had grown on me. Rather than returning to my apartment, I decided to stay at the hospital. We had an on call room rarely used by the radiologist on call. It was a relic of the old days before teleradiology made it possible to have a home station. But, to his credit, Murray had insisted on keeping the one at Fairmont Central. He said we might need it for an office later on. Such was the ongoing struggle for radiology to keep its territory.

I had packed a bag prior to leaving the apartment and I had stopped at Best Buy to purchase what was popularly known as a "burner phone". I had left my cell phone in the apartment. The on call room was musty with a desk, a squeaky desk chair and an old hospital bed with a bare mattress. I had stopped in the holding room for sheets and a pillow.

I locked the door and dumped the contents of my bag on the bed. In the backpack were the photo frames from Janice's office and the rather abstract turtle. While moving the items, the turtle slipped off the bed and shattered on the floor. Bits and pieces of fired clay spread across the floor. I swore and began to try and remember where in radiology I could find a broom. Then, I saw something protruding from the broken stump of the turtle's "neck". The mouth was open, and Janice had pushed something through the mouth and down into the neck region. I slowly teased the object from the stump of the broken neck. It was a tuberculin syringe, a tiny syringe that held only one cubic centimeter of fluid. The syringe was capped off at one end and the plunger had been pulled out and taped into place. The syringe was filled with a dark liquid. The dark contents seemed to sparkle for a moment in the glaring fluorescent light. What was in the syringe? And why had she hidden it in the turtle? It was as if she had to find a hiding place in a hurry and the turtle's mouth was the closest thing. That realization strengthened my paranoia.

I placed the syringe on the desk and returned to the contents on the bed. Now that I had found the syringe, I wondered what else might be hidden. Janice's smiling face made it difficult to remove the photos from their frames. There were inscriptions on the back of the photos with place and dates but nothing surprising. I emptied the cigarettes from the case into the trash. Nothing inside. I searched through the cosmetics and ended up dumping them into the trash. What about the backpack? Every pocket inside and out was empty. I turned the backpack inside out and was about to give up when I felt something stiff in the edge of one of the shoulder straps. A black stitch closed off the hem of the strap. Given this was a very expensive Vera Bradley backpack with bright colorful images, this tiny black stitch defied the otherwise trendy appearance. I pulled on the thread, and it slid out of the fabric exposing a hole. Inside I found a rolled-up piece of paper hidden in the strap.

With trembling hands, I sat in the wobbly chair and carefully unrolled the piece of paper on the surface of the desk. It measured about two by three inches and written in black ink on the paper were five numbers, 73482. What did this number mean and why did she have to hide it? I found the charger cable and plugged it into the wall. When I attached the iPad to the charger, it began to charge.

Before I pushed the power on button, my paranoia kicked in again. I closed my eyes and tried to recall the opening screen. Was the tablet just on Wi-Fi or did it have a cellular connection? If it did and I turned it on, could I be tracked? After I opened my eyes, I pressed the power on button.

The screen powered up and I was pleased to see the words, "no service" in the upper menu bar. That was the first time I was glad for poor cellular service in the hospital! If it picked up the hospital Wi-Fi connection, I should be safe as the hospital's service was hidden behind a tightly secured firewall to protect patient privacy. I typed in the password and immediately went to the settings icon and put it in airplane mode. Now, no one could track me.

The hexagonal icon pulsed. I touched it and a window opened asking for a PIN number. Smiling, I glanced at the paper and typed in the number. The app opened and Janice's secrets stared back at me!

The tablet's image contained a red background with six squares arranged in two rows of three icons. Each icon had a descriptor beneath composed of six numbers and letters. On each icon there was a capital letter "V" followed by a two-digit number with one decimal place. V1.2, V2.5, V3.7, V4.1, V6.1, and V7.2 were the numbers on each of the icons. What did it mean? I touched one at random and the V3.7 icon exploded into a new screen. A plethora of numbers and letters filled a table on the screen. Version number. Date of initiation. Density. And, a strange set of letters, probably abbreviations.

At the bottom of the screen was a big red button. I stared at the button and drew a deep breath and pressed it.

The screen's background flashed red and white as a window appeared with the words, "Cannot connect to the main server. Check internet connection." After pressing the "OK" button the flashing window closed. I sat back in the chair. If I wanted to find out what this was all about, I would have to take a chance and connect to Wi-Fi.

"Dr. Merchant, call the operator. Dr. Merchant, call the operator." Sounded over the hospital paging system. Great! They had just announced I was in the hospital!

As I left the room, dizziness hit me hard. I leaned up against a wall and tried to focus. The dizziness lessened. Probably my blood pressure! The stress was getting to me and I wasn't even in a deposition. Keeping one hand on the wall, I made it to one of our reading rooms. This one had only one reading station and was reserved for a radiologist who could read without interruption. To that end, there was a lock on the door. After keying in the combination, I stepped into the room and dialed the operator on the landline.

"Operator, how may I direct your call." A woman said.

"This is Dr. Merchant." I whispered.

"I have a Detective Sanchez on the line for you sir. Can I put her through? Please." Her voice cracked.

I rolled my eyes. "Yes. Put her through."

The line clicked and I heard heavy breathing. "Merchant?"

"Yeah, how did you find me?"

Sanchez laughed. "You're a doctor. If you're not at home, I figured you'd be at work. Taking call or something since you're no longer going to die. Every time I look for you, I start with the hospitals. What's wrong with your cell phone?"

"I turned it off. I wanted to be left alone."

Sanchez was silent for a moment. "Look, I need to do something that is very hard for me to do. I need to apologize."

"Apologize? How much is that going to hurt you?"

"Hey, I'm trying here. You remember where we last met in Colorado?"

I thought back to the pancake house. "Yeah."

"We need to talk and not over the phone. I have a hankering for pancakes." She hung up.

I looked at the phone and sighed. There was one of those chain pancake restaurants close to Fairmont Central and I realized for the first time that day, I was hungry. With the dizziness still affecting my balance, I made my way carefully out to my car.

THIRTY

With the windows darkened by the misting rain I could imagine I was sitting in the same restaurant in Colorado. It was after ten o'clock and Sanchez sauntered in chewing on her toothpick. She motioned to the back of the restaurant as she came in.

"Back here. Away from the windows." She spoke sharply to the receptionist and then she marched to the table in the back. I slid into the booth across from her.

"Aren't you being a little paranoid?"

"Look who is talking. Buying a burner phone to hide." She motioned to a harried server and ordered coffee and her usual. She had to explain to the server what her usual was.

The server glared at me, and I shrugged. "Just a short stack and decaf coffee." I glanced back at Sanchez. "How did you know about the burner phone?"

"I have traces on your credit cards. Saw you went to Best Buy and purchased a cell phone. Went by but they wouldn't give me the number. Said I needed a warrant." The server plopped a carafe of coffee between us and slid two empty mugs in front of us. "We don't have no decaf." She blurted out and turned and left.

Sanchez smiled. "I like her already."

"Sanchez, what you did is illegal." I massaged my temples. The dizziness still gripped me. Maybe caffeine would help. I poured a cup from the carafe.

"Yep." She shrugged. "But I had to find you. And if you're trying to go off the grid, don't use a credit card!" She chugged some coffee and wiped her lips on her sleeve. She glared at me and drew a deep breath.

"You okay?"

"Sanchez, I've faced death twice since you came into my life. I'm tired, stressed out, and have a headache." I guzzled the black coffee.

"Okay, look, Dr. Merchant, I was wrong about your wife. I did some digging of my own on this Dr. Korskin like you suggested. Your buddy, Jerry, was right. His background is a little too clean. Your friend, Keri, may be on the right track. If this man is the shadow man or the other man who survived, then he is one of the most wanted men in America." She drank more coffee. "Aw, man, that's good. Louisiana has much better coffee than Colorado."

"What should we do?"

Sanchez leaned back as her meal arrived. "*We* do nothing. You need to let me handle this."

She was right. I needed to back off. "Okay, I will get out of the way of this." My head buzzed with a sharp pain and then the dizziness was gone. I shook my head in confusion. As quickly as it had come on, the dizziness and headache were gone.

"Jack, I have authority to do some more digging." The waitress arrived and slammed plates on the table before us and walked away without a word. Sanchez raised an eyebrow and smiled.

"Yep, she's a keeper." She dug into her eggs. "What I need from you is more information on your wife. When did she start working with Korskin? Did she ever say anything about him?"

I leaned back and thought of the turtle and the syringe. "I really don't know exactly what Janice was working on. It had something to do with nanotechnology. I haven't learned anything useful. And, she's been working with Korskin for the last six or seven years."

Sanchez slid her cell phone across the table in front of me and tapped the screen. "Well, here is a real problem." She turned the phone. On the screen the face of a man with red hair stared back at me. The photo was blurry.

"Who is this?"

"That, mi amigo, is Keri's red-haired man. Pulled it off a security camera in the stairwell. They thought all of them were shut down, but that camera had a short and kept working. The photo was saved in a buffer on the camera."

"How did you get your hands on this? The FBI agent said they had no images of any of the men."

"This photo was only for those with the need to know. They didn't even show it to Theresa Douglas according to the records."

"The sealed records?" How had Sanchez gotten her hands on a photo from years ago? She hadn't earned the nickname of jaguar for nothing!

"I ain't afraid of no sealed records!" She said and chuckled. "There is no photo of the Shadow Man as Keri called him. This red-haired man looked nothing like Korskin."

"Could Keri be wrong about Korskin?"

Sanchez slurped more eggs and salsa. She retrieved the phone. "I had the photo analyzed along with a photo of Korskin from the Institute website. The facial structure of the red-haired man is very similar to Korskin's. You take this red-haired guy and alter his facial features, dye his hair, and give him contacts and he could be Korskin."

"Plastic surgery?"

"Possibly." She emptied her coffee cup and poured more from the carafe.

"He had someone in his office today. David Boone."

Sanchez almost dropped the carafe. "The David Boone? Interesting."

I nodded. "And it was weird. Boone told Korskin to give his regards to his daughter. Korskin sort of looked, I don't know, sad?"

Sanchez sat back and nodded her head. "His daughter? Get out of here!" She smiled. "I was looking into his financials and there is a monthly fee paid to a long-term care facility in Austin, Texas. I might need to check that out. Maybe he has a daughter with special needs. If I can find this daughter of his, it might give us his real name."

"Why would he have a daughter in a long-term care facility? Maybe that is how Boone has leverage on him. Korskin needs money to keep paying for the care of his daughter?" I shrugged and rubbed my face. "What does Boone have to do with this? Unless it's his nannomemes Janice was developing for him. Whatever those things are. In fact, things are getting all mixed up."

"Merchant." Sanchez said quietly. "Jack. The last time we had breakfast, you were a suspect. You're not anymore. Don't be a hero. It's time for you to back off and get out of the line of fire. Go home. Stop trying to dissect this thing like you're a medical examiner or something. You're a radiologist, not Sherlock Holmes. Forget about Korskin for now and let the big guys take care of it."

Sanchez's cell phone warbled. She looked at the screen. "What the deuce?"

"Something wrong?" I asked.

Her face turned red, and she stood up abruptly. "I have to go. Now."

"Sanchez, what's wrong?"

Sanchez glanced at me. "An ugly moment from my past just popped up." She retrieved cash from her pocket. She tossed it on the table. "I'll buy this time. See you, Doc." She hurried out of the restaurant.

THIRTY-ONE

It was close to midnight by the time I arrived back at Fairmont Central. The front doors were closed at 8 P.M. and I had to enter through the emergency room. A security guard posted at the entrance asked for my I. D. card and scanned my bar code into the system.

Dr. Moore looked up from behind his desk as I walked by. "Jack?"

I stopped. Uh oh! He would want a curbside consult instead of waiting for the interpretation from the virtual radiology group that covered for us at night. I should have changed out of my scrubs! "Hey Rich."

"You on call?"

"Not really. I'm in one of our on-call rooms. Had a, uh, leak at the apartment. Carpet's flooded." I paused and tried not to look him in the eyes.

"We've been waiting almost two hours for a report on a CAT scan. You know sometimes your virtual radiology group is slow."

I had heard this complaint for too many times. Our group

was considering using another service. "Two hours is the limit." I said.

"And you guys have told us to call the rad on call when the report is late. I was about to call Montana but you know how he is." Rich frowned.

Montana was anything but polite if he got called. "I'll be glad to look at it for you."

We went into a back room where the ER had its own PACS station. I sat before the computer monitors and looked at the work list. Moore pointed to the patient's name in the list. "Belly pain. Bane of our existence. Maybe kidney stones."

I opened the patient's CAT scan file and started going through the images. "Fatty liver, looks like."

"Yeah, she's a drinker." Rich said. He stood behind me with his arms crossed. According to my urologist, my liver looked like this.

"No gallstones. Pancreas is okay. Spleen's a little large. Might be getting cirrhosis already. But no ascites yet." The thought made me shudder. Was I looking at my future? I scrolled through the images from the liver down toward the bladder. The right kidney was larger than the left. Gray smears around it indicated inflammation or obstruction. The ureter draining the kidney was huge and as I scrolled down, a white dot popped up in the middle of the ureter. "There it is. Right hydronephrosis and a mid-ureteral stone. There's your kidney stone."

"How big. If it's greater than 5 millimeters, she won't pass it easily."

"It's 7 millimeters."

"You didn't even measure it." Moore said.

"It ain't my first rodeo." I glanced at him over my shoulder.

"Bet you a strawberry pie from Strong's Diner you're wrong." Moore said.

"You're on." I opened a menu and pulled up the ruler tool and measured the small kidney stone. "Would you look at that! Seven millimeters." I turned in my chair and smiled at Moore.

"I should have known better than to bet with a gambler like you, Jack." Ugh! Another kick in the gut!

Before I could reply the dedicated radio squawked and Rich hurried over and started talking. "Dr. Moore here. What's up?"

"Gunshot wound to head. You guys up for a neuro case?" The EMT said on the other line. "We're less than five minutes out."

"Neurosurgery on call tonight is at GUT. I just talked to them about thirty minutes ago. Besides, they are the level one trauma unit." Rich said, turning to look at me.

"Their ER is on diversion. They are closed to trauma cases." The EMT said over the radio.

Moore rolled his eyes. "Right!" He glanced at me and the look on his face told me everything! "In other words, they are short on some interns and residents to work the ER, so they go on 'diversion' at the drop of a hat and dump their patients on us. What's new? Who's been shot?"

"Some cop from out of state. Found her under the Texas Street bridge. Two shots to the head." The EMT said.

I stood up so fast my chair shot from under me and crashed into the wall and I ran over to the radio. "What's her name?"

"Who is this?"

"Dr. Merchant, radiologist. Is it Sanchez?"

Moore looked at me. "How do you know?"

"Just tell me!" I said over the radio.

"Yeah. Last name Sanchez." I stumbled back from the radio and grabbed Moore. "You've got to take her, Rich."

"Jack, we don't have a neurosurgeon here tonight. It will take them thirty minutes just to drive here."

"Then get them on the phone and have them get their butt over here, Rich. Please."

Moore nodded slowly. "Okay. We are slow tonight Or, at least we were." He turned back to the radio. "Bring her in now and I'll have neurosurgery get over here."

I waited at the ambulance entrance, my heart racing. The sound of sirens meant the ambulance was approaching and I saw the oscillating red and white lights as the it arrived. The sliding doors opened, and I ran out to the back of the ambulance. The doors opened from the inside.

"She's crashing." A tall, blood covered EMT hopped down, his hand automatically snagging the gurney. The other EMT released the gurney from the deep end of the ambulance, and they slid Sanchez into sight.

I leaned over her head. It was covered with clotted blood. "Sanchez, it's me, Jack. Hang in there." Her skin was pale and the EMT grabbed a ventilator bag and breathed for her as the legs of the gurney dropped to the ground. Her blood-soaked hair splashed red drops onto my glasses.

"Bro, we got to get her inside. She's flatlining." The EMT pushed me back with his blood covered blue gloved hands. I stepped back as more blood splashed from the gurney across my scrubs. They wheeled the gurney into the ER and down the hall to the trauma room. A police car pulled up with flashing lights and Jerry Langley hopped out from the passenger side.

"Jack? Is that you?" He shouted at me. I whirled and ran to him.

"Jerry? What happened?"

"Got a call for gunshots heard on the river front. I was filling in for a sick partner and riding with a rookie, Collier. Good thing, too or they would have had no idea who she was."

Jerry followed me into the ER, and he paused at the security desk. I went down the hall and tried to push my way into the trauma room. A dozen people scurried around Sanchez's body hanging I.V.s and attaching EKG leads and taking vital signs. I glanced at the monitor. Her EKG was indeed flatline. No heartbeat.

"Jack, get out of here! You can't help her right now." Moore said.

He was right. "She'll need a CAT scan."

"When she's stable."

"I'll get the techs ready." I said with trembling lips and stumbled down the hall toward radiology. They didn't need me to get them ready, but I couldn't stay. Images and memories of Janice's body kept surfacing and I shut my eyes to keep the horror from taking me. "No! This can't be happening!"

I ran into the CAT scan control room and Damian glanced up at me from his cell phone. "Hey, doc. What happened to you? I was just watching the latest Marvel stream." He paused and stood up. "You're covered in blood."

"Gunshot victim in the ER. They're bringing her around here for a scan." I managed. "She's my friend." My friend? Was Sanchez really my friend? It didn't matter. She did not deserve what had happened to her.

Damian moved quickly into the CAT scan room and got the table ready for a new patient. He came back into the control room as I sat in a chair.

"Doc, you got a name?"

"Gloria Sanchez." I mumbled.

"I don't suppose you know her birth date?"

I shook my head as Damian put in all the available information into the patient identification screen. They came down the hall and six people pushed her gurney into the CAT scan room. Moore trailed them all, his gloved hands and yellow safety gown covered with blood. "She's stable. Normal sinus rhythm. Neuro is pulling into the parking lot."

I helped Damian get her onto the table and strap her head down. Blood was everywhere across her shirt and her face and her neck and throughout her hair. Damian slipped a blue surgical hat over her hair after donning a pair of blue gloves. He slid the table into the scanner and motioned to everyone. I looked down at my hands. Sanchez's blood was soaked into my palms.

"Out of the room if you value your valuables." Damian said returning to the control room. No one wanted to get "zapped" by radiation.

Jerry Langley appeared behind me in the control room. "Anything yet, Jack?"

I looked up at him. "Just getting her scanned now."

Damian ripped off his bloody gloves and tossed them into a red box. He tapped on the keyboards and the table moved in and out obtaining a "scout" study in order to plan the scanning pattern. He pushed buttons and there was a clicking and whirring sound as Sanchez's head moved in and then back out of the huge donut of the CAT scanner.

Damian nodded. "We're good. You can get her off the table." The ER team scrambled back into the room and moved Sanchez back onto her gurney.

The images of Sanchez's brain scrolled on the monitor in front of me. I took the mouse and began to study one image at a time. Her brain tissue was gray and dark. Metal fragments on the surface of her skull caused white streaks as the metal attenuated the CAT scan Xray beam. I calmed my mind and examined each slice from the top of the brain to the bottom of the skull. I almost smiled.

"I can't believe it! Sanchez is one hardheaded bulldog."

"What?" Moore said, leaning over me.

"The bullets lodged in her skull. But she has an epidural hematoma. It's causing midline shift and that is why she stopped breathing." I pointed to a white crescent shaped collection along the outer surface of her brain. "There's the blood and its pressing down the brain." I took the mouse and pulled up a ruler and made a measurement. "Almost a centimeter of midline shift." The pressure of the bleeding epidural hematoma was pushing one side of the brain across the middle to the other side. This was dangerous and could kill Sanchez even though the bullets did not enter her brain tissue.

Three people hustled into the room behind me. Two neurosurgery fellows and their P.A. "What's up?"

I glanced at them. "Epidural. Midline shift by one centimeter. Temporal bone fracture."

"Any bone fragments?" The tall, dark hair man said. I had no idea who he was.

"No. Just a depressed fracture."

"Let's get her to the OR." He turned to the other two. "I need a formal report and I need those images in the OR."

"I'll take care of it." I said with a shaking voice.

Damian tapped on the keyboard. "The images are sent over to the PACS system, doc." He said to the neurosurgeon. "You have them in the OR now."

I stood up and almost stumbled. "I'll go dictate a report now."

In ten seconds, everyone was gone except for Damian. He looked at me. "Doc, you know how to bring the excitement. Better than Marvel."

As I walked through the CAT scan room, I noticed a toothpick on the floor. Moisture blurred my vision and I managed to find my way to the solitary reading room. I sat in the chair and signed into the PACS system. Sanchez's name showed up in the patient list. How many times had I actually known who the patient really was? To me, they were just names and possible diagnoses based on their symptoms. Faceless but not nameless.

I had been on a stretcher not too long ago and I had died! I was more than just a name!

Sanchez's brain images filled the high resolution monitor. I scrolled through each "slice" more slowly, trying my best to be professionally objective. My vision blurred from moisture. No time for this!

I checked and double checked my measurements and made sure there were no other abnormal areas before picking up the microphone and recording my report. Our PACS system used voice recognition and a "template" opened in the report window and I began speaking and the words appeared in the report.

"Two metal fragments from gunshot are noted in the soft tissues overlying the right temporal bone. Bone windows reveal a depressed skull fracture involving the temporal bone and the depression is 4 millimeters. No bone fragments are present in the brain substance. Underlying the fracture is an epidural hematoma with a typical convex appearance measuring almost two centimeters at its widest. Midline shift is noted with a one-centimeter midline shift from right to left with compression of the lateral ventricles. No evidence of bleeding in the brain substance is noted. No evidence or herniation of transtentorial herniation of the brain is noted. These findings were discussed with the attending neurosurgeon at the time of the examination."

I paused and caught my breath. The words came so mind-lessly, so rote. But these words were about Sanchez, not some faceless patient. I swallowed and read my transcribed report and made a few minor changes to some of the words. The system wasn't flawless.

"Impression, right sided gunshot wound with bullet frag-ments in the soft tissues overlying a depressed skull fracture of the temporal bone. Number two, an epidural hematoma with measurements as noted in the body of the dictation. Number three, no intraparenchymal hemorrhage or transtentorial herniation. Number four, midline shift from right to left as noted in the body of the dictation."

I sat back and checked the report one more time before signing off and allowing the final report to make its way into the hospital system. It was only then I noticed Sanchez's blood all over the microphone.

THIRTY-TWO

After a quick shower in the surgeon's lounge, I put on clean scrubs and tossed my bloody scrubs in the laundry. In the main surgery hallway, I spied the on call charge nurse and asked him about Sanchez.

"They are just now getting her under anesthesia. It will be a while before we know anything."

I went back to my room and collapsed on the bed around 3 A.M. I tossed and turned most of the morning waiting to hear some more about Sanchez. She was still in surgery when I woke up at 5:30 A.M. That shouldn't have been! Epidural drainage doesn't take that long. Was there other damage we didn't know about? This was common to focus on one injury only to discover another injury. She might have been shot elsewhere.

If I had been at home, I would have logged into our PACS system the next morning beginning at 7 A.M. But I decided to stay in the call room until time to start work. I packed up Janice's things into her backpack. The tablet, the syringe and the password went into my overnight bag. Once in the single reading station room I locked the door behind me. No one was supposed to be using it that day so I could work as if I were at home. I called the ER and asked for Rich.

"I don't know anything else, Jack." Moore said. "The dam broke after Sanchez came in and we've been overwhelmed. I know they called in Ron Berch."

"The surgeon? I was wondering if she was shot somewhere else."

"Maybe. Don't know. I never got a chance to finish our evaluation. Wish I could tell you more, but I got to go. Got a code coming in the doors right now." The line went dead.

With work to be done, I didn't have any more time to focus on Sanchez. This rotation was long and hard in the early morning hours. We set it up that way so one of us could log on early before we started having to do procedures and interpret most of the studies from the night before. The list contained over 150 patients done in all three hospitals since 6 P.M. the night before when we ended our latest shift. This included plain Xrays of the chest, joints and bones all from the emergency rooms. The list included all radiology studies from both Fairmont hospitals. There were also many imaging studies from inpatients such as ultrasounds and CAT scans from the evening before. Our practice group had an arrangement with a virtual radiology group to interpret our emergency CAT scans and ultrasounds done after hours or one of us would have been up all night looking at those studies! Rumor had it that some radiologists in the virtual radiology practice worked during the morning hours of their favorite Pacific islands while we slept! What a life that would be! Now, sitting in front of the usual morning dump, it would take me an hour just to read half of the list.

My head pounded from lack of sleep. My office phone rang right at 8 A.M. when the remaining radiologist rotations began. I answered it tentatively.

"Dr. Merchant, this is Mattie." Mattie was one of our secretaries. Someone had seen me go into the reading room! "I have a friend of yours, Jerry, who wants to talk to you."

"Sure. I'll take the call."

"Jack, it's Jerry. I was hoping I could catch you at the office. You aren't answering your cell phone."

"Jerry, I didn't get a chance to talk to you earlier this morning."

"I never left. Had to do all the paperwork for Sanchez. Can you meet me in the cafeteria? I need coffee."

"Sure. I'm caught up and I'm on my way."

Jerry was still wearing his full regalia as he walked up to my table in the hospital cafeteria. He slid into the seat opposite me and took off his mirrored sunglasses. His eyes were surrounded by black circles of fatigue. "Jack, I'm sorry I didn't ask you earlier, how are you feeling now that you know you're not dying?"

"Yeah, that was an ordeal! I'm much better. In fact, I feel better than I have in a long time. With the exception of not getting any sleep." I ate some of the biscuit and milk gravy the cafeteria was famous for. It was like eating at my mother's breakfast table and way too high in calories. But I didn't care. "So, what happened to Sanchez?"

Jerry leaned forward onto the table and glanced around. "Jack, where were you last night before Sanchez came in?"

I paused in mid chew and studied my friend's face. His eyes were filled with suspicion. "Why are you asking?" Wham! The dizziness hit me again. I blinked and tried to focus on Jerry. Forget a contrast reaction and leukemia. The stress and lack of sleep would kill me first.

"Just answer the question."

"Okay, so I stayed here at the hospital. We have an on-call room." I drew a deep breath and the dizziness began to abate.

"Can anyone testify to that?"

"Testify?" I wiped my mouth with a napkin. "Jerry, am I being accused of something? I don't even own a gun! Sure, there were times I wanted to shoot Sanchez, but this is crazy!"

Jerry studied my face and sat back. "Did you eat at a Pancake Palace last night about eleven?"

"Yeah, I did. Sanchez asked me to meet her there. She was asking me questions about Janice's connection to Dr. Korskin. She ended up telling me to go home and forget about Korskin. And she apologized for accusing me of murder." I paused. "Right before she was shot!" My heart sank. "Wait a minute! She got some kind of phone call. Said it was someone from her past. She almost ran out of the place."

Jerry sighed and sat back. "Where did you go after meeting that?"

"Here. I was checking a CAT scan with Dr. Moore when Sanchez came in. What's going on, Jerry? What happened?"

Jerry frowned and looked away. "Sanchez is dead."

I stiffened. "What?"

"They took care of her head wound but didn't realize she had a round in her belly. She bled out during surgery. I'm sorry, Jack." He sat back. "Last night, shots fired were reported near the river front. We found her down by the Texas Street bridge. Conveniently located away from any traffic cameras."

My hands started to tremble, and nausea hit me as the dizziness worsened. "Jerry, what is happening? Who would want to kill Sanchez?"

Jerry sighed and rubbed fatigue from his eyes. "We found her cell phone. She had a text from a Roger Thornton to meet her by the bridge. That must have been who she heard from right before she left. Turns out Thornton is from Colorado. He's a petty thug who moved here to handle some of the prostitution business down by the casinos. We figure she met the man, got in an argument and he shot her."

"I can't imagine her letting someone do that to her." I rubbed my temples.

"He probably caught her by surprise. We have an all-points bulletin out for him."

I swallowed back bile and the dizziness began to fade. I closed my eyes and breathed deeply.

"What's up with you, Jack? You getting sick again?" Jerry asked.

I slowly opened my eyes and the pain and dizziness were gone. "I keep having dizzy spells and headaches. Lack of sleep and too much stress."

"You need to back off." Jerry said.

"Yeah, Sanchez told me the same. Still, I have to ask, do you think Sanchez's death had something to do with Korskin?"

Jerry crossed his arms and studied me for a moment. "I have been warned by my superiors to drop any further inquiries into Korskin. Or the Institute. They said that the Secret Service had it all under control." He relaxed and rubbed his face. "They want to keep this quiet, or the secret service might be spooked."

"I'm spooked, Jerry. I stayed at the hospital last night because I'm scared to go home. Sam found out some information and warned me to be extra careful."

Jerry nodded. "Yeah, she shared some of that with me, too. Look, I can see if one of my buddies can sit outside your apartment for the next couple of nights. Or you can stay here in the hospital. Although their security would make Barney Fife look like a SWAT team member."

"She didn't deserve that, Jerry. Sanchez irritated the crap out of me, but she didn't deserve to die." I glanced at him.

"If you know anything that might change things, now is the time to say it."

I opened my mouth. I could tell him more about Korskin, but he had already been warned off of Korskin. "I don't want you to end up like Sanchez. I've been wallowing in the mud and self-pity for months and you are the only person who has tried to lift me out of the dumps. I owe you a lot, Jerry. I think we should both take Sanchez's last advice to me and let it go."

Jerry looked like he had swallowed acid. "Something I definitely need to do, but don't want to do. Stay here in the hospital until the President's visit is over, Jack. I'll speak to hospital security about keeping a closer eye on you." He stood up and pushed the chair under the table. "And I'm sorry about Sanchez." He walked out of the cafeteria.

I studied the cold, coagulated pile of gravy and biscuits and shoved it away.

THIRTY-THREE

With a great deal of difficulty, I finished my reading responsibilities at three. I could not concentrate. Fortunately, the home shift radiologist didn't have to take a night of call during the week. Which was good because I was distracted. What was I going to do? I needed to tell someone about Korskin's and Sanchez's suspicions. But who?

I went back to my call room and sat at the desk, staring at the syringe and the tablet. How could I get cellular or Wi-Fi coverage without the danger of being tracked? Maybe there was someone who could help me.

"What's up, Doc?" Gill said when I stepped into his cubbyhole. "I've always wanted to say that."

I looked around at the shelves covered with wires and circuit boards and pieces of machinery. Gill moved something large, gray, and greasy off a chair beside his workstation. "Have a seat. You may need to dry clean your scrubs later."

I sat down. "This is amazing. Looks like Scotty threw up."

Gill grinned. "Hey, I like that one. Can I use it?"

"I thought it up while I was peeing." I said lamely. Gill just lifted an eyebrow and waved my hand. "Sorry, I don't quite have your panache."

"It's a good thing. I need my panache. What's eating you, besides no longer having to stare eternity in the face?"

I looked away. "I have given that conversation some more thought, okay?"

"Well, I wouldn't look a miracle in the mouth." Gill said and chuckled. "Sorry about mixing metaphors. But what's a meta for?" He grinned again, and I didn't respond.

"Gill, I'm not here to talk about that." I placed the iPad on a clear spot on his workstation.

"No, thanks, Doc. I'm not an Apple man."

"It's my wife's, Gill. There is something on it I don't understand. It may have had something to do with her death."

Gill froze and glanced at the tablet. He got up, walked around me, and shut and locked his door. He crossed to a piece of equipment on a shelf and flipped a switch. My ears itched for a second. He sat back down. "Now, no snooping. No one listening."

"That's paranoid."

"No, that's so I can listen to my worship songs while I work without the Fairmont PC Police objecting. We're not supposed to proselytize. Just a precaution so we can speak privately."

"You remember the detective from Colorado?" I said.

"Yep. I heard she was harassing you."

"She's dead, Gill. After talking to me last night. Someone shot her." I leaned toward him. "She showed me a picture of someone on her cell phone she thought might be connected to my wife's death. An hour later, she was dead. It's a little too much of a coincidence."

"I don't believe in coincidences." Gill said, massaging his beard. "What does this have to do with this tablet?"

"I'm trying to sign in to one of my wife's apps. But I have to be connected to Wi-Fi and I don't want to be tracked. I don't want a professional killer showing up at my bedside." I resisted the urge to tell him about Baldy.

Gill grinned. "You came to the right place, Doc. I work with IT every day on our PACS connection. It is crappy. They don't understand how important it is to have bandwidth. You know how big these data sets are from MRIs and CTs and tomosynthesis." Tomosynthesis was a multi-layered mammogram and the 'datasets' contained tons of information, often overloading our work stations.

"Yeah, I remember fighting with IT when we put in our home stations. They couldn't see why we had to have rapid speeds out of the hospital. Those first few months, it was taking ten to fifteen minutes just to access a simple CT with only a hundred images."

"I was there, Doc. Who do you think solved the problem? Took a bottle of Jack Daniels and a whale of a hangover the next day, but I talked the director of IT at the time into making the changes." He picked up the tablet. "When we were having problems, I had a dedicated line put in so I could get around the hospital network. I put in a few tweaks myself for the firewall. I use an encryption method that routes the connection information all over the country. But we have to make a hardware connection."

He rummaged through a nearby bin of cables and pulled one out. "Here we go. An old ethernet cable with an adaptor that fits this tablet. Lucky for you this is an Apple tablet. It has ethernet support built in."

"I thought you weren't an Apple man." I said.

"Doesn't mean I can't appreciate their tech." He plugged the cable into a router behind him and slid the other end into the tablet. He handed it to me. "You're good to go for about ten minutes. After that, the rerouting gets hinky and unreliable."

I opened the app and signed in. Now, the icons showed a green outline, meaning we were connected. I glanced at Gill and then touched the V3.7 icon. The screen changed again to the tablet settings, and this time I didn't pause before hitting the "go" icon.

The tablet beeped and a four quadrant window filled the screen. In the upper left-hand corner was a typical map with a pulsing locator pin. In the upper right-hand corner was a list of commands. The lower left-hand corner showed an ever changing list of moving lines similar to an oscilloscope.

Gill leaned over my shoulder. "What the hey?"

"I don't know." I studied the screen. The location pin pulsed, and I tapped on the window and it filled the screen. I enlarged the map view until I could read the streets on the map. My heart froze. "Gill, this is Fairmont Central." I pointed to the map. I enlarged it some more and the map view changed to an architectural drawing of the hospital.

"That's more than just the hospital, Doc. That's right here in this room."

I retrieved the syringe from my pocket and glanced at it. "Could it be focusing on this?"

Gill lifted an eyebrow as he held the syringe up to the light. "Looks almost like liquid carbon."

"What?"

"Liquid crystals, maybe. Can I put some of this on my microscope?"

"You have a microscope?"

"Sometimes you need it to read the inscriptions on these tiny circuit boards."

His router beeped and Gill reached over and pulled the cable loose. The screen flashed and went back to the icon view. "Time's up, Doc."

I powered down the iPad mini. Gill moved more pieces of

equipment, exposing a large binocular microscope. He looked around and found a glass plate from the screen of a broken instrument and placed it on the microscope cradle. Gill took the tape off the syringe handle and removed the cover from the tip and placed a small drop of the black substance on the glass and recapped the syringe.

Gill pulled his chair over and bent over the microscope. He backed away and glanced at me. "Take a look, Doc."

I slid over, then put my eyes against the lenses. It took a moment for me to focus on the tiny, black nodules in the field of view. I gasped. They looked just like the nodules in Janice's tissue sample. But there was one difference. These nodules moved!

Gill hunched over his laptop. "Doc, I've seen these things somewhere before."

The sight of the things stunned me. I held up the syringe and resisted the urge to tell Gill where I had seen them before.

"Ah, here it is." He pointed to his laptop screen. "Now, Doc, you gotta understand something about me. I'm not a conspiracy nutcase. But some people I meet down at the casino are. Their lives are turned upside down and they want someone to blame besides themselves. So, I read up on what they talk about. And this was something I heard from a group of homeless guys. Seems one of their buddies got some money for trying out a new medication. The next day, he jumped off the bridge."

I gasped and sat back. "I heard about that from Jerry. He's a friend of mine, a police officer."

Gill turned the laptop so I could see the screen. "This is one of those conspiracy webpages. I looked it up after Neal died. He kept mentioning Nanny Means. Didn't know exactly what he was saying, so I kept experimenting with the word until I found this."

I looked at the screen. The title of a blog post from the "Hidden Cypher" was "Nannomemes Will Change Your Mind".

"Nannomemes!" Korskin and David Boone came to mind. They had talked about nannomemes. Korskin told me practical use was years away.

"That's right. Hidden Cypher talks about the development of some kind of nanoparticle that can affect the mind." Gill raised an eyebrow. "Like make you want to jump off a bridge."

I sat forward and read the blog. Most of it was ranting drivel, but I came across a name. "David Boone."

Gill frowned as I sat back. "The David Boone. The Eliminator? Great movie. Didn't care for the two sequels."

"He's more than an actor, Gill. He's an entrepreneur now, a billionaire, and he is here in town." I looked at Gill. "Boone said he invested money in my wife's invention." I held up the syringe. "She named them nannomemes. Could this be it? Gill, could this be a syringe full of nannomemes?"

Gill sighed. "If it is, your wife just changed everything."

THIRTY-FOUR

Around five that evening, I called Jerry and asked him if he would meet me in the hospital cafeteria that evening. I know he had warned me off but this new information could change everything. Jerry showed up around six. He wore jeans and a bright, ugly Christmas sweater. He sat across the table from me in the cafeteria.

"You didn't have to dress up for me." I said, picking at my spaghetti and meat sauce. Jerry had grabbed a cup of coffee.

"Ugly sweater party tonight at church." He mumbled. A very obese Santa stuck in a chimney on the roof of a house covered most of his chest. Across the lower part of the sweater were the words, "I'm stuck on Christmas".

I smiled and shook my head. "Who picked out the sweater?"

"Oh, I did." He sipped coffee. "If Sally insisted I get an ugly sweater, I went all the way." He pushed on Santa's bulging belly and it squeaked.

I finished my meal, if you could call it such. "I asked you to run by because I wanted to see what you had learned about Sanchez's killer."

Jerry glanced around the cafeteria. It was half full, and he leaned toward me. "Remember Baldy?"

"Yes." I said and an icy wave passed over me. "Don't tell me."

"We found Thornton's body this morning with the cell phone that he used to call Sanchez. He was killed and mutilated just like Baldy."

A chill ran down my back. "What is going on, Jerry? We have a serial killer or a professional killer in our midst?"

"A little of both." Jerry studied his coffee cup and finally looked up at me. "Jack, I'm going to tell you once more to stay out of this. Stay here and you will be safe for now. That's all I can say." He stood up and finished his coffee.

"Wait! I found out some more information today." I said.

Jerry shook his head. "No you didn't, Jack. Go lock yourself in your room." He walked out of the cafeteria, leaving me speechless.

THURSDAY, the next day, was a blur. The reading list was huge and by three o'clock, my mind was muddled from reading over three hundred and fifty cases and from lack of sleep. I had to get out of the hospital. The President was scheduled to speak at five the next day and I had a ticket to attend. I couldn't show up in scrubs. In Janice's memory, I would wear my suit. That meant another trip to my apartment.

Just in case I was being watched, I wouldn't take my car. I went down to the front of the hospital. Ralph, a security guard, sat behind the wheel of his car just outside the front doors. His job was to give a ride to anyone who was afraid of walking to the employee parking lot. The three o'clock shift had already switched out and there wouldn't be many employees leaving the hospital until the seven o'clock shifts switched out.

"Hey, Ralph." I bent down and glanced in the passenger window of his car.

Ralph was overweight and balding, with a cloud of nicotine that swirled around him most of the time. "Hey, Doc." He smiled at me after rolling his window down. "How's it going?"

"Good. How's your ulcer?"

"Better. I still say that barium you made me drink cured me." He rubbed his belly. "But I still haven't gotten the weight off. You need a ride?"

I glanced around at the parking lot. People moved in and out of cars, passing in and out of the hospital doors. Was the killer among them? "Ralph, I need a big favor."

"You talking about what Jerry Langley told us? Keeping you safe, and all?"

I groaned. If this was common knowledge for security, then the killer would probably know it, too. "Thanks for that but I need a ride to my apartment to pick up some clothes. Then back here again."

"Hop in." Ralph unlocked the door. I slid into the passenger side of the car and Ralph drove out of the parking lot. He looked in his rearview mirror after I gave him my address.

"Got it, Doc. I'll just take the scenic route." He glanced at me with a glint of mischief in his eyes. "Just in case we are being followed."

I didn't want to pop his bubble. The killer knew where I lived so it would be unlikely he would follow us. It took twice the time to get to my apartment than what I was capable of driving. Ralph climbed out of the car and looked around us, surveilling the parking lot. "Now, Doc, I don't got a gun. But

I've got pepper spray. I'll walk with you up to your place to make sure there are no surprises."

I started to protest. Chances were if there was a problem, I would be protecting him, not the other way around. My apartment was on the second floor at the top of the stairs. I unlocked the door and Ralph went in before me, holding the pepper spray like it was a pistol.

"Clear!" He said loudly. I rolled my eyes and followed him inside. Ralph looked around at my trashy apartment.

"Doc, my wife has a good cleaning person if you need it." He said. "Dependable and fair price."

"Sorry for the mess, Ralph. I've been sick in the hospital and haven't been home that much. I just need to grab some clothes and then we can leave."

I went to my bedroom. In the back of the closet still wrapped in dry cleaner plastic hung the only suit I owned. An overwhelming sense of loss hit me when I took the hanger off the rod. No time for this, I argued. I grabbed more underwear and made sure I had a tie and a clean shirt along with my dress shoes. I paused once looking at the box from my aunt. I took it down and retrieved the New Testament from within and tucked it into my scrub shirt pocket.

Ralph insisted on checking out the parking lot and his car before allowing me to follow him down from my apartment. He even opened the hood and studied the motor and then looked under the undercarriage for a bomb.

His vigilance paid off. We made it safely back to the hospital.

THIRTY-FIVE

Janice's tablet lay before me on the call room desk. I picked up the syringe of what were surely nannomemes. What was happening? Someone was killing people who were getting too close to a truth. What was the truth that costs lives? Korskin was somehow involved. If Korskin was associated with the vaccine affair, then what was he doing here in Shreveport? I took the pass for the President's speech from my coat pocket and studied it. It allowed me, by name, into the viewing area and then to the reception in the Institute afterwards. Members of the cabinet associated with health care would be on the dais and would be present at the reception. Along with David Boone, who had donated millions to the Institute. What did Boone have to do with all of this?

My mind was tired and muddled, and I heard a knock at the door. Instantly, my heart raced, and I froze. The knock came again. I cracked the door. A figure in a white coat, surgical mask, and a puffy surgical cap stared back at me with eyes I instantly recognized. Keri pushed her way into my room.

"Keri! What are you doing here?" I said.

"I had to track you down. I've been looking for you for days." She said as she pulled the cap and mask off. "I heard about Sanchez, and I was worried sick. You haven't answered your cell phone, and no one has seen you at your apartment. And the techs during the day said you are working from home."

I shut the door and locked it. "Keri, you were supposed to go back to Colorado! How did you find me?"

She sat on my bed. "I remembered when you were a resident, we spent an evening in your on call room. You got call after call after call and we didn't get to spend much time together. I wondered if you had an on call room in the Fairmont system. It only made sense you would have one here, since this is the busiest hospital. So, I borrowed some surgical garb and pretended to be a neurosurgery resident and coaxed the room location out of the operator." She put a hand on my arm. "I'm sorry, but I had to see you. I'm scared and when I heard about Sanchez, I started thinking that they may watch the airport."

"Why would they even suspect you might be here?" I sat beside her as the dizziness hit me again. I really needed to do something about my blood pressure before I had a stroke.

Keri sighed and shuddered. She pulled a card from her scrub shirt pocket. "I've been staying at a cheap motel in Bayou City, not far from one of the casinos. I've been taking the bus everywhere and paying for everything in cash. Last night, I found this card outside my door."

The business card was wrinkled and dirty, as if someone had accidentally dropped it and stepped on it. I tried to focus on the words through my dizziness. "Zachary Williams" was the name across the top. On the bottom was a symbol and some words. "U.S. Secret Service." I said.

"Yes, Jack. Why was someone from the Secret Service at the motel? I asked the manager about it, and he said some big guy from Secret Service was checking out the motel for security reasons."

"Seems pretty routine." I said as the headache began.

She shuddered again. "Yeah, but he also asked specifically if a woman matching my description was staying at the motel."

I stiffened and looked into her frightened eyes. "What?"

"Why would a Secret Service person be asking about me?"

I stood up and paced around the small room. "You were at the hospital with me. But why would that trigger an investigation?"

Keri looked up at me with fright filled eyes. "I don't know! But if the Secret Service was looking for me, then how can I possibly leave the city? They'll be watching every way of leaving. Airport, buses, train station, you name it."

I looked at the locked door. Could they be coming for her right now? What could we do? I could call Jerry, but he was emphatic I leave all this alone. The only other person who knew about Keri was Sanchez. She was gone. We were on our own.

"Someone must have overheard us talking. Jerry is very discrete and Sanchez is gone." I rubbed my temples. "Wait! Sanchez said she accessed the sealed files on the trial." I glanced at Keri. "That must have triggered something. It would be just enough to make someone start asking questions about you."

"But I'm supposed to be dead." Keri said.

"Whoever is behind this has resources way beyond what we have suspected. It would be child's play to look into the witness protection program for someone matching your description right after the trial." My headache was leveling out. "Why are they involving the Secret Service? Does this thing go all the way up to the President?"

Keri gasped. "President Mitchell! Wasn't he on the cabinet of the president at the time of the vaccine debacle?"

"Yes." My dizziness disappeared in a wave of realization. "He was the Secretary of Health and Human Services! He would have been in charge of Medicare and health care." I shuddered at the thought. "Could he have been involved in the pharmaceutical company that developed the virus?"

Keri drew a deep breath. "I never had the opportunity to study the company. It was months after my relocation that I could even begin to process what had happened, Jack. But if President Mitchell is connected to the vaccine debacle, it stands to reason he would do anything to find me."

"And what would he have to gain from Janice's nannomemes? Or maybe there isn't a connection with that." I said. I rubbed my tired eyes in exasperation. All the moving pieces floated around in my mind. I looked at Keri. "The President is speaking at the dedication of Janice's wing of the Institute tomorrow. Something is going to happen. I'm sure of it." I didn't tell her about the tablet or the syringe. "If the Secret Service is looking for you, then it stands to reason you are considered a threat to the President no matter what the reason."

Keri hugged herself. "I wonder, who is the Shadow Man?"

"Not the President." I said. "If he was involved, he never would have taken a chance to expose himself. He would have sent a lackey."

She leaned in to me. "I'm scared, Jack. More frightened than I've ever been."

I hesitated and put my arm around her. The old feelings were still there, but so far away; so far in the past. She must have sensed my discomfort, and she stood up and moved over to my desk. "I don't mean to bring up old feelings. You're still not over Janice's death." She said as she sat in the chair.

"I've had a hard time the past year." I said, examining my

hands. Anything but looking into Keri's eyes. "I've ruined my life and now I have a chance to get it all together again. I just had a brush with death."

"Two." Keri said, as she picked up my New Testament. "What is this?"

"My New Testament. Mother and Daddy gave me that on the day I was baptized."

Keri smiled. "You never told me you had been baptized. Were you a baby?"

I shook my head. "No. In the Baptist church, you only get baptized when you walk down the aisle and commit your life to Christ." Even as I said it, the distant and foreign memory surfaced. I remembered sitting at the end of the pew during the revival service. That day I had realized I couldn't be good all the time when I had thrown a rock and hit Michelle Talbot in the head. It had scared me to realize I couldn't be good all the time. Even as a ten-year-old, the implications of that frightened me. I was out of control and wanted somebody else in control of my life, and that had to be God. I recalled running down the aisle during the invitation and praying with my pastor. And just like that, the distant memory blossomed inside, filling me with a remembered warmth and peace and tranquility that I was in the hand of my Savior, Jesus Christ. When had that memory gone away? When had I forgotten all of this? I swallowed hard and tried to embrace that memory; tried to pull it back into my present.

Keri opened the New Testament and smiled. "Your mother wrote in it?"

I nodded. "I haven't looked at it in years. But, yes, she made some notes throughout the Bible for me."

Keri put a hand to her mouth. "Did you see this?" She held the book open.

"No. What did she say?" I said hoarsely.

"She said 'My son, always be prepared for the battle for good against the forces of evil.' And she highlighted some verses."

"Read them." I said.

"For our struggle is not against flesh and blood, but against the rulers, against the authorities, against the powers of this dark world and against the spiritual forces of evil in the heavenly realms. Therefore, put on the full armor of God, so that when the day of evil comes, you may be able to stand your ground, and after you have done everything, to stand."

Keri wiped a tear from her eye. "Jack, you don't know what it was like when I had to leave you. Those men were evil, and they took my life away from me. There I was in Colorado, trying to live off a meager stipend with a whole new identity and my old life just gone. And there was no one to help me." Keri looked back at the Bible. "If I had only reached out to God. He was there for me, and I never knew it."

I stood up and put my arms around her shoulders while she sobbed. "I'm so sorry. I did not know. I went through my own crisis thinking you were dead. Wondering why God would let you die when you were trying to do the right thing. I guess that is when I put God away. And when Janice and I lost our babies, I couldn't even be mad at God because I had pushed God out of my life."

Keri put her hand on mine and wiped her tears with the other hand. "Maybe it's time we ask for a little help from a divine source. Will He hear us?"

"I think God will, Keri. If we are in the service of good, I have to believe God will be there with us. First, I have to get you to someplace safe. And then, I have to confront Korskin and put an end to this."

THIRTY-SIX

Dr. Sam Francisco answered her front door. It was close to midnight, and she squinted at me through her cat-eye glasses. Her green hair was rolled up in purple rollers and she wore a large, shapeless moo moo. "Jack?"

"Sam, I need a favor." I said.

She looked at Keri shivering beside me. "Is this your mysterious friend?"

"Yes. Keri, meet Dr. Sam Francisco."

Sam motioned past her into the living room. "Come in." She looked beyond us into the yard of her small house. "How did you get here?" She closed the door behind us and locked it.

"I had one of the hospital security give us a lift. He swears they did not follow us." I said.

"Jack, what is going on?" She asked.

"The less you know, the better. Keri is in trouble."

Sam nodded and took her by the arm. "I have a spare bedroom you can have for the night. I'll call Langley and ask him to put a uniform out front. He doesn't have to know why." She glanced at me. "One perk of being the medical examiner."

"Thank you, Sam. My ride is waiting."

Keri reached out and hugged me. I held her close for a moment. "Be careful." She said in a shaky voice.

"I will." I looked over her shoulder at Sam. "I need one more favor."

THE SECURITY GUARD took one look at the I.D. Fortunately, it had no photo on it. "Dr. Francisco? You're the new medical examiner?"

I lowered the credentials and nodded. "I have been called to pronounce a patient."

The security guard looked over his shoulder at the waiting room for the emergency room at GUT hospital. "I'll have to check with Secret Service. They're everywhere."

I nodded and tried not to let the nervousness show. "Of course. The deceased is a prisoner brought here under very suspicious circumstances." I leaned toward him. "They think someone got by you and killed him in his sleep."

The guard had picked up a phone at the desk just inside the doors of the emergency room. "What?"

"But I can see you are very conscientious. Very thorough. No one could have slipped by you. I'll be glad to tell the Secret Service that fact."

The guard looked at the phone and placed it back in its cradle. "No need to tell them anything. Go on in." He waved me past. When he saw the backpack slung over my shoulders, he stopped me.

"What's in the backpack?"

"Autopsy tools." I said. "I prefer my own bone saw. Want to see it?"

The guard's eyes widened, and he swallowed. "No! Go on."

After Theresa had died and I had finished my residency in radiology, I had been approached by an old friend in Talako who said a local radiology group was looking for a new partner. I had contacted Montana. His first question was if I hunted or fished. I said 'no'. "Good" he said. That meant I could work the weeks he was off hunting and fishing. Louisiana looked good compared to the bad memories of Houston, Texas where I had lost Theresa. At Montana's request, I had gone to GUT's radiology residency program for a year's fellowship in body imaging before taking the position with the group.

While at GUT, I had stayed in the residents' on call room. It was not nearly as nice as the one at Fairmont and had a double-decker bunk bed. Often, other residents from different services would share the room and their beepers and cell phones ringing all night would keep me from sleeping. It was then I had discovered the secret passageway.

I called it a secret passageway, but in fact it was just an old abandoned hallway that once connected the oldest wing of the hospital with the medical school. When the Institute had been built between the medical school and the hospital, they left an underground utility tunnel intact so students could pass back and forth between the medical school and the hospital until they completed the Institute. Now, all conferences were held at the Institute which had elevated walkways connecting it with both the medical school and the hospital. But the tunnel was left intact and abandoned.

I remembered once taking the old stairway down from the tenth floor of the hospital to the second floor walkway to the Institute and accidentally bypassing the second floor. I ended up at a door in the basement and was paying attention to something on my cell phone and walked right through the door into the abandoned tunnel. It creeped me out. But when I heard some moans of passion down the hallway, I realized where some of my fellow residents had been meeting for their midnight "rounds".

What I discovered a few months after starting my fellowship was a utility access door off the tunnel leading to the basement of the Institute. I often would wander through the tunnel during my lunch break just to escape the stress of my fellowship days. Now, the question remained if the tunnel was still open or if the Secret Service had sealed it.

I made my way up to the tenth floor, and the elevator stopped on the second floor. A transporter person wheeled someone in a wheelchair into the elevator. No doubt the patient was coming from radiology back to their floor. The patient's head was swathed in gauze, and a warm blanket covered their shoulders.

"Seven." The transport said. I punched the button.

The transporter glanced at my lab coat. "Hey, doc? Don't think we've met."

"I'm from Fairmont radiology." I said before I realized it. "I've been consulted on a case."

"Radiology, huh?" He said. The patient tilted their head toward me for a moment then back down on their chest.

"Yes." I said.

"Hey, my name is Tyrone. I'm applying for a job at Fairmont. Maybe you could put in a good word." He smiled at me.

"If you're good at what you do, I will." I tried to end the conversation.

The patient tilted their head toward me again. "He's a little rough." A hoarse voice came from the gauze.

Tyrone rolled his eyes. "It's not me. It's the floors. They are ancient."

The door opened at seven, and Tyrone nodded at me. "Nice talking to you, Doc."

My finger stabbed the door close button, and I held my

breath until the doors closed. I reached the tenth floor and as I stepped off the elevator, I felt something beneath my foot. I raised my foot and saw a toothpick on the floor of the elevator. I drew a deep breath! It reminded me of Sanchez. Trying to push the horrid memory of her death from my mind, I hurried past the nurses' station for the east wing. Psychiatric inpatients stayed on this wing. Ironically, the west wing was reserved for on call rooms.

I passed the on-call room and went directly to the stairs. According to my watch, it was after midnight. After the walkways with the Institute had been installed, the stairway was locked at all floors but ten where the walkway connected to the Institute. It was a testimony to Korskin's arrogance that he made sure everyone had to pass through his fancy penthouse foyer on their way to other floors of the Institute.

I hurried down the stairs, hoping and praying I wouldn't meet anyone on the way up from midnight rounds in the tunnel. When I finally reached the basement level, I breathed a sigh of relief. The door to the hidden tunnel was still intact. Several boxes were stacked in front of it, and it took me a few pulls to open the rusted doorway.

The dank, musty odor of the tunnel filled the stairwell. It would seem the hidden rendezvous point for personnel in the past had been forgotten. The tunnel was moist, and the odor of mildew and rat poop made me sneeze. I used my flashlight to work my way along the tunnel until I reached the midpoint. Now, where had the access door been? Right or left?

The walls were nothing but bubbled, peeling paint with a patina of mildew and moisture. The floor squished beneath my shoes. I found a hole in the wall and realized the door handle had broken off. How to open the door, then? And if I did, would an alarm sound? The rusted door handle lay immersed in a puddle of goo at the base of the door. I picked it up, and it slipped from my hand and clattered across the tunnel floor behind me. Something scurried across my feet. A rat! My scream echoed down the tunnel. It took several tries, but finally, the door handle fit into the hole. I twisted, and with great effort, got the latch to open. After several shoves and a sore shoulder, the door creaked inward toward the utility access tunnel beyond. Squeezing through the small gap, I stepped into a much more modern and clean tunnel of the Institute. I pushed the door shut behind me for no other reason than to keep the rats at bay.

The tunnel before me smelled of ozone and hot metal. Pipes and cables ran to my right and left, the modern infrastructure of the Institute. To my right I found a stair access. If I was right, it should lead up to the foyer and hopefully beyond.

I walked slowly up the well-lighted stairs to the first floor. A window in the stairwell door looked out into the foyer. In the distance, a lone security guard sat at a desk. A shadow passed over the window and I stepped back just as someone moved to look through the window. As I ducked to the right, out of sight, my heart raced. A pair of eyes peered into the stairwell and the door handle rattled. I heard a voice in the distance and the man's face turned away from the stairwell.

"Yes, I want some coffee." He said to the distant security guard. He moved toward the foyer and I glanced through the window. The man walking away from me wore a suit with a visible earpiece in his right ear. Secret Service! I had to be more careful!

Nine flights later I encountered no further interruptions. The stairs opened onto the hallway leading from the elevators to Janice's wing. The hallway down the wing was dark and I moved quietly along the hallway to Janice's office. I slipped into her office and shut the door behind me and locked it.

The sight and residual smells of the office hit me hard. The blood from my nosebleed was crusted on her desk. I drew a deep breath and made my preparations for the next day. Once I was finished, I glanced at my watch. It was now almost two in the morning. I had to hurry now to get back to my on call room and spend the night. I made my way down the stairs and back to the old tunnel without incident. At the exit to the emergency room, I checked out with the security guard.

"How'd the autopsy go?" He asked.

"Bloody." I said. "And lots of pus."

He gagged and I walked out into the parking lot and called Ralph at Fairmont to get a ride back to the hospital. Once I collapsed onto the call room bed, I was instantly asleep. I had already asked Montana, who was off this week, if he would cover my home rotation since I was invited to the President's speech and reception. He was more than glad to work for me as Debra had a "honey do" list a mile long. It wasn't hunting season or he would have been in Argentina!

THIRTY-SEVEN

The next day, the weather was perfect, and the sky was cloudless, with the temperature in the mid-fifties. The event took place in the parking lot in front of the Institute with the towering glass and chrome Institute as a backdrop. I had to check in with a Secret Service person waiting at the entrance to Fairmont Central, and she gave me a ride to the presentation.

My pass gave me a close view of the stage area, but I sat in the fourth row behind many politicians, dignitaries, and local hospital administrators. Dr. Lamb, Fairmont Chief Executive, sat on the stage beside David Boone.

I didn't recall much of the speech by the president. He touted his party's health care plan and spoke fondly of Janice, as if he had known her. Korskin beamed throughout the entire speech from the seats behind the President. The President and a few members of his cabinet were escorted off the stage at the end of the speech and we were told to remain seated. My chauffeur agent tapped me on the shoulder.

"Sir, if you would come with me, please." She said.

My paranoia kicked in, but I followed the agent behind the

stage and through the main doors of the Institute. I had to pass through a metal detector and an airport Xray unit and a wanding before I could proceed. The Secret Service let me keep my burner phone. We took a service elevator to the top floor. The agent was stoic and silent the entire way. I dared not ask where I was going.

The elevator opened onto a kitchen area. Ah, this was the penthouse dining room for visiting dignitaries and wealthy donors. I had heard about it from Janice. The kitchen was a typical steam filled hot room with scurrying cooks, a chef, and servers. The agent took me along the outer rim of the kitchen and into a small office.

Dr. Korskin sat at a desk and looked up with a smile. "Dr. Merchant. Jack." He extended his hand, and I shook it without enthusiasm. "How did you like the speech?"

"I don't like the government coming between me and my patient, but other than that, it was mostly forgettable." I said tersely, rubbing my temples. A headache began at the top of my neck. Elevated blood pressure again! Calm down, I told myself. "Sorry, I am grateful you invited me. It was a fitting testimony to Janice."

"Yes, well, I wanted you to meet the President and his party. It was the least I could do." He motioned for me to follow.

No, the least he could have done was to not make the opening of the Janice Manning Nanotechnology Wing a political dog and pony show. I followed Korskin to a lounge area. Two agents stood outside the doors, and they motioned us in. President Mitchell regaled his entourage with a story about his latest colonoscopy. He turned and smiled at me.

"Dr. Manning, it is so good to meet you." He shook my hand. I did not correct him.

"Thank you, sir. Thank you for honoring my wife's memory."

The President smiled vacantly. He was looking right at me but looking right through me. I was nothing to him. He motioned to the men and women around him. Three cabinet members whose names and positions I did not catch. Nor did I care. But the last person caught my interest.

"This is Dr. Gladia Stovall, head of Health and Human Services."

"Jack and I know each other." She said. Stovall stood just a few inches short of me and was a heavyset woman, looking rather snappy in her business suit. Her hair was pulled back in a tight bun. "I was one of Jack's professors oh so many years ago."

"Dr. Stovall taught microbiology at my medical school." I fought a frown. "I still haven't forgiven you for that true false test."

Stovall chuckled and nodded. "One of my worst mistakes." She turned to the President and Korskin. "I gave them one hundred true-false questions. You should have seen the class agonizing over the answers."

"They were all true." I said. "No one does that on a test. We all believed that at least a third of the questions had to be false."

"After their protest, I threw the test out." Stovall said.

"Only because of the protest." I said.

Stovall's smile faded. She cleared her throat. "Well, the next day when I came into the auditorium to lecture, they released five hundred marbles at the top of the auditorium."

"They rolled down and ended up around her feet. She couldn't move without falling." I said.

Stovall managed a smile. "Medical students are a little strange, Mr. President."

The President had listened to the exchange with what appeared to be genuine interest, but he was already plotting his next speech. "I'm glad to hear that about Gladia. Now, if you'll excuse me. I'm hungry."

He was gone toward the exit of the lounge, headed to the dining room. I followed, and Korskin barred my way. "Uh, Jack, there isn't room at the table for you, I'm sorry to say. But I wanted you to meet the President."

"And Gladia." I almost spat her name. "She's a snake in the grass, Korskin. Her Medicare and insurance guidelines have just about killed private practice physicians. You know that." My focus narrowed to his beady eyes. "Wait a minute! She's the reason you're getting a grant for the PET/CT scanner, isn't it? You're still trying to lure me away from my practice."

"You have to play the game, Jack." Korskin said. "Besides, I'm hoping that after today, we can change her mind about reimbursement rules."

"Oh? And how are you going to do that?"

"I have my ways, Jack."

I don't know what made me snap. Maybe it was the entire charade. Maybe it was the cold and uncaring leader of our country. Maybe it was seeing Gladia again. "Will you threaten to kill her like you killed Janice?" I blurted out.

Korskin froze. "What?"

"I know who you are, Korskin. I know about your past. I can't prove it, but I know you had something to do with Janice's death. And, I wouldn't have put it past you to take out the only other person who agrees with me, Detective Sanchez."

Korskin licked his lips and smiled. "Now, Jack, I know you've been ill. You've been under a lot of strain with the first anniversary of Janice's death. I'm going to give you the benefit of the doubt on your outrageous and unfounded accusations.

Just calm down and I will have an agent escort you from the building quietly."

He reached for my arm, and I jerked it away. "No need for that. I'll just wait in Janice's office for my escort." I turned and walked out of the lounge before he could stop me. Janice's wing was on the floor below. It was deserted. The Secret Service had cleared out the entire building for the President's visit. I ran down the stairway and down the hall to her office. Once I was inside, I closed and locked the door.

"You fool." I said out loud. Why had I blurted out like that? Now I had lost the element of surprise. Korskin would be free to carry out his plan and there was little I could do to stop him. There was a knock at the door. It was not a pounding, just a quiet knock. I looked through the side window. Korskin.

"Jack, let me in. Let's talk. You've got it all wrong."

I opened the door. Korskin was alone. His face was pale. "Can we talk? You seem to have some wild idea I had something to do with Janice's death?"

I retreated into the office and sat behind her desk. Reaching into the drawer before me I took out the tablet I had left there the night before. "I had to sneak into the building last night to put this here. I knew the Secret Service would examine me when I entered the Institute." I held up the tablet. "Are you looking for this?"

His eyes bulged at the sight of the tablet. "Where did you get that?"

"From Janice. She hid it. I'm wondering why."

"Jack, you have no idea what that tablet can do. It is the final step in Dr. Manning's plan."

"Oh, and what would that be?"

Korskin studied my face and he changed. He stood a little taller and cracked his neck. He reached into his mouth and removed a false set of teeth sitting on top of his own. He ran his red tongue over his teeth. "Oh, that feels so much better." His voice changed. "I get so tired of the facade. Now, if you would be so good as to call Dr. Francisco on what I assume is your unregistered phone."

With my heart racing, I dialed Sam on the phone. "Sam?"

"Jack, where are you? This afternoon, they came. Home invasion. They took Keri." My heart almost stopped I glanced up at Korskin and he only smiled and shrugged.

"What?" I managed. "What about the police watching your house?"

"I sent them home after lunch. I did some paperwork from home, and I was about to go to work and take Keri with me. Before we could get into my car, a man showed up. Flashed a Secret Service I.D. and grabbed Keri and threw her into his car before I could react. Knocked me in the head and left me unconscious in my own garage. But I'm hard headed. After I called the police and the ambulance came, they cleared me, but I wasn't going anywhere until I talked to you. They tried for hours to get in touch with Secret Service. When they finally did, they denied any knowledge of this Agent Williams who took Keri."

Before I could answer, Korskin jerked the phone out of my hand and ended the call. He backed away and turned the phone off. "Now, if you'll just hand over that tablet to me, I'll make sure nothing happens to Theresa Douglas."

I flinched at the name. "Where is she?"

"With a certain operative of mine with remarkable skills he acquired in Russia. Now, of course, he is legit and a member of the Secret Service."

"He killed Sanchez, didn't he?"

Korskin shrugged. "No, Jack, Sanchez was killed by an old nemesis of hers. At least that's the official story."

I held up the tablet. "And what does this do?"

Korskin smiled. "Well, you have the right to know. Janice wasn't just developing those nannomemes for Boone. She went a step further. Nanorobots or Nbots. It's all the rage in medical research. Imagine microscopic robots traveling throughout your body promoting wound healing, repairing genetic defects. The problem has always been power and longevity. Janice made a breakthrough on powering up the Nbots. And the key to that power solution is in your hands, Jack."

Like pieces of a puzzle falling into place things began to gel. "You had Baldy inject them into my veins, didn't you? What did you do, Korskin? Put some kind of chemical in my coffee to make it look like I was having a contrast reaction? And, then, during the code you had your assassin put Nbots into my blood stream?" I stood up from Janice's desk. "My leukemia, my nosebleeds, my weakness it was all from the Nbots, wasn't it?"

Korskin reached into his jacket pocket and pulled out a small, black tablet. "And a miracle in my hand. One minute, I've mobilized your white cells to look like leukemia and the next, everything is back to normal. I had to confiscate the first bone marrow aspirate because it would have looked normal. I found out about Theresa from you."

"What?"

"If you send the Nbots to the inner ear you can eavesdrop. Problem is their presence made you very dizzy. I couldn't use that feature very often. But I heard enough to put it all together. Theresa Douglas had a boyfriend when she was alive. After a little digging, I found out it was you. Leading you along by the nose was simple enough and led me right to the only woman alive who could identify me."

"I thought it was my blood pressure." I hissed.

Korskin activated the tablet and a green screen glowed. "Now, back to the tablet. We've simplified the interface, Jack.

But there was so much missing we could learn from Janice's iPad. But, with this, I can still make you have a heart attack. I can make you fall asleep on your feet. I can change your mood from sunny and happy to suicidal."

"Like the people who jumped off the bridge?"

Korskin shrugged. "Trial and error. Mostly error. We have better control now. Jack, listen to me. You want to keep medicine in the right hands? Give me that control."

I froze as the realization washed over me in a cold panicky wave. "The President? You're going to put Nbots in the President?"

Korskin laughed. "Of course not. I'm going to put them in Dr. Stovall. You have to be focused, Jack."

"Like you were with Janice? How did you kill her?"

For a second Korskin's face softened, and he shook his head. "Her death was just as much a shock to me as it was to you. Something went wrong with the Nbots, Jack. Something caused them to overload their tiny power cores. Normally, that wouldn't have been a problem but there were so many of them it caused spontaneous combustion. That is why we need that tablet. We need to know what she learned."

"Or, what? You'll burn up the next victim?"

Korskin sighed and studied the black remote. "Okay, Jack. Let's see if you can reason your way through this." He pressed a button.

THIRTY-EIGHT

The pain in my head exploded in intensity and I fell to my knees. I dropped the tablet and gripped my head. Korskin reached for the tablet, and I lashed out with my trembling hand and snagged it. Through my blurry vision, I opened the control panel on the tablet and stared at the screen. One of the icons was pulsing. I stabbed it with my finger and the pain suddenly stopped. I could control my own Nbots! But, I didn't relax. I kept moaning in pain. I focused on the tablet. A window opened with the message, "Welcome, Dr. Manning. Now connected to your private server." I wasn't sure what that meant but it had to be better than what Korskin had planned for me. Still gripping my head, I stood up. "Korskin, if you don't back off, one press of a button and I erase this entire tablet's content." I poised a finger over the screen.

Korskin frowned and pressed his tablet's screen. The pain was already getting better but I relaxed and blinked tears from my eyes.

"You made your point, Korskin. You can make me do anything." I studied Janice's tablet and noticed that another of the icons was pulsing. I touched the icon, and a screen sprang open with a big, red, blinking "Activated" in the middle of the screen. A name appeared in the upper corner. "G. Stovall." So, Korskin had already given Stovall the Nbots.

I sat down in Janice's chair. "What do you want from me?"

Korskin leaned on the desk. "That's better. Cooperate and I will let Theresa go. I can give her a set of Nbots that will erase her memory. She'll go on living with a new identity. Again." He laughed. "See the power of Janice's invention?"

"Once I give you this tablet, I'm a dead man."

"But Theresa will live." He said.

"If you kill me, you'll never be able to open the tablet. I changed the password and set up an erase after three attempts features. Looks like we are at an impasse."

Korskin's cell phone rang, and he answered it. "What? I am taking care of last minute details. I'll be right there. Could you send Agent Williams to Janice Manning's office?" Korskin ended the call and glared at me.

"Agent Williams will stay outside this office until I can introduce the President for his dinner address. This is not over." A knock on the door and Korskin slipped out. I heard a muffled conversation and then silence.

I paced around the office. Korskin had no idea I had some measure of control over the Nbots from Janice's tablet. Question was, how much control?

I sat down and began looking through the different icons. There were a dozen of them. There was the blinking icon that represented my Nbots. Stovall's icon still blinked but the controls on the screen with her icon were cryptic. How could I disable them? Two more icons pulsed. I opened a window on the first icon and noticed on the map it was right outside the conference room. Now I knew how Korskin had control over Agent Williams. I played around with the controls and found a drop down menu with those cryptic commands. One said, "XOut". What did that mean? Deactivate, perhaps? My fingers trembled as I pressed the button beside it. It began to blink, and a window came up. "Do you wish SV42 to exit?" Did I? I pressed the Y for yes.

Now what? I walked carefully over to the office door and pressed my ear against the wood. Agent Williams was silent for a moment and then began to cough. The coughing grew more violent and suddenly the door flew open. The man standing before me was covered with blood leaking from his mouth and nose. He stared at me as he coughed a fine spray of blood onto the carpet. I backed away and he lurched toward me like a zombie.

"What. Did. You. Do?" He said between gasps. He coughed one last time and a cloud of blood shot from his mouth and ignited in blue flames. Williams fell forward onto his face, twitched a couple of times and grew still. What in the world had happened? I glanced at the tablet.

"SV42 self destruct sequence completed." Flashed on the screen. I knelt over the man and pressed my hand on his neck. He still had a pulse, so he wasn't dead, but he needed help. However, if I called for help, Korskin would know. I had to stop him from controlling Stovall and I couldn't take the chance on cancelling her Nbots with the tablet given the results of my last trial. If I could get Jerry, but Korskin had taken my cell phone. I looked around for a land line but realized I had no idea of Jerry's number. I picked up a landline and pressed operator.

"All lines are temporarily disabled as a security measure for today's Presidential visit." A mechanized voice said. I slammed the receiver back onto the phone cradle. Williams gurgled behind me, and I knelt and turned him on his side to clear his airway. A cell phone slid from his suit jacket. I grabbed it but when I touched the screen, it called for a password to continue.

With his bloody blistered face, facial recognition was out of the question. I would have to get out of the building and find Jerry somehow.

"Williams, report in." A voice echoed from underneath the man. I rolled him forward and retrieved a walkie talkie from his belt connected to an earpiece. The earpiece had pulled out of his ear and lay on the carpet. I picked up the bloody earpiece, wiped it on Williams' suit and slid it into my ear. When I touched the earpiece, I heard a click. That was how to talk.

"Status unchanged." I growled.

"Korskin is on his way." The other voice said.

"Copy that." I stood up and glanced out into the hallway. If Korskin was coming up the elevator, I had to use the stairway. I ran back to the drawer and removed the syringe and pocketed the tablet and the syringe. But where was Keri? I keyed the walkie talkie again. "Is the other package secure?" I said hoarsely.

"What package?" The voice answered. So only Williams was in on Keri's abduction. I found the stairs and closed the door behind me just as I heard the elevator ding on arrival. Hurrying down the stairs as quickly as possible I almost fell twice.

"We have an intruder." I heard Korskin say over the radio. "Williams is down. Cover the stairway."

He had called the Secret Service on me! I halted on the fifth floor. Far below, I heard footsteps coming up the stairway. I pushed through the door onto the fifth floor. Of all things, it was the radiology suite! And it was empty. Wouldn't want patients to muck up the President's proceedings! The elevator dinged in the far corner, and I slid down a hallway pausing to peek back. Korskin got off the elevator, his gaze fixed on his remote.

"Cancel that alert. Williams slipped and fell. No intruder.

No need to bring in any more agents." He smiled and addressed the air before him. "Jack? You can't hide. I know where you are from your Nbots. I don't know how you did that to Williams, but it tells me that tablet is far too dangerous. You know, I can do the same thing to you?"

Several Christmas trees lined the long hallway, and I hid behind one as I retrieved the tablet. My hand brushed the syringe. I pulled it from my pocket and slid it out of the bag. Could I do this?

"Korskin, I'm coming out. I don't want to end up like Williams." I touched the icon on the tablet, and I felt a vibration in the syringe from the activation of its Nbots. I slid the tablet into my pocket and palmed the syringe. Korskin stood in the center of the hallway as I approached.

"Ironic, isn't it? Radiology. This is your world, Jack. And, yet, you have no control over it."

I had to buy some time to get closer. "What will you do to me? Erase my memory?"

Korskin shrugged. "Truth is, the Nbots have a flaw. Boone knew about it with his nannomemes we were developing but he insisted on securing them anyway in spite of their flaw. The Nbots are the same. You see, the secret to fixing that flaw is on that tablet you have. And so, Jack, I appeal to you as a physician."

"What is the flaw?"

"Twenty eight days pass before the nannomemes' power source dies out and the body breaks them down. Boone's nannomemes only last a matter of days. But, if we could find the solution to the power problem, Nbots would revolutionize medicine, Jack. We wouldn't have to worry about them losing their power."

I drew closer "And, that is why you have to control Stovall."

"Yes, to funnel funds into key projects around the nation. To overcome FDA constraints. To cut through the paperwork."

"Key projects you have some control over?"

Korskin shrugged. "I'm not alone, Jack."

"I know. There is another man, the Shadow Man. Were you the red-haired man?"

Korskin grew very still and smiled. "Since you ask." He touched the remote and his face began to writhe and seethe with unholy motion. Muscles relaxed and moved, and his features settled into the familiar image of the red haired man I had seen on Sanchez's phone. "No need for plastic surgery anymore."

"Only lasts 28 days?"

Korskin pressed his remote and his face morphed back into its familiar pattern. "I have to replenish my Nbots every four weeks. Originally, we had two tablets like that one. However, Janice had not updated her software interface on the second tablet." He massaged his lips as they settled back into place. "It is really a dirty shame, Jack. Because I lied to you. When I found out Janice had an MRI that revealed her Nbots, I had to do something before someone else found out. I used that older version of that tablet to try and access her Nbots on the day after her MRI. I was hoping to eliminate the evidence before she discovered I had infested her."

The light from his remote tablet illuminated his face. "The programming was buggy, not at all at the level you hold in your hand. Janice was holding her new version back because she suspected I was up to something. How was I to know the MRI had affected the Nbots? The self destruct directive was only supposed to turn off the power and allow the body to break down the Nbot."

"The Nbots exploded when they left Williams." I stepped

closer, my mind reeling under the implications. I had been right all along! "You killed her, didn't you?"

"It wasn't what I planned, Jack! I had no idea the self destruct would set off her new power modifications. But the results were not a complete waste. Now we know we have a new alternate action at hand." He drew a deep breath. "Problem was that other tablet reset itself and erased all contents after I used it. Janice was a little too smart for her own good. We had to start from scratch when we couldn't find the prototype in your hand and came up with this tablet."

Korskin's gaze was directed at the tablet, and I saw my chance. I took three quick steps and grabbed the back of his head and pulled his face toward me. He gasped and I shoved the syringe up his nose and drove home the plunger. He shoved me away and fell back onto the floor. I grabbed the tablet from my pocket. I opened the blinking icon. "I'm guessing with your new and improved tablet you don't have control over the old Nbots, do you?"

Korskin gasped as the Nbots coursed down his throat and he hacked and tried to cough them up. His eyes filled with fury and his face changed again. "What have you done?"

"I'm in control now, Korskin."

He stood up slowly and began to tremble. His new features began to change again. The Nbots were at war. Korskin slapped at his face as if he were being attacked by bees. I stumbled back into the Christmas tree and tripped over it. Korskin glared at me through red rimmed eyes and stabbed at his tablet.

I felt something tickle at the back of my throat. I turned and ran, holding the tablet before me and I frantically stabbed the icon for my Nbots. A separate control window opened and showed the self destruct directive had been initiated for my Nbots!

Turnabout was fair play! I opened Korskin's Nbot control

window and touched the self destruct sequence. These Nbots were the older version. Would they behave as Janice's had? The icon of my Nbots showed up in the corner of the screen. I tried to pause the countdown, but I couldn't stop the process. What was I to do?

I paused at the end of the hallway and heard Korskin's foot-steps echo down the empty hallway. "Jack, where are you? I triggered your Nbots' self destruct. You can't stop the process. But I can. All you have to do is surrender the tablet and open the security page for me."

"Once it has begun, it can't be stopped, right Korskin?" I shouted down the hallway.

Korskin paused and silence fell over the hallway. "Well, I guess I'll just have to go back to the drawing board."

"You won't have that option. I have control over the Nbots you just received. I triggered their exit and self destruct program. You stop my countdown and I'll stop yours."

Korskin roared in anger, and I bolted down the hallway deeper into the department. Ahead, I saw the MRI suite. I slid into the Christmas tree right outside the MRI room door and it fell on top of me. Tiny flashes of light sparkled before me as the tinsel reflected the green exit sign to my left. Flashes of light? What had been different with Janice's Nbots? Janice had an MRI before we went on our trip. On Mickey's birthday! The magnetic field had damaged her Nbots. If the MRI could damage my own Nbots, maybe I could buy some time.

I shoved the tree off me and stood before the huge, copper lined doorway into the main MRI room. Inside, the huge machine sat humming and hissing from the liquid gases that kept the magnet cooled. This MRI was a research machine with a 5 Tesla magnet, the strongest magnet available. A warning sign on the door mentioned the damage the magnetic field would do to pacemakers and all electronic devices.

"I'm counting on it." I shoved open the huge door and stepped inside. An eerie blue and red light oscillated behind the magnet from the gas tanks. The magnetic field immediately tugged on the keys in my pocket and the tablet flew out of my hands and banged up against the outer shell of the magnet. I swore. I hadn't thought about the tablet. Chances were now it was damaged beyond repair from the magnetic field. Something black flew past me head. Korskin's tablet joined Janice's on the magnet. I felt the Nbots begin to boil inside me.

"Smart, Jack. The MRI should damage the Nbots." Korskin shoved me aside and towered over me in the doorway. His face writhed and moved in an unholy display. His eyes filled with fiery hatred. "You'll have to get closer to stop the Nbots. Yes, that is why Janice's Nbots malfunctioned. But, Jack, you'd have to go inside the bore of the magnet to disable them. And, right now, you won't get any closer."

"Hey! Face freak?" Someone shouted from out in the hall-way. I glanced over Korskin's shoulder. A figure in a wheelchair wheeled toward us. The wheelchair stopped and the figure stood up. A hand pulled away the gauze. Detective Sanchez stared at us with raccoon eyes. She lifted her right hand, and it held a pistol.

"Sanchez?" I said.

"The rumors of my death were greatly exaggerated. When I saw you in the elevator I figured you were up to something. Funny how everyone ignores a patient rolling down the hall-way. One of the Secret Service guys even offered to wheel me here for my MRI." She pointed the pistol at Korskin. "What's up with your face?"

"You're supposed to be dead." He said.

"Nice try. No one is expecting a person to show up from the dead."

Korskin slid to the side in the control room and grabbed for something. He lifted a large metal tank of oxygen above his head. His eyes filled with fear as the tank moved of its own accord. Now was my chance!

I stood up and ran for the magnet and dove into the long, cylindrical bore sliding through to the other end. I felt the Nbots pulse with the effects of the field. Slamming up against the back wall I turned to look down the bore at Korskin.

Something moved behind him and Sanchez lumbered into view. Green and gold flashed around her and the Christmas tree writhed in midair and hurtled toward the MRI. It caught Korskin in the face and he fell toward the magnet. The field grabbed the oxygen tank and pulled him across the room. The Christmas tree wrapped itself around Korskin's body like a prehistoric spider. I lurched up from behind the magnet and ran with all my might through the door just as Korskin and the oxygen tank slammed into the magnet and the metal frame of the Christmas tree molded itself around Korskin's body. In slow motion I saw Sanchez lift the pistol. I screamed 'no' but it was too late. The pistol jerked as it fired and the bullet hit the oxygen tank.

I glanced back and saw the panic and fear on Korskin's face as the tank ruptured with the impact and a lone spark shot into the cloud of escaping oxygen. With sudden strength, I shoved the thick, heavy door closed just as the explosion took place. The floor shook and the explosion blew out the glass shield between the MRI chamber and its control room. I rolled out into the hallway and fire filled the control room. Sanchez stumbled back and fell into her wheelchair.

I pushed her ahead of me running down the hallway and made it to the bend in the hallway when the other tanks ruptured, filling the air with helium and cold mist. The smothering mist extinguished the fire but also deprived me of oxygen. I slid into darkness.

THIRTY-NINE

"We've got to stop meeting like this."

I opened my eyes. Keri hovered over me. My mouth felt dry and pasty. My eyeballs were lined with grit. I looked around at the hospital room.

"What happened?"

"Well, let's just say you've been out of it for about twenty-four hours. There was an explosion at the Institute and they had to evacuate the President. There are a number of people waiting to talk to you."

I swallowed and tried to sit up. Every muscle in my body ached. "The Nbots?"

"Yeah, about those." She reached over and picked up my original cell phone. "You received a text with a link to a video on your phone. Before we go any further, you need to watch it."

With shaking hands, I took the phone. On the screen an arrow sat in the middle of the video, and I touched it. Janice looked back at me. I gasped.

"Hey, honey. If you're watching this video, something has happened to me. I recorded this while you were running to the

store to get me some snacks. I will upload it on my server and if you ever activate my tablet, this text would be sent to you with the attached video." She paused and swallowed. "Let's get the elephant out of the room. I found out from the MRI of my pelvis I can never have children. It's not your fault. And I need you to know that I had some of my eggs harvested for the future. Your suggestion of a surrogate is a good one. I'm sorry I messed on that suggestion." She laughed. "Now, since you found the tablet I hid in our secret drawer, you obviously found the PIN number in the turtle, or it wouldn't have activated. I need to tell you that your life may be in danger. I have suspected for months that Dr. Korskin and David Boone have something planned for my Nbots. I wouldn't put it past Korskin to infest you. When I looked at my MRI I knew I was infested also. I've written a new exit program for my Nbots and I've encoded the one sample in my office. If you get infested, don't worry. The new exit protocol will be uploaded tomorrow to those Nbots and they will not self destruct on exit unless you tell them to. I hope my Nbots will act the same way. Whatever you do, do not allow my tablet to fall into the hands of Dr. Korskin or David Boone. If something bad has happened to me, I love you forever, I'll love you for always. We can get through this, Jack. Take care."

My chest heaved with sobs and tears blurred my vision. I looked up at Keri and she showed me an emesis basin filled with black residue. "I guess this is what she was talking about? They say you coughed this up during the night."

The basin was lined with a dark, swirling liquid. "Yes." I said wetly.

A nurse came into the room pushing a wheelchair. "I see that you are up and awake, Dr. Merchant." He said. "Once you were awake, I was requested to escort the two of you to the examining room down the hall. That is, if you feel up to it."

I sat up slowly and every bone in my body ached. "But,

Keri, how did you get away from Williams? What happened to Sanchez?"

"You're about to find out." Keri said.

Keri helped me into the wheelchair and the nurse pushed me down the hallway past busy doctors and nurses to an examining room. The room was set aside for private consultation between a patient and their doctor prior to complete admission to the floor. Sometimes, the room was used for counselors in the event of the death of a patient. When the nurse wheeled me into the room I was confronted with a group of people.

Detective Sanchez sat in her wheelchair to my right. One half of her head had been shaved and the blonde hair on the other half hung from beneath gauze around her head. Beside her Jerry Langley stood while he examined his cell phone. Two Secret Service members, a man and a woman flanked the other person sitting in the room, Dr. Stovall. One of them was Tyrone, the transporter I had met in the elevator.

Stovall motioned to the only other empty chair in the room. "Please have a seat Ms. Douglas." She said to Keri. Keri flinched at the mention of her real name.

Stovall leaned over to Tyrone and whispered. He nodded and left the room taking the nurse with him. Stovall sat forward.

"Jack, I don't need to tell you that yesterday was a fiasco. The explosion down on the radiology floor totally disrupted the reception. The President was whisked away, and we were left behind to pick up the pieces." Tyrone returned and handed Stovall a computer tablet. Stovall studied it, swiping through screens.

"It seems that you were in your wife's old office when you were accosted by Agent Williams. Is that right?" She looked up at me.

I nodded. "He was working with Korskin. He was going to

confine me while Korskin completed his plan to infest you with the Nbots."

Stovall looked at me and removed her glasses. She rubbed her eyes. "So, now I'm infested, Jack?"

"I saw your Nbots on Janice's tablet. They were active."

Stovall motioned to the other Secret Service agent, and she removed a plastic bag from her pocket. It contained the ruined remnants of the tablet. "This tablet?"

"Yes. It contained all of Janice's control parameters for the Nbots. Korskin had infested Williams with them to control him and force him to do certain tasks."

"Such as killing a hired assassin and attempting to kill Detective Sanchez?" Stovall said.

"It was him, all right." Sanchez said.

"But you were pronounced dead." Stovall said.

"That was my call." Jerry looked up from his phone. "I was suspicious of someone in Korskin's hire and when it was obvious Sanchez would recover from her epidural hematoma, I decided to allow everyone to think she had died. If the killer knew she was still alive, he might come after her again. We had Sanchez moved to the University Hospital where no one knew her."

"And why did someone want to kill Sanchez?" Stovall asked coldly.

"I had uncovered evidence that Korskin has a daughter in a long term care facility and was being blackmailed by someone with lots of money and power. I was sloppy. Korskin found out I had accessed the sealed files of the vaccine trial and he sent someone to kill me." Sanchez said slowly. "Korskin sent me a text that an old perp I had been searching for was in the area. When I arrived, Agent Williams showed up and started firing at me without any preamble. I don't know what happened after that. I think a homeless person stumbled onto the scene and

Williams ran thinking the deed was done. Jerry tracked down the homeless person." She pointed to Jerry. He held up his phone. A video was playing that showed a woman slumped against a twisted grocery cart filled with her "junk".

"I interviewed the woman and she identified Williams as the assailant." Jerry said.

"Why didn't you bring that to the Secret Service?" Stovall said and then held up a hand. "Never mind. It would seem you couldn't trust anyone, right?"

"Neither could you." Sanchez nodded to Tyrone. "You were on to us from the start."

Stovall studied me. "Tyrone was ordered to keep an eye on you and let you lead us to Dr. Merchant's tablet. He was NOT supposed to let you take his pistol."

Sanchez shrugged. "He took me over after I told him Merchant was up to something. When the ruckus about Williams broke out, I managed to get away from him."

Stovall glared at her and then cast one glanced at Tyrone.

"She's sneaky." He said.

"Like a jaguar." Sanchez hissed.

Tyrone swallowed hard, keeping his eyes averted from Stovall's steely gaze. Stovall held up Janice's ruined tablet. "We managed to recover much of the information. Enough to reprogram one of Korskin's tablets. We need the password, Jack. If what you claim is true, the reprogrammed tablet will show if I have been infested." Stovall nodded toward me, and the other agent handed me the new tablet. The screen awaited my input. I put in the password and the program opened up and I entered the PIN. I glanced at the screen and before I could touch it, the agent pulled the tablet out of my grasp and returned it to Stovall.

Stovall studied the tablet and began tapping at the screen. She held it so I could see it. "That diagram shows I have Nbots just as you surmised, Jack." She turned the tablet away and began tapping again. She stood up. "If you'll excuse me, I need to step into the restroom."

She disappeared into the restroom and soon we heard her coughing and retching. She returned to the examining room with an emesis basin in her hands. She wiped her mouth with a cloth and walked over to me. She pushed the emesis basin under my nose and the smell made me gag.

"Are these the Nbots?" She said hoarsely.

I glanced at the swirling black content of the emesis basin. "Yes."

"Secure them." Stovall handed the emesis basin to Tyrone. He left the room. Stovall sat down.

"Korskin said he wanted to control you." I said.

"Jack, you need to know that Dr. Korskin was not one of the men who initiated the vaccine debacle a few years ago as Theresa claims."

I glanced at Theresa and she shook her head. "But, his voice was so familiar."

"He was not the 'red-haired' man." Stovall said.

"It was his face. When I changed the setting on his Nbots, his face returned to the face of the red-haired man. He all but admitted to that." I said.

Stovall leaned forward. "You don't understand. He was NOT that man. Officially the red-haired man is still at large."

I glanced at Jerry and he shrugged. Sanchez laughed. "Another noble lie?"

Stovall wiped her mouth again. "Let me just say that this entire affair is far deeper and more widespread than you think. We are looking for the man behind the vaccine fake."

"The Shadow Man." Keri said.

"What about David Boone?" I said. "He gave money to Korskin. And, the Institute."

Stovall grimaced. "And he is also a major contributor to President Mitchell's re-election campaign. Forget he was involved. Jack, your wife's invention is solid. I will personally see that it is further developed for the good of the country."

A cold chill ran down my spine. "What? For the country? She designed it for patient care."

Stovall frowned. "Your vision is short sighted, Jack. We will allow the research to continue in the Manning Nanotechnology wing, but it will have to start from scratch. We're appropriating this technology. It is too dangerous in the wrong hands." She stood up. "I'm sure you can agree on that."

I gasped. It was then I realized Stovall had no problems working with the tablet. She had used such a device before! "You were far too familiar with Janice's tablet." I said loudly. Stovall raised an eyebrow and shrugged.

"I'm a quick study." She headed for the door with the agent in tow. "Also, Ms. Douglas, a U. S. Marsal will be here shortly to begin the process of creating a new identity. You are in more danger now than before, I am afraid." She left the room.

"Well, that's crappy." Sanchez said as she put a toothpick in her mouth. "What gratitude?"

I was stunned and glanced at her. "How did you show up just in time?"

"I recovered pretty fast from the surgery. Just had a splitting headache. Made me irritable."

"And that was new?" I said.

"Hey, if I hadn't seen you on the elevator I wouldn't have wondered what you were doing in the hospital posing as Dr. Francisco. Yes, don't look at me that way. I talked to the security guard you fooled. You went up to the tenth floor and then disappeared."

She leaned forward. "I found an ancient nurse who remembered the hidden tunnel connecting GUT to the Institute. She said all the murder victims who died at GUT became ghosts who wandered the abandoned underground passage." She touched the short hair on the shaved side of her head. "It itches." She scratched. "So I asked myself what you were up to. First, I remembered telling you to stay out of things. Then I remembered you don't listen to reason. What's in the Institute that would interest you? Well, the President, for one thing. Your wife's wing, the other. Why would you sneak into the building and go to your wife's wing? Hiding something? Looking for something?"

She sat back in her wheelchair. "I figured either you were looking for something that might break this whole thing open. Or, you were hiding something from Secret Service you couldn't get past the security the day of the President's visit. I had Tyrone wheel me over to the Institute for my supposed MRI. He heard about Williams and the search for a missing assailant and he bolted. But, not before I appropriated his poorly hidden pistol. Once I was alone I just wheeled myself to your location."

"My location?"

"Your new burner phone? On that night before we met at the pancake restaurant, I went to the convenience store and pulled my badge on the clerk. Told the clerk who sold you the phone to give me the number because of a threat to our national security. After surviving an assassination I was pretty ticked off. I started tracking your whereabouts the day before the President's speech while I was recovering. Had a little double vision for a few hours and a heck of a headache." She moved the toothpick to other side of her mouth. "Pain meds took care of that. Better living through chemistry. So, when I found out you were not at the reception and on the fifth floor, I knew something wasn't right." She leaned forward. "I'm weak from surgery, not dead."

"Thanks for saving my butt." I said. "But you shouldn't have shot the oxygen tank."

She shrugged and winced again. "Blame it on the brain swelling." She pointed to her head. "I was aiming for Korskin."

I glanced at Keri. "How did you get free?"

"That Agent Williams told another agent to guard me for my own protection. That agent wasn't in the bed with Korskin. Listening to his conversations he had with other agents, it dawned on me Williams was working on his own. I convinced them to let me call Jerry."

"Once I heard from her it wasn't long before the explosion took place." Jerry said. "The Secret Service agent guarding Keri, I, mean, Theresa, gladly turned over her protection to me." His phone beeped and he glanced at it. He frowned. "Just got a text to escort Theresa down to the elevators. They are waiting." He looked up at 'Theresa' and I she stiffened. She looked at me with moisture filled eyes.

"I don't want to go."

I swallowed hard. "If you stay, your life is forfeit. You know that."

"You could come with me?" She reached for my hand then pulled it back, covering her eyes. "That would never work, would it?" She sobbed quietly and I put a hand on her shoulder.

"I hate this, Theresa. But I can't live with the possibility that I could cost you your life." The tears were filling my eyes now.

"I know." She said and wiped her eyes. "Jack, you have to stay here anyway. We are the only ones who know about those Nbots Stovall just took out of here. Who knows what the government will do with them? You must see that Janice's research is legit and truly helps people."

"Good call." I said lamely. I felt hot tears on my cheeks. "But we haven't had enough time."

Theresa smiled. "You had time to put on that armor and stand in the gap. You beat those evil idiots, Jack. Don't forget that." She held up my New Testament and pressed it into my other hand. "I've been clinging to this since they found you yesterday. You are a good man, Jack. And we need more good men to stand against the evil of our times. Read the Bible. Find a new life. That's what I plan to do. Who knows, I might get baptized one day."

I couldn't find the words as she stood up, leaned over, and kissed me on the lips. "They have to move quickly before they can recover from Korskin's death. Rushing me out of town makes the only sense of this whole mess." She smiled at me one last time. "Goodbye, Jack. I love you."

"I love you too." I said as Jerry ushered her through the door.

"Well, that sucks. Like my new hairdo." Sanchez said. "Let's get some breakfast."

FORTY

"I never dreamed when I retained you as a consultant that you would be the person to bring me such horrific business." Dr. Sam Francisco said as she pulled off her face shield and tore off her disposable gown and tossed them into a red container. She pulled a blue surgery cap off her hair. Her hair was snowy white with scattered gold and silver sparkles.

"Your hair is, uh, interesting." I said.

"Winter Wonderland." She smiled. "Jack, it took everything in my power to keep the feds from taking my patients before I could do an autopsy. Three days to wrangle the authorities into letting me do the autopsies on Korskin and Williams." She wore white cat-eye glasses with golden highlights. "Four agents watched my every move. One passed out." She smiled. "It will take a few days to get the micro back on the cells, but grossly, I saw the Nbots you described in the tissues of Agent Williams and Dr. Korskin. And in your bone marrow, by the way. Not contaminants, but Nbots. How are you?"

"I had a CT and an MRI. No evidence of the Nbots.

Thanks to Janice's reprogramming, they exited my body safely." The memory of the video hit me, and I was silent. It took me a moment to recover. "Sam, imagine what we could do with these Nbots if they really worked. Korskin gave me leukemia and then took it away. Or at least, he made my blood look like I had leukemia. What if these things could cure any disease?"

"It would bankrupt the country." Sam said. "No more health care dollars for the government. Everyone would live a long, long time. Where would we get all the food?"

I pointed to her green swill. "Not that, for sure."

Sam laughed. "Now you know why Stovall confiscated the Nbots. She'll make sure the right people stay healthy and alive."

"And what about the 'wrong' people? What will happen to them? Will they die of mysterious diseases? These things are a dangerous weapon in anyone's hands."

"Like my drink." Sam smiled and picked up her green slop and sipped it. "I've got to find a better recipe." She removed a gift wrapped box from a nearby counter and handed it to me.

"What's this?" I studied the package wrapped in shiny paper covered with snowmen.

"Your Christmas present." Sam beamed.

I tore away the paper. The white, shiny box carried a picture of a MacBook Pro. "A laptop?"

"Not just any laptop." Sam tapped the box. "It's already set up for you and you alone." She pointed to a pile of folders on a nearby desk. "All the backlog of cases are loaded on the laptop for your review. Highly secure, of course."

"You're giving me my case load for Christmas?" I raised an eyebrow.

Sam frowned. "You said you'd help. You're on the clock, now. There are at least three dozen cold cases that could use your input. The best cure for you is to get back in the saddle and get back to work."

I sighed and managed to smile. "I'm dying to please you."

Sam smiled. "Merry Christmas."

I PULLED into the casino parking lot. It was early. Way too early to be drinking. Way too early to be gambling. But tell that to the hundreds of people already seated before their slot machines and blackjack tables across the gangway on the river boat casino. I got out of my car and took the escalator up to the entry level. An outer balcony overlooked the city of Talako and wrapped around the sides to give a view of the river. It was a cool, misty morning and the sky was a dull gray threatening an afternoon rain. Pulling my jacket closer around me I stood at the railing looking down the river.

Theresa was gone. Lost to me now until they could identify Korskin's boss, the Shadow Man. But, for the first time in over a year, I felt almost whole. I missed Janice but I now knew what she had done to protect me and to stop Korskin. Now, what to do with her eggs was a totally different issue. Can't think about that right now with Christmas almost upon me. I had to honor her memory by moving on and trying my best to look outside myself and try to do my job as a doctor to help others through interpreting the "shadows" of their Xrays and to help Dr. Francisco unravel the mystery of the dead. And, I had to do what Theresa reminded me to do. Stand in the gap against evil. In fact, I had already planned to go to church the next day with Jerry. Time to heal!

I couldn't do that seated at the bar or the blackjack table. That was not the reason I was here. I spied the group of people huddled under one of the riverside pavilions and standing on the stage, Gill spoke. I had no idea what he was saying but I decided it was time to turn back to God. The New Testament sat in my pocket. I made my way down the stairs to the riverside pavilion and, hopefully, into a better future.

ABOUT THE AUTHOR

Bruce Hennigan grew up in Northwest Louisiana and became a physician practicing in the field of radiology. He was a church drama director for 15 years and wrote over 150 plays. He is a certified apologist, or one who defends the truthfulness of the Christian faith with Reasons to Believe and with the North American Mission Board in the role of a Certified Apologetic Instructor. He speaks on this topic on a regular basis. Bruce is also the author of nine books in the supernatural thriller series, "The Chronicles of Jonathan Steel" as well as "Death by Darwin", "The Homecoming Tree", "Our Darkness, His Light", and, with Mark Sutton, "Hope Again: A Lifetime Plan for Conquering Depression."

Together with Mark Sutton, he participates in a seminar based on the book entitled, "Conquering Depression". For more information on the book and tool, "LifeFilters" go to www.conqueringdepression.com.

To find out what David Boone did with his Nannomemes, check out Book 5 of The Chronicles of Jonathan Steel, "The 9th Demon: Time of the Cross".

Dr. Jack Merchant in his near future appears in Book 7 and 8 of The Chronicles of Jonathan Steel, "The 7th Demon: The Pandora Stone" and "The 5th Demon: Demoneyes".

Dr. Merchant will appear in the upcoming mystery, "Slice Fatigue", a Jack Merchant Mystery.